CXVI

DESPERATE MEASURES

Angie Smith

CXVI

INSPIRED BY LITERATURE

Ange Smith

Copyright

Copyright Angie Smith 2016

Angie Smith asserts her rights under the Copyright, Design and Patents Act 1988 to be identified as the author of this work.

All rights reserved. No part of this publication may be reproduced, stored in a retrieval system, or transmitted, in any form or by any means, electronic or mechanical, including photocopying, recording or otherwise, without the prior permission of the author.

This novel is a work of fiction; names, characters, businesses, organisations, places and events are either the product of the author's imagination or are used fictitiously. Any resemblance to actual persons, living or dead, is entirely coincidental.

Acknowledgements

With special thanks to my husband for his endless support and input, to Laura (a star beta-reader) and to countless other beta-readers, bloggers and fellow authors – you know who you are. A special mention must go to Tracy and the members of THE Book Club on Facebook and of course Nicky Handcock (Pentire proofreading) and last but not least Karri (Cover Art by Karri Klawiter) for her tremendous covers. Without all of you this would not be possible.

Prologue

Monday 23rd February 2015

He drifted slowly in and out of consciousness. No longer aware of the time or the day, he lay in the foetal position, the hard, damp, concrete floor painful and uninviting. He'd tried to keep track on his days in captivity, but isolation and complete darkness made this virtually impossible. Several days ago, or it may have been hours, minutes, or even seconds ago, he'd reassured himself this was his thirteenth day. He cared little for the accuracy of this assumption. He knew at some point within the next twenty-four hours Gravel-voice would come and give him half a glass of water. If he was lucky he might not get beaten this time, but Gravel-voice would always ask the same question, "Have you decided to tell me where your daughter is?"

In the first few days, when he'd been asked that, he'd been strong, almost cocky, and resolutely refused to answer. This resulted in such severe beatings that he'd lost most of his teeth, received a broken nose, and dislocated his left shoulder. His whole body was bruised and sore. Since then each beating became so painful that most occasions he lost consciousness before the punishment concluded. The irony of this was that he had no idea where his daughter was. Even if he wanted to tell Gravel-voice what he so desperately wanted to know, he couldn't.

He'd considered lying, just to have a break from the beatings, but knew that once the lie had been uncovered the punishment would be increased. He concluded his only chance of staying alive was to remain silent, hoping against hope that someone might rescue him from this purgatory. But who would do that? And where exactly was he?

He thought he may be being held in one of the rooms in the basement of an old disused warehouse, somewhere south of London. The echoing footsteps he heard prior to Gravel-voice's arrival indicated a large hollow barren space, and the slight cockney accent gave a hint to its location, but there was no guarantee his deduction was correct.

Because his body entered starvation mode days after incarceration, almost all his fat reserves were now exhausted, and his cells were beginning to selectively break down body proteins. He'd managed to catch a few spiders and the odd beetle by blindly feeling around in the edges and corners of the room. Other than this he'd not eaten a thing. He knew that at some point the loss of body protein would affect the function of his vital organs and that death would follow. That point was fast approaching and he needed to do something, otherwise he would be no more. The problem he faced: what could he do?

Suddenly he heard echoing footsteps approaching, although this time there appeared to be more than one pair. He closed his eyes tightly because he'd learned that the sudden shaft of light from outside the room would blind him. He heard the key being placed in the lock and prepared for the kick to his ribs. He could no longer defend himself; in fact he could no longer move off the floor.

The door banged open and he was aware of two people entering.

"Goodness me, what on Earth have you done to him?" a woman's voice asked.

"You want to know where his daughter is. Eventually he'll tell me," Gravel-voice responded.

He felt the man's hands on his torso and he was dragged up into a sitting position and propped against the wall. He saw the woman look away, obviously disturbed by his appearance, She was young, blonde, and dressed in business attire.

"Have you decided to tell us where she is?" Gravel-voice asked, holding him and preventing him from slumping back onto the floor.

He opened his mouth and tried to speak. He could form no words; he was too weak.

"He's going to tell us," Gravel-voice shouted. "Get some water."

The woman disappeared, returning a few moments later with a dirty-looking glass. She gave it to Gravel-voice who attempted to tip some into his mouth, but he passed out and went limp.

The woman bent down and felt his pulse. "You stupid idiot, he's dead!"

Gravel-voice quickly let go of him and he fell down. "That wasn't supposed to happen."

"You told me you could make anyone talk," the woman said.

"He isn't anyone. He's Maria Barnes' father."

"He *was* Maria Barnes' father, and you *are* a complete imbecile." Two shots from a semi-automatic pistol rang out and sent Gravel-voice crashing to the floor. The echoing footsteps of the woman walking away could be heard.

He opened his eyes, and — although unsure how long since he'd tasted it — he had a chance of freedom. She hadn't locked the door, and even though she'd turned the light off, there was some minimal illumination from the adjoining room. Most importantly, she'd left him fresh protein; approximately 95kg of fresh protein.

He used what little strength remained to crawl to Gravel-voice. He licked the blood from the head wound. It was a start. His plan to feign death had worked; now he could regain some strength and try contacting his daughter. Someone was going to a great deal of trouble to find her.

Chapter 1

Tuesday 1st September

Woods' attention wavered as he glanced across at the intercom receiver. He considered whether or not to ignore it. According to the clock on the mantelpiece it was just after 9.00 a.m. and he had not expected anyone so early. In fact he didn't expect anyone at all today. People who usually called at the flat generally rang his mobile first to check he would be there. He struggled up out of the chair and hobbled across the room. As he reached the receiver it fell silent. He cursed, but now that he was on his feet he decided on a coffee. Before he made it to the kitchen door the intercom sounded again; persistent people irritated him. He snatched up the handset. "Yes," he barked. "What do you want?"

"Greg Woods?" a young female voice enquired.

"What's it got to do with you?"

He heard the softest of laughs, then, "Well, they said you were grumpy."

"Well *they* were right. And whatever you're selling, I don't want it. So get lost!"

"Is this how you spoke to Maria Barnes?"

He hesitated and his attention held. "Do I know you?" he probed.

"If you invite me in I'll be able to answer that."

"Goodbye!" He banged the receiver down and limped into the kitchen. He immediately felt the cold on his bare feet, from the solid tiled floor. He switched the kettle on and rattled the top drawer searching for a teaspoon. The jar looked empty, but if he scraped around in the bottom there would be enough for one weak black coffee. It would save time to make it in the jar and drink from that. He knew he would have to go to the convenience store at the end of the road later, where he could also buy some milk. Maybe he ought to go to the supermarket and stock up. He decided he might just do that.

His eyes narrowed when a knock on the flat door sounded. Had someone let the woman in? He struggled over to the door and peered through the spyhole. He couldn't spot anyone. He looked to the sides, attempting to see if they were trying to hide out of sight. Then the knock came again, only this time much louder. Still no-one was there. He yanked the door open and rushed out, stumbling and falling on the floor; the woman had been crouching at the base of the door and he'd tripped over her.

"What in God's name are you doing?" he bellowed, trying to get up.

The young woman — dressed all in black — dashed into his flat. "Fancy a coffee?" she shouted.

He went back in and found her in the living room.

"God, what a mess," she said, tut-tutting. "Is this how you live?"

"You have five seconds to tell me who you are."

"Or you'll try to throw me out?" she scoffed.

"Or I'll call the police."

Now she laughed cynically. "I don't think that would go down well with your former colleagues…" Then, almost as though it was an afterthought, she added, "but it might give them something to discuss between doughnuts."

Far from impressed, he decided to take matters into his own hands. He lunged out and tried to grab her right arm. In lightening quick time she stepped back, avoiding him.

"Not as sharp as you used to be," she taunted, grinning.

The observation unsettled him and he bent down to seize at his walking stick, which was propped at the side of the sofa. Again her speed outwitted him, and she kicked it across the room.

"There's no wonder you've not found Maria. I'm surprised you can find anything in here. When was the last time you tidied up?"

"What are you, some kind of door-to-door housekeeper?"

She smiled, her dark blue, almost black eyes turning friendly.

Now he sighed, and flopped in the chair. He needed to rest. "Just get out of here and leave me alone." The pathetic nature of his demand appeared to soften her persona.

"I'm sorry," she said, picking up his stick and leaning it against his chair. "Can I make some coffee?"

"There's barely enough for one cup. I need to get some."

"Tea then?" she suggested, flicking her long, blond ringlets over her shoulders.

"I've no tea bags. I'll have to go to the shop."

"I'll fetch you some provisions."

"I don't need your help."

"You do! Just look in the mirror."

He squinted. The headache had returned. He closed his eyes briefly and then looked around for the painkillers. Where were they?

The young woman, appearing oblivious to his discomfort, continued, "We'll need gallons of coffee, if we're going to work together, and something to eat. It looks like you haven't had a decent meal in weeks! Give me twenty minutes and I'll have your fridge and cupboards stocked. Then I'll tidy up. Disorganisation exasperates me."

"Why would I work with you?"

"Because together we're going to find out what's happened to Maria Barnes."

Woods leaned on the window sill, watching the young woman walk away from the flats towards Horbury Road. He noticed her slight build mirrored Barnes', and the more he thought about it, the more he realised there were other similarities: her height, hair style — although hers was way longer, almost to the middle of her back — and of course her attitude, this being the primary reason he'd decided to send her across to the store and then hear what she had to say. Something about her intrigued him, and that particular spark of interest hadn't flickered for so long that it barely registered. Today though, things were different; the headache had subsided without intervention from his medication, and strangely he felt energised by her visit - he wanted this to work. Maybe she could assist him. Nevertheless, while she was out he needed to hide some sensitive documents; until trust had been established he couldn't risk them being seen. In actual fact, if he did not get a move on, she would be returning with the provisions, and the window of opportunity would have vanished. He needed to move fast, something that proved difficult these days.

As he turned away from the window he caught sight of a man stepping out of a dirty-looking dark green Volkswagen Passat, and seemingly following the young woman. He hobbled across the room, grabbed his binoculars and, returning to the window, focused on the man, who by now was disappearing from sight. He switched to the Passat: another male in the driving seat held a mobile phone to his ear and was speaking into it. I wonder, he thought, shaking his head and scratching at the stubble emblazoned on his chin. He fished out his mobile and pressed the speed dial button.

"Hello Pete, it's me," he said, as soon as it answered. "Get a squad car to come down to the flats and check out a dark green Passat. It's in the car park now. I've just witnessed the occupants paying an unhealthy interest in an elderly woman on Park Grove Road. It appeared they were intending robbing her, but something spooked them. Now they are waiting outside the flats for their next victim."

"Aye, do we have a registration number?"

Woods obliged, adding, "The driver looks to be in in his early thirties. He's wearing a dark shirt. The passenger, who appears slightly older, is wearing a grey hoody, blue jeans and red trainers. He's just followed a young woman towards Horbury Road."

"I'll put the call out."

"Tell them it is a priority. The young woman appeared vulnerable," he lied.

"Will do."

The call ended as Woods refocused on the Passat. He caught sight of the driver watching *him*, also through binoculars. They locked on each other's stare for nearly a minute. He couldn't resist and waved. "In for a pleasant surprise, are we?" he said, to himself. He could hear sirens in the distance. Two minutes later he spotted the young woman heading back across the road carrying two shopping bags. The man in the dark hoody appeared fifty metres behind her.

As she strolled into the car park Woods noticed the driver of the Passat photographing her. The sirens were now screaming down Lawefield Lane; another twenty seconds and they would be here. The young woman reached the entrance and used the button to call the flat. Just at that moment a couple of police patrol cars screeched up blocking the Passat in. Two uniformed officers leaped out of one and grabbed hold of the man in the grey hoody, while the occupants of the other confronted the Passat driver.

"Hello," Woods said, answering the intercom. "I'll let you in."

"There's a right commotion going on down here. What kind of area do you live in?"

"Welcome to Wakefield." He pressed the button on the receiver to open the door and then went to greet her as she stepped from the lift.

"Let me help you with those," he said, trying to take one of the bags.

"I can manage," she replied, indignantly.

He followed her to the door and when she stepped aside, he opened it, allowing her to enter. She placed the bags on the kitchen worktop and peered out of the window.

"I suppose you orchestrated that?"

He tried to appear nonchalant. "What?"

"I'm capable of looking after myself."

"That's what Maria used to say."

"I'd seen him following me. Now they'll start taking an interest in us. Why couldn't you leave them alone?"

He frowned. "Who are you?"

She pulled the well-worn black leather jacket off and threw it over a chair. She switched the kettle on and looked around. "My name's Zoe Field. Don't you have any clean cups?"

"They get dirty."

She groaned and searched in the cupboard below the sink. "Is this why the flat is in such a mess? You don't have any cleaning materials either!"

He waved the comment away. "Do you have OCD?"

"Do you have a robust immune system?"

The kettle boiled. "I'll rinse two cups out," he said, nudging her out of the way.

"I could have bought washing up liquid if I'd known." She unscrewed the coffee jar, peeled off the foil seal and shook what he assumed to be a spoonful, in each of the cups he now held. Then she poured the boiled water in and took one from him. "We'll probably get dysentery," she chuntered, sipping it.

"A disease of the lower intestine caused by bacteria or parasites."

"So now you're a walking encyclopaedia. Try hovel, it might remind you of somewhere."

He smirked.

"What I'm having difficulty with is how you ended up like this!"

"It's a long story, Miss Field, and I need to sit down."

As she took the carton of milk, opened it, and poured some into her cup, he moved slowly to the lounge, with his coffee balancing precariously in his bony hand. She followed.

"Tell me what you do and what your interest is in Maria Barnes," he said, settling in the chair.

"You won't like what I do."

"As long as you don't work for MI5 I'm not bothered."

"I'm a freelance investigative journalist."

"You were right. I've suddenly lost interest in you. Drink your coffee and go."

She smiled. "You've been trying to find Maria for almost three years, and the sum total of your effort appears to be scattered around the flat. You are no nearer finding her now than you were when you started."

He nodded dejectedly. "It's hard finding someone who doesn't want to be found."

"I agree. But at least I have a lead, whereas you have nothing, apart from a mess!"

"What's your interest in her?"

"To be honest, it's not her I'm interested in. My interest lies in Faulkner-Brown."

"Why would *you* have an interest in him?"

"Can I make something crystal clear?"

He shrugged, more or less involuntarily.

"I'm not going to bed with you, unless you have a wash."

"Whoa, who said anything about going to bed?" Her comment had shaken him.

"You can't keep your eyes off my breasts. No matter how hard you try to disguise the fact, you appear obsessed by them. I assume you are fantasising about them right now."

"No I am not!" he protested, covered in embarrassment. In reality he'd been trying to avoid looking down her cleavage ever since she had arrived.

"Yes you are. Admit it."

He shook his head and immediately wished he hadn't; the pain temporarily blinded him. He attempted to change the subject. "How old are you?!"

"What has that got to do with it? I'm over the age of consent, and I'm happy to go to bed with you, but I can't make love to someone who smells."

Now he was totally thrown off course. He sipped his coffee, trying to think of a response. He couldn't. The best he could manage was to re-concentrate on her age. "Twenty-two?" he said, feebly.

"Twenty-four actually," she snapped.

"My daughters are twenty-three."

"I know that! In fact I know all about you. I've been researching you for the past six months. What a delightful experience that has been." He raised an eyebrow, but she continued. "I know you separated from your wife in 2013 and that you have little contact with both her and your daughters. For some weird reason, that I can only guess is your fixation with Barnes, you're now living in what used to be her flat, presumably trying to form some invisible bond with her."

Her knowledge forced the false façade to crumble. In an attempt to restore some limited dignity, he asked, "How do you know Faulkner-Brown?" although his voice was etched with emotion.

"I don't personally, but I know all about him, and his dealings with Russia and what saved both him and Barnes."

"How could you possibly know anything about that?"

"Celia Schrotter."

"She's in prison, serving fifteen years."

"Ten out of ten. Go to the top of the class."

"How come you've been able to speak to her?"

"She's my mother."

"Ah…" he nodded. "Now I understand."

"Credibility, I think is what you'll call that," she smirked.

He nodded agreement. "Join me at the top of the class."

"My mother was made a scapegoat!"

Woods sighed. "Yes, I know, while Faulkner-Brown walked away scot-free."

"If you think finding Maria is hard, try searching for him."

Woods had attempted to do just that; unfortunately all his leads had proved fruitless. He had given up and concentrated on Barnes. "Is your view that if we find Maria she'll be able to throw some light on his whereabouts?"

"Partly, and I'm hoping she'll be able to confirm what evidence he used to secure the deal with Russia."

"Back then she claimed it would turn everything on its head, but she wouldn't give me details because the phone line wasn't secure."

"My mother thinks she knows. But, if she's correct, it hasn't been exposed."

"What were her thoughts?"

"The death of Vladimir Peshkov. . ."

"Let me guess," Woods butted in, rubbing his greasy, grey, matted hair. "The British poisoned him to discredit Russia."

"Correct. And Faulkner-Brown held the evidence. As you know, the inquest is ongoing and there's no indication of the truth emerging. I've been following the story."

"The Russians will wait for the verdict and then act."

"You could be right. The last thing they need is another scandal. Their standing has been damaged by their antics in the Ukraine. They need something to redeem them and discredit their adversaries."

Woods finished his coffee and noticed she hadn't touched hers. He looked around the room. She was right, he needed to clean up and sort through the paperwork. It would give him time to think, but first he had to delve deeper. "Do you believe Faulkner-Brown is in Russia?"

"When we find Barnes we'll ask her."

"Are you suggesting she's with him?"

"No! But there is no doubt that MI6 want to get their hands on both him and her."

"Hence the numpties sitting in the car outside. Why are they following you?"

"They think I'm on to something. My priority is to make sure they don't find out what. I assume that once they've explained who they are to the police officers they'll be left alone. Then I'll have to deal with them."

"Tell me about the lead you claim to have."

"You'll know that her father was kidnapped and nearly starved to death."

"He was lucky to survive, but he claims not to know where she is."

11

"He also claims not to have had contact from her. But he's lying. He has regular contact, and I know how."

Woods' senses heightened and he couldn't help leaning forwards. "Tell me more."

"Ahh… So now I have your full attention." She placed her cold cup of coffee on the table and looked long and hard at him. "Get yourself washed, shaved and suitably dressed. Then I'll tell you! I presume you have some clean clothes here."

"A few."

"Get all the dirty ones together and I'll start washing them. I dread to ask, but when was the last time you washed the bedding?"

His lacklustre expression gave the answer.

"Strip the bed and I'll wash the covers."

"I don't have any washing powder."

"Then I'll borrow some from one of the neighbours. I hate dirty bed sheets."

"You're not sleeping here!"

"Yes I am. We'll need to work long hours over the next few days. After I get rid of the idiots tailing me I need somewhere to lie low. Like it or not, this is where I'm staying. I'll sleep on the sofa if you don't want me in bed with you."

"I need to check out what you've told me before I agree to work with you."

"Then ring McLean and Jacobs. Get them to do it. You're never off the phone to them. I don't know how they have the patience to deal with you."

"How do you know all this?"

"I'll explain later." She looked uneasily towards the bedroom. "I don't suppose Maria's clothes are still here?"

He nodded, thinking she might want to make use of them. As soon as he saw her expression he knew he was mistaken.

"I thought as much; why haven't you thrown them out?!"

"I haven't had time."

"In all of two years, you haven't had time to dump them in the bin?"

"Well, no." He realised the stupidity of the claim.

"You need help; psychiatric help!"

"No I do not! I accept it's strange, but it's not what you are thinking."

"And just what do you suppose I'm thinking?"

"I don't know, something like I surround myself with her belongings to satisfy some desire I have on her."

She scowled and he sensed she was thinking again. An awkward silence followed. Eventually she asked, "Then why did you keep the clothes?"

"I've never got round to sorting them out. And I suppose if I'm brutally honest, there is part of me that thinks one day she might return. In reality I know that will never happen. I'm not an idiot."

"Then why don't you stop acting like one?"

"Why do you want to stay here if you think that?"

"Because I've been told that under that filthy mixed-up smokescreen there is a brilliant detective, who can help me find exactly what I'm searching for. In return I'll use my skills to assist you."

"What kind of skills?"

"I can hack phones, computer systems and networks, and I can source information that even your chums in the police force have difficulty getting."

"Have you hacked my phone?"

"Of course. How do you think I know Jacobs and McLean have been leaving messages in your mailbox?"

"So you're not afraid to break the law?"

She smiled. "I call it uncovering the truth."

Now he did something that he hadn't done in a long while; he too smiled. "Probably the wrong time to mention this, but I don't have any shower gel or shampoo!"

"It's a pressure washer and some carbolic soap you need."

Zoe sprinted out of the flats to her silver Smart car, her long dark blond ringlets bouncing as she jumped in. Then she started it up and sped off from the car park. As she did this she noticed the driver of the dark green Volkswagen Passat hurriedly starting his vehicle and coming after her. He caught up as she waited, indicating left, at the junction with Horbury Road. She looked in her rear view mirror and spotted the passenger in the Passat speaking on a mobile phone. She grinned and paused, patiently judging the volume of approaching vehicles on the main road. Due to the speed-camera, less than one hundred metres from the junction, traffic obeyed the thirty mile per hour limit. She must time this to the absolute second.

Now! She floored the accelerator and her car flew straight out in front of an approaching double decker bus which had to break hard, the driver blasting the horn in annoyance. Zoe wasn't in the slightest way bothered and accelerated away. She immediately indicated right, and then made for the supermarket car park. She knew the Passat driver would have seen which way she headed, but he would have to wait at the junction for a gap in the slowing traffic - caused by the sudden breaking of the bus.

As she entered Asda's car park she swung quickly to the left and went around the back of the building to where an articulated lorry was delivering goods to the store. The size of the car allowed her to get through a small gap and she screeched to a halt out of sight of the Passat, which she could hear driving at speed through the main car park and heading to the Dewsbury Road entrance, presumably assuming that she was going to the motorway. "Yes!" she said, gleefully to herself, knowing the plan had worked. Now she could buy the necessary cleaning materials and head back to the flat. The Passat meanwhile would no doubt be speeding along Dewsbury Road.

Ten minutes later she drove calmly back into the car park at the flats, where she had left Woods sorting through paperwork strewn on the floor. She parked at the far end, tucking the Smart car into the tightest of spots alongside a transit van, which Woods had said hardly ever went out. If the two men in the Passat returned looking for her, unless they drove to the back and viewed every parking space, they would not see the tiny Smart car.

She strolled over to the entrance and pressed the intercom.
"Hello," Woods said.
"Hi, it's Zoe."
"Did you lose them?"
"Does the sun rise in the morning?"
"Excellent." He laughed. "I'll let you in."
The door latch clicked open. She carried the two full carrier bags and her laptop over to the lift, and requested the fourth floor, her elbow

nudging the appropriate button. When she'd ascended and the lift door opened Woods was waiting to meet her.

He grinned. "Nice work, Miss Field. I trust you avoided the ANPR camera at the bottom of Westgate. And that you parked the Smart car out of sight."

"I don't like being patronised," she snapped. "Of course I avoided the camera. And Biddy is tucked away behind the van."

"Biddy?"

"That's what I call her."

"I see. Well, whatever floats your boat."

"Stop calling me Miss Field. My name's Zoe."

Woods' nod signposted his acquiescence and they made their way into the flat.

"Is it okay if I call you Greg?"

"Yes, you call me whatever you want. I respond to most things."

"Good. I've bought some large bin liners. We can fill them with Maria's clothes. Then I'll ring a taxi and take them to a charity shop in one of the small suburbs where there isn't any CCTV."

"That's what Maria would have wanted. There's a couple in Horbury on the High Street. It's only ten minutes away."

"Right, you get yourself clean and disinfected, and I'll start on the washing and clearing out Maria's stuff."

"Then you can explain how she's communicating with her father."

"The *how* is not an issue, it's the *where from* that is the problem." She glanced at him and sensed he had gained new life; working together with him no longer seemed in doubt. Perhaps they would form a beneficial partnership after all. Time would tell, and as always, was of the essence.

Chapter 2

Tuesday 1st September

Beth Luthi glanced at the chirping telephone, positioned on the right hand side of the desk in front of her. She placed the report she had been reading down and picked up the receiver. "Hello, Colette."

"Devon Coleman is here. He would like a word. Is it convenient?"

"Send him in, and hold all my calls for the next fifteen minutes."

Luthi set the receiver back in its hold and quickly hid the report in her desk. The sharp rat-a-tat, immediately followed by Coleman's entrance was an indication of the man's brimming confidence. She deliberately and purposefully, rather akin to a headmistress reviewing the intake on the first day of term, regarded his attire. She motioned that he should be seated. "Well?" she said, as he settled in the chair, brushing a fragment of fabric off his immaculately pressed trousers with the back of his hand.

"So far so good."

"Meaning?"

"She's still in the flat."

"Good. Now all we need is for him to take the bait."

"He will," Coleman replied, grinning.

Her eyes narrowed. She shook her head slowly. She disliked cockiness, and that word perfectly described his persona. "And what exactly are you basing that assumption on, Mr Coleman?" she asked, currishly.

"Field's young, vibrant, spirited and she resembles Barnes. And at this moment in time she's his only hope."

His smugness did little to sooth her mood. "Woods may be seriously ill, however, he's not your normal run-of-the-mill police detective. . ."

"Former police detective," he corrected.

"Mr Coleman," she emphasised each word. "I don't want to remind you how much is riding on this operation, or the consequences of its failure. That should be emblazoned deep within your soul. This has to work! Understood?"

"I'm fully aware of that."

"Then be under no illusions. If Woods or the Field girl gets the slightest indication that we are manipulating events, they will react. It is imperative that we appear to be doing everything within our powers to track and hinder their progress. The harder we make it for them the more resourceful they will become."

He nodded. "And we allow them to lead us to Barnes and Faulkner-Brown."

"Yes, we do."

"You'll realise that eventually we'll reach the point where our involvement becomes apparent to every single one of them."

This time she nodded. "Yes, and by then we'll have a hold that will ensure Barnes' compliance."

Now he sniggered. "And that's the point when the wheels fall off. The words Barnes and compliant are an oxymoron."

"Do you have any other suggestions, because I'd love to hear them?"

His indifferent shrug answered for him.

"Right, Woods is the only person Barnes is likely to allow anywhere near her. We need him for the access to her and we need her for the access to Faulkner-Brown."

"And we need Field for her wizardry with mainframes."

"Precisely."

"Okeydokey, just checking we're on the same page."

His response, combined with the smirk, sealed it. She decided to terminate the meeting - ten minutes with him was enough for anyone. "Keep me informed," she demanded. "The next twenty-four hours are crucial."

Woods stepped out of the bedroom and waited for the comment that he'd hoped would be heading his way.

"Wow, I'm impressed. You do belong to the human race. And I love the suit."

He grinned. In truth, he felt cleaner, smarter, and more like his old self. "What do you think to the head?"

"Cool."

"It'll grow back. I don't have clippers."

"Seriously, I like it. I find bald men sexy."

He forced an unconvincing smile, and moved on. "What can I smell?"

"Lasagne; it'll be five minutes."

"I suppose you also eat like a horse and don't put on any weight."

"Stop comparing me to her. It's creepy."

He took the point and viewed the living room. He counted at least six bin liners which looked to be full of various bits of paraphernalia and Barnes' clothes. "Been busy, I see."

She shrugged. "I can't find the photographs of Faulkner-Brown's wedding, or his children."

"You are well informed."

"My mother," she pointed out, but he'd already guessed that.

"I assume he took them."

"That's a pity. I could have made good use of them."

"How?" he asked, scowling.

"I have photographic recognition software; the sort MI5 use. If I could find his family it might assist in locating him."

He nodded. From the limited knowledge he held on the software he knew advances were being made in its capabilities and success rate.

She must have noticed him pondering because she added, "That's what has given me the lead on Maria."

"Tell me more."

"Let me dish out the food and I'll explain while *you* eat."

Five minutes later they were sitting together on the sofa, and as he made the most of the piping hot lasagne she elaborated.

"I spent several months watching her father."

"This is probably stating the obvious," he managed to say, between mouthfuls. "I assume you know about Pendleton the Aardvark, and how they used to communicate?"

She rolled her eyes, and, his embarrassment clearly visible, and his mouth full, he mumbled, "Sorry, carry on."

"I knew Maria's grandmother had passed away and that her father would no longer have access to the laptop in the nursing home. So therefore I looked at other ways they might communicate."

"The intelligence services have been monitoring his movements for the past three years; they claim he's not in contact with her."

Her eyes rolled again, only this time much more slowly. "The people who undertake MI5's surveillance aren't Oxbridge's elite. The surveillance teams are just dogsbodies who report back."

"Did you go to Oxbridge?"

"Of course not. I went to Bristol, but that doesn't mean I don't have a brain."

He smiled. "Go on. Tell me what you've discovered."

"Each week her father shops at Tesco. Nothing peculiar about that, you might think, but if the dogsbodies had paid particular attention they would have noted that, unlike most people, he doesn't follow convention."

He got the distinct impression this was leading somewhere and his interest in the lasagne waned.

"People generally go down the fruit and veg aisles first - that's how most supermarkets are designed. Entice you in with fresh produce and get you in the mood to shop. However, the first thing he does is stroll down the end of all the aisles, where the tills are located. Then he shops in the opposite direction to everyone else." She raised her eyebrows and paused.

This time he kept quiet. He guessed there was more to it than that.

"While he's first walking past the tills he's paying particular attention to one cashier, a friendly, elderly gentleman. If the elderly gentleman doesn't make eye contact with him, he completes his shop and then pays by debit card at the first available till."

He nodded, and remained silent.

"That's it," she said, abruptly.

He frowned. "It can't be!"

"Eat the lasagne before it goes cold. Otherwise I'm not telling you."

He shook his head and momentarily considered arguing that he was no longer hungry. Begrudgingly, he scooped up a fork full and held it close to his mouth. "Tell me what he does if the elderly cashier makes eye contact with him."

She pointed at the fork.

"This is worse than being a child."

"You're skin and bone. You need to eat."

He obeyed, and she continued. "If eye contact is made, he completes his weekly shop and goes to pay at the elderly gentleman's till. Even if there is a queue and other tills are available he always waits patiently in line until his turn. Then he pays using his debit card, but this time asks for fifty pounds cash-back." She stopped and nodded at Woods' plate.

He scooped in another mouthful.

"The elderly gentleman takes two twenty and one ten pound note out of the till and hands the money over to her father, along with the receipt."

He hurriedly swallowed the food. "Between the ten and twenty pound notes is a small slip of paper," he said.

"Correct. Her father places the money, the small slip of paper and receipt in his wallet and goes out to the car with his shopping. When it's loaded in the boot he sits in the driver's seat, opens the wallet and reads the message."

Woods attempted to get up from the sofa. "Right!" he announced. "We need to go and see him!"

"Stay down," she ordered, pulling him back. "Finish the food."

"I haven't got time. We must go and see him."

"What? So he can tell you to get lost and call the police. Just like he did the last time you pestered him. He won't tell *you* anything. You truly burnt that bridge. Besides, I've got all the messages, but I haven't been able to decipher them."

"I know how they communicated. I can probably help."

"No you can't!"

He scowled.

"Please hear me out before jumping to conclusions!"

He scooped the last forkful off the plate and ate it.

"I developed a programme that would translate the messages into every conceivable language, and then look at all the permutations of the letters in each word. They're using a different code this time. It's impossible to crack."

"Let me take them to Horbury Library. The librarian might be able to work it out."

"NO! She won't. Besides, I have a lead, but first I need to explain who the elderly gentleman is, and how he receives the messages."

Woods produced a resigned, half-hearted grimace. "Go on," he said, frustrated. He already knew he liked her and sensed that they'd be able to work together. He had a good feeling about this. Could they really find Barnes? He sincerely hoped they would.

"When she was nine years old, the elderly gentleman taught Maria to play the piano."

"Who else knows?"

"What? That she learned to play the piano?"

"No! About the way they communicate."

"You're the only person I've told."

"And how did you get the messages?" He thought he knew the answer.

"I hacked into the old guy's computer. I wanted to see what sites he visited."

"And?"

"Watch your fledglings grow, dot com. It's a social media site for parents with young children. Mainly used in the US. You post on your child, or your children, and share photos, problems, solutions, and comment on how they are developing."

"I've never heard of it," he said, rather puzzled.

"That's because you haven't got young kids."

"Can I see the messages?"

She reached over for her laptop, which she'd placed at the side of the sofa. She turned it on and a few seconds later handed it to him. He noticed her fingernails were bitten almost down to the cuticle – was she really the nervous type? He didn't think so, but he said nothing as she continued. "The old guy checks the site each day. When the post he's interested in arrives, he prints it and then the next time Maria's father goes shopping, he hands it to him."

Woods carefully read the messages: nineteen in total. Each contained a photograph of a small child, obviously showing its development over the past two years, with a message below, appearing to refer to the child's wellbeing, or what it had been doing. He looked up and noted Zoe's gaze. "I don't understand," he said. "Is the child hers?"

"Good question. Although I can't see any similarity; can you?"

He shook his head. "I can't imagine her having a baby. She has certain views about men. Are you sure these posts are from her?"

"As you can see, they're uploaded by Ms Toplenden."

He stared at the name on screen for several seconds. "Toplenden is an anagram of Pendleton," he declared, smiling.

Zoe nodded. "I can't trace where they're being uploaded. The IP address is from Venezuela; she's obviously using proxy-servers to hide her true location. And, as you'll see, there are never any responses to the posts. It appears to be one-way communication from her, and she doesn't have any friends, so there are no comments from anyone else either."

"Is the picture a clue to the key for the code?"

"No. I don't think so. If you look closely you'll see the background is bland and unspecific. Care has been taken not to show anything that might give away the location. Although the picture is what's finally given me my lead."

Woods stared at her. "Your photographic recognition software?"

"Yep."

He shook his head. "Maria's not stupid. She'll be using images that are freely available, and she'll be doctoring them."

She appeared dismayed by the comment and shook her head. "How many billion images are posted on the web every single day?"

He rose and went over to the window. He held his hand up to shield the bright sunlight. "I don't know," he answered, feeling the headache returning. "I would imagine quite a lot."

"Well, the software compares every single one with the quintillions of images it has in its memory banks, then it compartmentalises and stores them."

He thought he should look impressed, but the headache wasn't subsiding and he was frantically searching for his medication.

"Are you looking for these?" she asked, holding up a packet she'd pulled out of her pocket.

"Yes," he snapped. "What the hell are you doing with them?"

She threw the packet across, and miraculously he managed to catch it.

"Why are you taking those?"

He quickly swallowed two capsules. "None of your damned business."

"I found them down the back of the sofa. I was going to Google it."

"I suppose if I don't tell you, you'll hack my medical records."

He sensed she was holding back the smile; he had to say something. "They're for headaches."

"They're strong opioids, controlled drugs, only available on prescription; that much I've gleaned from the information inside the packet. What kind of headaches?"

He went back to the sofa and settled next to her. The medication started to take effect and he knew the pain would eventually recede. His problem was that he would begin to feel sleepy. "I get bad headaches; the doctor gives me these. They are the only thing that helps. Satisfied?"

"You are rubbish at lying."

"I know. But let's leave it there for now. In the meantime, please tell me about the child's photograph and the match you've found."

"I see you used the singular, rather than the plural. You've realised that there is only one *single* match. That's virtually unheard of in the modern day. Guess how many images there are of you?"

"Hundreds."

"Tens of thousands, actually."

"I don't believe you."

"Think about how many times you are recorded on CCTV."

"Yes, but that footage doesn't make it onto the internet."

"No, but it does make it on to GCHQ mainframe."

He managed a silly laugh, aware that the oxycodone was taking effect. "And you can hack into their database."

Her smugness gave him the answer.

"Tell me about the match, before I drift off to sleep."

"Are you alright?" Suddenly she sounded concerned.

He nodded slowly. "The tablets make me drowsy."

"Then go to sleep. I'll tell you later." She got off the sofa and he managed to pull his feet and legs up, stretching out and making himself comfortable. Three minutes later he was asleep.

Woods blinked his eyes open and heard the washing machine completing its final spin. He looked round. Zoe was nowhere to be seen. Relieved that the headache had subsided, he noted that the bin liners were also gone. Perhaps she'd taken them to the charity shop. He stared at the clock. It was 1.20 p.m. He'd been asleep for a couple of hours, but he felt better.

Slowly, he got off the sofa, stretched out and walked gingerly into the kitchen. He snatched up the note from the worktop and read it.

Gone to Horbury.
Should be back by 1.30.
You have some explaining to do!

He screwed up the paper, threw it in the bin, and switched the kettle on. He needed a caffeine fix and at least now he had coffee and milk. He quickly made the beverage and went back into the lounge to sit on the sofa. As he did so he noticed his latest hospital appointment letter had been placed on the TV. Instantly he knew what she would want explaining. He overheard the key turning in the flat door and realised it was truth and consequence time.

"Hi," she said, as she entered. "How are you feeling?"

He managed a single nod. "Fine," he said; nevertheless his reserved appearance must have conveyed his discomfort. He saw her glance at the appointment letter and then she stared knowingly at him.

"Why didn't you tell me?"

He sighed and sipped the coffee before placing the cup on the table in front of him. "I have difficulty talking about it. I'm embarrassed, feel inadequate, and I don't really know how to react to it." He looked at the floor, desperately trying to hide the emotion.

She came to sit beside him. "How many people know about this?" She placed her hand on his.

"My GP, the consultants, and the staff at the hospital clinic, and now you."

She squeezed his hand. "Why haven't you told Pamela, or Holly and Laura?"

"Because I'm stupid. Plus, I don't want to worry them. There's nothing anyone can do about it. They gave me one to two years, and that was eighteen months ago. On the positive side the last two scans have shown the tumour's growth has slowed."

He heard a long drawn-out sigh, but still he couldn't look her in the eye. Then he felt her arm going round the back of his shoulder and the slight pressure from the hug as her head nuzzled into his side. Her sweet, mellow perfume filled his nostrils as she held him close.

"I had no idea. I wish I hadn't come here," she said. "It's the last thing you need right now."

"NO! It's exactly what I need right now. Your visit has energised me. It's given me new life and something else to focus on. You're the best thing that's happened to me in a long time. I want to work with you, Zoe. Believe me on that. I know that together we can find Maria and Faulkner-Brown." Finally, he made eye contact and smiled. "We can do this. I won't let you down."

Very slowly she released her hold and her smile reassured him.

"Please tell me about the child's photograph and the match you found."

She appeared hesitant, and he instantly worried that she was going to leave. However, eventually, after what seemed like an age, she fetched the laptop and slid down beside him. "Look at this," she said, positioning the screen so that he could see. "This was posted on Facebook three months ago. The toddler sitting at the far side of the table is the one Maria uses in her posts. The other five children at the birthday party are of varying ages and I've managed to identify the four-year-old boy whose party it was. I've also identified his parents and where they live."

"Excellent, if we can speak to the parents we should be able to discover who attended the party. And if we discover the toddler's parents we'll be one step closer to finding Maria."

Zoe cleared her throat. "Travis and Melisa Hayden are the parents of the four-year-old boy - both are American citizens who live on Long Island, which is a private island two miles off the north-east coast of Antigua." She touched the mousepad and another tab opened detailing the location. "On the three hundred acre island are a mixture of fifty-six private multi-million pound homes and forty hotel suites which are part of the Jumby Bay Resort complex."

Woods whistled. "Wow. Have you got a list of the home owners?"

"Does the sun rise in the morning?" She pulled the laptop back onto her knees and started typing in the search bar of yet another tab. Within seconds a list of names appeared. She turned the screen and Woods quickly read it. "You'll be interested in this one." She tapped her finger on one particular name. "Iveta Dubova is the only single female owner. And, before you ask, I can't find any images of her on the internet, or any details on her, not even her age."

"You think that's Maria?"

"I think we need to go to Antigua and find out."

"Can we use Google Earth to view the property she owns?"

"We can do better than that. We can utilise the satellite imagery GCHQ have access to. They're much clearer and more detailed." She fiddled around with the laptop and forty-five seconds later he gazed in amazement at the latest images. According to the dateline, they'd been recorded sixteen hours earlier, and, considering Antiguan time was five hours behind British Summer time, that indicated they were taken the previous day at 4.40 p.m. local time.

"How does a single, presumably Russian, female own that? Look at the private mooring and the catamaran. Jesus!"

"Just because it's owned by her doesn't necessarily indicate she lives there. She could be a billionaire and it might be rented out."

"To Maria?"

"Perhaps, or perhaps it's the parents of the toddler who live there. Either way, that's what we need to find out. Maria might work on the island and be employed at the resort; she may know the parents of the toddler."

He noticed her gaze fixed on him.

"Are you sure you are okay to travel?"

"Why shouldn't I be?" He feigned a smirk.

"The problem is how to reach Antigua without MI6 knowing about it."

"If you're worried they'll be watching out for you at the borders, you can use Laura's passport and we'll travel together. They've lost all interest in me these days."

"Yes, right up until the moment you called your former colleagues this morning and nearly had them arrested!" She shook her head and then continued. "Have you not listened to a word I've been saying? Photographic recognition! The second I go through passport control, no matter whose passport I'm using, they'll be on to me."

"Then we need a way of avoiding border control."

"Alleluia! Or we fly to a neighbouring island and bribe a yacht owner to sail us to Antigua."

He nodded, although he was deep in thought. "There is another way, and it's a lot less cumbersome."

Zoe smiled. "We use Pauline Crean's jet."

"But we'd have to fly to somewhere that doesn't have an international airport, or twenty-four hour immigration control."

"Somewhere like one of the smaller islands in Turks and Caicos."

"Been doing your homework, I see."

"Thankfully, Pauline Crean is one of the few people who you haven't managed to ostracise."

"Good. We'd better head over to Hawes. It'll be nice to see her again."

Luthi's mobile buzzed. She fished it out of her handbag and looked at the screen. Then she immediately pressed the green answer button. "Well?"

"Woods has just telephoned for a taxi to take him to Hawes," Coleman said.

"Excellent. They'll be going to see Pauline Crean. Where's her jet?"

"Heathrow. In one of the hangers."

"I would suggest it will be flying up to Yorkshire shortly. Keep me informed." She ended the call and smiled inwardly. She replaced the phone in her bag and leaned forward. She tapped on the Hackney cab's dividing glass panel. The driver turned his head. "On second thoughts, please could you drop me off at The Savoy? I think I'll treat myself to some vintage Dom Pérignon this evening. It's been a good day."

Chapter 3

Tuesday 1st September – Thursday 17th September

Woods and Zoe arrived at Pauline Crean's farmhouse just after 7.00 p.m. Prior to leaving the flat, Woods had spoken to one of his neighbours and arranged for Zoe to store the Smart car out of sight in their garage, which was located just off the car parking area. As the garage was used only for storing odds and ends, there was plenty of room for Zoe's tiny car. Once that had been secured and locked out of the way he had packed a small travel case, making sure to include his passport and medication. Meanwhile Zoe had said that she would purchase clothing in Antigua, as what she wore was all she had with her, and luckily she carried her passport in her bag.

As the taxi driver drove off, Woods held the travel case in his left hand and pressed the intercom button with the other. On the way to Hawes he'd asked the driver to stop at the services on the A1(M) for a quick comfort break, where he had taken the opportunity to telephone Pauline from one of the payphones and check that she was at home. Consequently, they were expected and the intercom was duly answered. Pauline opened the gates automatically and allowed them to enter. As they approached the farmhouse the entrance door opened and Pauline's three chocolate Labradors bounded out to meet the visitors. Zoe froze, the frantic barking clearly unsettling her.

"They're friendly," Woods reassured her. "This is Isambard, Kingdom and Brunel." He bent down to stroke them. He didn't really like dogs, but he made an effort to fuss them so that they wouldn't take much notice of Zoe, who, despite the wagging tails, still appeared uneasy.

Pauline called the hounds to heel and they sped back to her. She sent them inside, and came out to meet her guests.

"Hello Pauline," Woods said. "Are you well?"

She hugged him. "It's been a while."

"Yes it has." Woods introduced Zoe and together they made their way to the farmhouse. "So how have you been keeping?" he asked.

"I'm good. How about you?"

"I'm fine," he lied, noticing Zoe giving a disapproving side-glance.

They went inside and he left the travel case in the lobby area. Pauline showed them into the sitting room and then disappeared off to make coffees.

"Wow," Zoe said, looking around at the exquisite ornaments and expensive furniture.

He smiled. "As you can see, Pauline has good taste. Everything here is top drawer. Wait until you see the grounds, the stables, and the vehicles she owns."

"My ears are burning," Pauline shouted from the kitchen. "What's he saying about me, Zoe?"

"We're just commenting on what a beautiful house you have," Zoe replied.

"Where are Sarah and Scott?" Woods called out.

Pauline appeared with the drinks. "Sarah's working in London, for an investment bank, and Scott's currently in America. He's part of the pit crew for a Moto GP racing team; he loves it. He travels all over the world."

"Nice," said Zoe.

Pauline handed the coffees out and as she gave Woods his cappuccino she asked, "So how is the search for Maria going?"

"We have a very promising lead."

"Just like all the other promising leads you've had."

"Pauline, this one is different. Believe me, this is the strongest lead so far." He looked to Zoe for support, and she didn't disappoint.

"I'm sure we're close to finding her," she said, "and if I find her I'm certain she'll be able to point me in the direction of Faulkner-Brown. It's him I'm interested in."

"Why would you have an interest in that snake?" Pauline probed.

"My mother is in prison because of him, and of all the people on this planet, if anyone needs bringing down, it's him."

Pauline nodded, presumably in agreement. "I share that view. He was the one who murdered Jonathan." She paused for a moment and then said, "so how can I help?"

Woods took a quick sip of the coffee. "We need a big favour. But we'll understand if you don't agree to this."

"Now I'm intrigued."

"We'd like the use of your jet, please," Zoe chipped in.

"What have you got in mind?"

"We need to get to Antigua," Zoe replied. "But we'll have to take an unconventional route. The problem, as always, is the British Intelligence Service. They have an unhealthy interest in finding both Maria and Faulkner-Brown, and they keep tabs on our movements. We have to play cat and mouse. If either of us goes through border control they'll be on to it."

Pauline nodded and Woods' perception told him she wasn't against the idea. "We'd like to do this without any interference from MI6," he said. "We still believe they want to murder both Maria and Faulkner-Brown." Pauline sighed, but he went on, "What we'd like to do is fly to Turks and Caicos, using the airport on South Caicos Island. This is a small — one runway — airport with no international flights, no immigration or customs personnel."

Pauline smiled. "I love Turks and Caicos; I have friends there. I haven't seen them in ages. They live at Conch Bar on Middle Caicos, and they have a yacht which they charter out."

Woods' attention picked up a notch. "Do you think they'd be interested in sailing us across to Antigua?"

Pauline appeared lost in thought and he assumed that she hadn't heard him. "Pauline, do you think they'd sail us to Antigua?" he repeated.

What she said next startled him. "We can all go. I'll come with you. I'll stay with Hillary and John. And if they can't sail you to Antigua, they'll know someone who can. I need Caribbean sunshine right now."

"Great," Zoe said, grinning at Woods.

"Are you sure, Pauline?" he checked.

"Yes, it will take me a few days to organise. The Phenom's currently at Heathrow, undergoing maintenance works. I'll sort out a flight-crew, have it fuelled and flown up here as soon as the work's completed. I'll put the dogs in kennels and ask Lisa to look after the horses. Hopefully by Friday, or Saturday at the latest, we can fly out."

"Sounds good," Zoe said.

Pauline looked at Woods as she spoke, "You can stay here until then. It'll be nice having some company. You can use the spare room and Zoe can have Sarah's old room."

Woods nodded appreciatively and then grimaced.

Zoe's reaction came at lightning speed. "Do you need your medication?" She was already standing and heading towards the door.

He shook his head. "No, Zoe, it's alright, it's just a twinge in my back. I need to get up and stretch my legs."

She returned to her seat and he spotted Pauline looking at her. "What medication?"

"Just painkillers," he replied, before Zoe had a chance to speak.

"Mmm," Pauline mumbled, looking anything but convinced.

Wednesday 2nd September

Luthi could hear her phone buzzing on the bedside cabinet. She fumbled around in the dark, trying to find the light switch. Finally she succeeded, and stared in disbelief at her watch. The name on the phone's display gave her an indication that the call would be important. "Hello Coleman."

"Sorry to disturb you at such an unearthly hour, but I thought you would be interested in this. By the way, where are you? I couldn't reach you at the flat, or at your house in the Cotswolds."

Her annoyance intensified. Whenever Coleman spoke, it always infuriated her. She sucked in her lips and then carefully chose her words. "Interestingly, I reread my job description the other day, and if my memory serves me correctly, nowhere did it specify that the Head of the British Intelligence Service should report to you."

"Maybe someone made a mistake and omitted that clause. It happens."

"Whereas, when I reread *your* job description, paying particular attention to the conditions appertaining to the termination of your employment, I did note that you, a Senior Intelligence Officer, should, in fact, and you may find this amusing, report to *me!*"

"So I've been getting it wrong all these years. I'll slap myself on the wrists and save you the trouble."

She shuddered. She knew she was wasting her time. "Just explain why you've woken me at 3.00 a.m."

"Forty-five million US dollars have been stolen from the CDT-Net National Bank in Venezuela."

"How and when?"

"Yesterday morning. CDT-Net is the largest internet bank in the Americas. The family of one of the managers was taken hostage and she was forced to go into work and transfer the money."

"Surely a transaction of that size has to be authorised."

"Correct. She produced falsified documentation and the transaction went through. Immediately the money disappeared into the ether."

Luthi sighed. "I presume her and her family were then murdered."

"Correct again."

She mulled over Coleman's news for a few seconds, and uncharacteristically he kept quiet. "Can you get someone to monitor the situation on the ground? Keep us up-to-date."

"Are you thinking what I'm thinking?"

"I very much doubt that."

"Well, I've already organised for someone to fly out there and keep an eye on things."

"Good. I might be off mark here, but this has the hallmarks of Faulkner-Brown."

"That's what I thought. You see, great minds think alike."

She groaned. "The first stage of any plan is to obtain sufficient funding for the operation."

"Just what kind of operation will forty-five million dollars fund?"

"Exactly," she said.

"Are the Americans any nearer identifying where and when the cyber-attack will happen?"

"No. The classification remains severe. The current thinking is that the financial markets could be targeted. Close down all the banks and within days the western world grinds to a halt. But there's no proof of that at the moment. However, I don't share that view. I think we should focus on protecting our intelligence-gathering systems. That's what Faulkner-Brown would be interested in exposing. I'm upgrading our own security as of now."

"I see."

"So, what's the latest on Woods?" she checked.

"He's at Pauline Crean's with Field. Crean's been making phone calls regarding the jet and speaking to some old friends in Turks and Caicos about a boat trip to Antigua."

"So it's definitely a green light."

"Yes, that part of your plan appears to be working."

"Good."

"So where exactly are you?"

She hit the phone's red button and threw it on the bed sheets. Coleman needed reining in; the problem was that she'd have to wait until control over Barnes, Field and Woods was in place. And she knew that wasn't going to be easy.

Friday 4th September

The Phenom 300 took off at 2.00 p.m. from the private airfield in North Yorkshire. The anticipated flight time, and the time zone difference, meant they would be scheduled to land in Turks and Caicos at around 5.00 p.m. local time, coinciding with the airport closing down for the day. The plan was that Woods and Zoe would remain out of sight on the aircraft while Pauline and the two pilots posed as the only people on board. The Phenom would be parked up, with the pilots staying overnight and flying out the next morning. Pauline would leave her details with the airport staff, which no doubt would be registered the following morning with immigration on Providenciales Island. Once the airport staff had left, and the area was quiet, Woods and Zoe would sneak out and meet up with Pauline. They would all head to Cockburn Harbour where the yacht and Pauline's friends would be waiting. It would then take twelve days sailing to reach Antigua, where reservations were provisionally confirmed for a three day stay at Hermitage Bay, a privately owned, boutique hotel, located on the west coast of the island. The reservations were in the names of Peter and Sofia McLean - Woods, knowing the hotel would need to register its guests' passport numbers, had contacted his former Detective Inspector and borrowed both his and his daughter's passports, the intention being they would stay at Hermitage Bay first, and then transfer on Sunday 20th September to the Jumby Bay Resort and one of the hotel suites, this being the first available vacancy on the privately owned island.

Woods had spent most of his time resting during the two days at the farmhouse, while their host and Zoe shopped and prepared for the trip. Pauline had insisted that she purchase everything, including Zoe's clothing requirements and travel incidentals. This meant Zoe would not have to use her own debit or credit card, thereby avoiding registering her presence in the area.

Now, as the aircraft reached cruising altitude, Woods looked across at his companions, who were relaxing, chatting, and obviously enjoying the whole experience.

Zoe must have caught his gaze because she mouthed, "Are you okay?"

He half smiled and nodded. He looked down at the glass of champagne and wondered what the next few weeks held in store for them. Would they find Barnes, or would this prove to be yet another dead end? At first he'd been sure it would take them to her; now doubts had crept in. Over the past three years he'd travelled across the globe searching for her and each time disappointment had crushed him, the result being the primary reason his marriage had crumbled and thereafter the separation from his long-suffering wife Pamela. She had been unable to cope with his obsession and the continual mood swings associated with it. He knew she was better off without him, particularly now that she had met someone else. That's partly why he hadn't told her about the incurable brain tumour and his present predicament. In truth, he still loved her. He knew what Zoe had said the other day was a perfect analogy of his behaviour - he should stop acting like an idiot. Maybe finding Barnes would mean he could do exactly that. But what if they failed to find her? How long could he keep this self-inflicted quest of his going, particularly considering his failing health? This would have to be his final attempt - all or nothing. Success or failure: his last hurrah.

Luthi grimaced when her mobile phone's screen informed her it was Coleman calling. For a split second she considered ignoring it, but she'd insisted she be kept up-to-date, so she pressed the green accept call button. "Hello, Coleman. What's the latest?"

"They are currently airborne and on their way to Turks and Caicos."

"How long will it take to sail from there to Antigua?"

"Depends on the weather."

She took a deep breath. "A week?" she proposed, calmly.

"Double that."

"Right, that gives you plenty of time to fly out and get yourself settled on the island."

"Do you want me to start looking for Barnes?"

"NO! We're not even sure she's in Antigua, and, if she is, let them lead us to her. If she gets wind we're snooping around, she'll disappear, whereas she'll at least let Woods see her. Do you know where they are planning to stay?"

"No, I've had someone keeping an eye on the reservations made over the past few days; there is nothing in their names, so unless they are using false ID's I suppose they'll find an available hotel when they arrive."

"Okay."

"Why don't you fly out with me? There's a nice secluded five star boutique hotel on the west coast, adults only, no children. You need a holiday and we could stay there."

"What *I* need is absolutely no concern of yours whatsoever. In fact, spending time in Antigua with you is probably the most unappealing option available to me at the present time."

"Oh well, suit yourself; it's your loss. I'm sure I'll find someone at the hotel who appreciates the finer things in life."

"Do that. Just remember, if you don't deliver on this, I'll ensure that you are completely ostracised from the finer things in life."

"Ahh, you want me all to yourself, I see."

"Goodbye, Coleman. Ring me when they reach the island." She tossed the phone on her desk in disgust.

Thursday 17th September

In an attempt to fend off the onset of hypothermia, Mike Cody pulled his legs up and wrapped the filthy duvet around his cold, shivering, semi-naked body. He'd been sitting on the soiled, stinking, bare mattress, which lay on the stone-flagged floor, most of the day. His bare ankles were securely shackled together, and a three metre heavy chain fixed the shackle to the cellar wall. With some degree of difficulty he was able to stand and shuffle around the room; he could just make it across to the opposite corner of the damp, musty, dimly lit basement, to use the bucket, which, because it hadn't been emptied so far today, smelt putrid. Merely the thought of using it now made him retch. Luckily he didn't need to at the moment, but he wondered when they would be coming with the food and a hot drink, because that is when they would empty it, and for some reason today's sustenance was late. He guessed it to be around 4.00 p.m.; the tiny amount of daylight flickering in, from what presumably used to be the coal shoot into the cellar, gave an indication of that. Of course the shoot had long since been sealed up by a tiny frosted window, which was now so dirty you could hardly see through it, and he had tried unsuccessfully to open it, thinking he might be able to call for help. Although by day three of his captivity he felt the possibility of any help coming may have completely evaporated. No-one would even know he had been abducted; he lived alone — his existence akin to a recluse — in a second floor maisonette flat in West Bridgford, which lay on the outskirts of Nottingham. His contact with his neighbours was nothing more than the occasional nod, to the young woman who lived in the flat below him, and to the elderly gentleman who constantly stared out of the window next door but one. He would see him every time he went to Abdul's convenience store at the end of the road. What about Abdul? Abdul might miss him, but then again it was a long shot. Would a shopkeeper really ring the police and say one of his regular customers had stopped coming to shop there? No chance; the police would probably arrest him for wasting their time. It was never going to happen. The others he had contact with were a small group of people who used the blog sites and chat forums he had visited. But would any one of them miss him? He doubted it, and even if they did, everyone on those sites used pseudonyms or nicknames, his being 'Fish'. They would simply not be able to trace him, which was the whole point of the sites he visited.

His thoughts halted swiftly when footsteps from above broke the silence. He listened carefully and estimated there were at least two, if not three, people up there. Then the light came on and he squinted against the brilliance of the double florescent tubes fixed up on the ceiling. The light switch must have been at the top of the cellar steps because its illumination usually preceded someone coming down and entering the locked room. He waited anxiously as the footsteps, and now muffled voices, descended the steps. The key was placed in the lock and the mechanism clicked as it unlatched and the door flew open. He held his breath as three men, wearing dark clothing, gloves and ski masks, carried an unconscious, scrawny-looking while male, into the room. The young man, dressed only in boxer shorts, was dumped unceremoniously on the floor. His ankles, too, were already shackled together, and the second heavy chain, which had hung from the same wall fixing as the one securing Cody, was used to secure the lifeless body.

"When he comes round, explain what will happen if he doesn't cooperate," the tallest man growled at Cody, in a strong Asian accent. "Are you listening to what I'm saying?" he demanded.

"Y... yes," Cody replied, his voice quavering.

The other two men went back up to the ground floor leaving the tall one, who Cody assumed to be the leader, alone with him. Cody tried not to shake, but the fear and the cold made this difficult.

"What is wrong with you?" the man barked.

"P... please, Sir," Cody's voice trembled, as he tried to produce a brave smile. "I... I'm so cold. I think I'm getting pneumonia. It's freezing down here."

One of the other two men returned with a pizza box and a thermos flask, containing a warm drink. "Here, you'd better eat this, before it gets cold." he said to Cody, also in a strong Asian accent. He passed the food to him and placed the thermos flask by his side, and then he went to the corner to retrieve the bucket. "I suppose we'll need another container, now there are two of them," he said, speaking to the tall one, who nodded agreement.

"Get a few more blankets from upstairs as well, and you'd better fetch another mattress down for the unconscious one. I had to burn the other. It was soaked in blood," the tall man said.

"Right, Boss." The second one disappeared off with the bucket.

The tall man bent down to within inches of Cody's face "I want you to decide what kind of equipment you need," he said, in a calm, cold voice, devoid of any emotion.

Cody wasn't sure what to say. "Err... Yes, Sir... err... what exactly do you want me to do?"

"I ask the questions, not you."

Cody fell silent, frightened to speak. His bewildered look must have prompted the tall man because he said, "You have a lot of equipment, computers, laptops and electronic devices, in your flat. Do you need something similar here?"

The realisation of why he had been abducted struck home. "Is that why I'm here, because of what I can do?"

"I've told you, I ask the questions. Start messing me about and I'll use the machete on you. Understand?"

Cody nodded and stared down on the stone floor at the dark staining. He felt nauseous.

"You comply and give me what I want, and you can go back to your flat unarmed."

The commotion coming down the stairs curtailed the discussion. The other two men appeared with another mattress, blankets and two empty buckets. "Now eat, and we'll see you tomorrow," the man instructed.

Cody nodded again. He opened the pizza box and looked inside. It wasn't his favourite topping, but anything would do; he needed brain energy and one meal a day wasn't enough. He tore a piece off the pizza and took a bite.

"Good," the tall one said. "Come on, we need to go," he told the others. He turned back to Cody. "Cover him up, to keep him warm until he regains consciousness, you've got enough blankets now, and you're going to need his help. His specialism will assist you with what I'm planning." He followed the other two out of the door, locking and securing it after them.

Cody stared at the new arrival, his companion, laid pale and lifeless on the cold stone floor. He moved closer to him and reached out to touch his shoulder. "Are you alright?" he checked. No response. He gently shook the young man. "Are you alright, Mate?" he persisted.

Still nothing. He took hold of the man's shoulders and pulled him back towards the second mattress. With some difficulty he managed to position him on it, and then cover him with a couple of blankets. He shuffled back over to his mattress and opened the flask. He poured some of the contents into the plastic lid, which doubled up as a cup, and sipped from it. It was black coffee, but it was hot and it would warm him up a degree or two. He took another bite from the pizza and stared across at the other young man. He wondered where his specialism lay. Whatever the abductors wanted them to do would be illegal and he had already worked out that no matter what they did neither were likely to get out of this alive. He needed a plan. The problem: he had absolutely no idea what to do next.

Chapter 4

Thursday 17th September – Friday 18th September

Coleman looked up from his Kindle and smiled across at the American woman sitting up at the bar speaking to the waiters. Like him, she was on her own, and she'd arrived the previous day. Since then he'd gleaned that she worked as a travel writer and that she intended spending a couple of days at Hermitage Bay, before moving to the hotels at Carlisle Bay. They'd agreed to have dinner together, this evening, in the restaurant. The food here was exquisite, and Coleman fully expected her to be imagining spending the night with him in his suite, or at least that was his plan.

"Gee, look at that! New arrivals." The woman pointed out to the waiters, looking across as a yacht sailed slowly in to the bay. The hotel's speedboat was already heading out from the beach to collect the guests.

Coleman glanced seawards. "Impressive way to arrive," he called across to her.

"Awesome," she shouted back, nodding. "Obviously British."

"The flag on the boat rather gives the game away," he replied.

"Gee, I hadn't seen it. Look at the guy, tall, skinny, stiff upper lip and reserved. He's got to be British. And the young woman, she looks embarrassed, I wonder if he's her father or if they are married."

Coleman flew up and stared over at the beach, where the new arrivals were being greeted by the hotel staff and given cold flannels to freshen up. *It's them!* He refocussed on the yacht, seeing two women and a guy as they prepared to sail off, waving at the new arrivals. *That's Pauline and her friends!* He knew the staff would bring Woods and the Field girl up onto the sun terrace, where he was, and present them with cocktails and ask them to complete the registration forms. He thought about moving over to the bar and chatting to the American woman there, but she, like most of the Americans at the hotel, had the propensity to speak rather loudly. It would draw their attention. He needed to move quickly. He hurried across to the toilets and disappeared off inside, locking himself in one of the cubicles. He waited, knowing it would take Woods around ten minutes to complete the forms and finish the cocktails, and then they would be shown to their suite.

Ninety seconds later he heard the sound of someone entering the male toilets. Was it Woods? He held his breath. He could hear whoever it was using the urinals and then washing their hands at the sinks. Then someone else entered.

"Nice yacht, Man," an American male voice said. "First time in Antigua?"

"Yes, in fact it's our first time in the Caribbean."

Coleman knew Woods had answered.

"You're kidding me! How long are you here for?"

"A few days." Woods must have finished drying his hands, because Coleman heard him pull the exit door open and add, "Will you be in the bar this evening?"

"That's the plan," the American replied.

"We'll see you there then."

Coleman looked at his watch. 2.45 p.m. He had to move to an alternative hotel. He'd wait ten minutes, go to reception and explain he'd just received an urgent call from home and that he needed to check out and head back to the UK. He'd then quickly pack and hopefully leave without being spotted by Woods or Field. Things like this were annoying, but the way you dealt with them was the important factor. However, he'd already decided not to mention anything about this to Luthi. He could also turn this into an advantage, which might impress her.

When the young man first stirred it was at least three hours since the abductors had left. The cellar's only illumination at this time came in the form of a small amount of borrowed street light, which managed to make it through the dirty, frosted glass windowpane. Cody shuffled over to him. "Hello, Mate. How are you feeling?"

The young man's head moved and he looked dazed. "What have you done to me?" He demanded to know, clawing at his short auburn hair.

"You've been abducted," Cody responded, trying to sound reassuring. "We are both being held here, we're locked in a cellar. There's no way out."

The young man managed to sit, propping himself against the wall. He pulled at the blankets and stared at his ankles. "What the fuck? Who are they? And who the hell are you?" he blurted out.

"My name is Mike Cody. What about you?"

"Harry Zen. Why have they brought us here?"

Cody sighed. "The truth is I don't really know yet. They won't answer my questions, but I get the idea they want us for our specialism, whatever that means."

Zen's eyes narrowed. "What is your specialism?"

"If what I'm thinking is the reason they've brought me here, I don't see it as a specialism; it's more of a hobby."

"What is it?" Zen's voice sounded irate, and why wouldn't it? No doubt he was still trying to come to terms with the predicament he found himself in.

"Computers, mainframes, networks, and the likes. They mentioned the IT equipment I have in my flat."

Zen's eyes were now wide open. "Have you ever been on the Unlimited Darkened Horizons site?"

Cody started at him. How did he know about that? "H… have you?"

"Yes."

"I'm Fish."

"Shit! I'm Buzz."

"I thought you were American. You're not what I imagined at all."

Zen gave a resigned grin. "I thought you were a *girl*."

Cody smiled. "So now we know why we are here. All we need to know is what they want us to do."

"How long have you been here?"

"Three days," Cody replied, shrugging.

"Are they terrorists?"

Cody nodded. "Yes, I think they are, and there is something you need to know." He paused and tried to compose himself. "When they brought me here, and I came round, there was another young guy shackled to the wall. A big strapping, strong and fit lad, and, like you and I, he was dressed only in boxer shorts…" Cody glanced at Zen, fear emblazoned on his face. "He told me his name was Thomas Shaffer. He said he hated Asians and that there was no way he would help them."

"What was *his* specialism?"

"We never got round to discussing it. And at that time they hadn't mentioned anything about specialisms. So it wasn't even on my radar. Anyway he wouldn't cooperate. He told them exactly what he thought and he made derogatory comments about their religion and the Quran." He looked around and again he was shaking. "The next thing I knew, three of them burst in and dragged him to the centre of the room. The one I think is the leader, forced him to his knees, took out a massive machete, chanted what a supposed were a few verses from the Quran, and then beheaded him." Cody looked down on the floor at the dark stained stone flags. "There was blood everywhere, and I thought I'd be next. I was absolutely terrified and I passed out. When I came to, he was gone and they were cleaning up the mess. I just kept throwing up in the bucket. Begging them not to do that to me and saying I'd do anything they wanted. I've never seen anything so horrific in all my life."

"How the hell did they find us?"

"I have no idea."

"Shit! What are we going to do?"

"Do you live with anyone, someone who'll report you missing?" Cody asked.

"Yes, but she's in New York for the next couple of weeks. What about you?"

"Archetypal geek. Live on my own and stare at my PC twenty-four/seven. No-one will miss me."

"Have you any idea where we are?"

Cody shook his head. "It was the middle of the night when they abducted me, around 4.00 a.m. I answered the door and they burst in, knocked me to the floor, gagged me and placed a black bag over my head. Then I felt a needle going in my arm and the next thing I remember was waking up in here a few hours later."

"They grabbed me last night, around ten, on my way home from the pub. A van pulled up, the driver asked for directions, and then three masked guys jumped out and threw me in the back."

"Where do you live? I'm from Nottingham."

"Reading."

"Well, we could be anywhere in the UK. They've all got strong Asian accents, but with a slight northern twang."

"Northern?"

"Possibly Yorkshire."

Zen shook his head, clearly rattled.

Cody thought he ought to clarify his own thinking. "They need us alive, and they need us to cooperate. While ever we do that, we stand a chance."

"A chance of what?"

"A chance someone might rescue us."

"Like who?"

"I've no idea, yet, but the alternative is not acceptable."

At 6.35 p.m. local time, Woods and Zoe strolled into the bar area. It was quite busy, mainly with raucous Americans having pre-dinner cocktails. He raised an eyebrow and smiled at Zoe. "What would you like?"

She looked at the list of drinks. "Margarita, please."

"Two Margaritas," Woods ordered from the cheerful, smiling barman, whose perfectly white teeth contrasted dramatically with his dark skin.

"I'll bring them over, Man, with some nibbles, if you care to sit on one of the sofa-seats looking out across the beach." The barman pointed in that direction.

Pleased, Woods moved away. "Is this okay?" he checked.

"Yeah, Man."

Zoe followed and they settled in a quieter area. It was too noisy at the bar: young Americans discussed what they had been up to that day; it appeared each one was intent on outdoing the other's achievements, their superlatives becoming more and more expressive. Woods noticed a woman sitting just across from them smile at him.

"Their moms and dads have paid for them to be here," the woman said, in an American accent, as she pointed across at the people over by the bar. "They all have very rich parents. It's about showing off. Gee, look at me and what I've got!"

Woods smiled. "Why do they have to talk so loud?"

The woman laughed. "I don't know what you mean."

"Something about empty cans," Zoe sneered.

"I saw you arrive in the yacht. Where did you sail in from?" the woman enquired.

"Turks and Caicos," Zoe replied, before Woods could say anything.

"Gee, you must be celebrities."

"We're going to Jumby Bay on Sunday," Zoe boasted.

Woods nudged at her leg with his foot and shot her a disapproving glare.

"Wow, millionaires as well?"

"Hardly." Woods said, shaking his head.

The barman arrived. He placed the drinks and a bowl of dried cassava on the table in front of them. "Enjoy," he prompted.

Zoe giggled. "Strange glass."

Woods had already tasted his. "Very nice," he said, munching on the cassava. "So what do you do?" he asked the American woman.

"I'm a travel writer. What about you?"

"I'm a retired detective. My daughter's an investigative journalist." He spotted Zoe holding back a smile.

"Ahh... that might explain what happened earlier today."

"Why, what was that?" Zoe asked.

"When you arrived, the guy I was supposed to have dinner with this evening, suddenly started acting strange, and then promptly checked out of the hotel. Perhaps he has some history and has crossed paths with you in your past life as a detective. You may well have saved me."

Woods squinted. "What was he called?"

"Devon, or at least that's what he told me."

"Surname?"

"I only knew him as Devon."

"What did he look like?"

"Tall, neatly cut dark hair, wore a tuxedo and a bow tie. James Bond type - drank Vodka Martini, shaken not stirred."

"You're joking."

"No I'm not. Anthony," she shouted over to the barman who was singing Pharrell Williams' *Happy*, much to the amusement of the Americans at the bar. "What did Devon drink?"

"Vodka Martini. Where is he tonight?"

"He's gone. Took one look at these two and hot-tailed it."

Woods' mind went into overdrive. The woman claimed to be a travel writer. Therefore there was a good chance she would have taken photographs in and around the hotel. "You wouldn't happen to have a shot of him on your camera?"

"Let me see." The woman started flicking through images on her iPhone. "Here's one, taken last night in the bar."

"Can you Bluetooth it to me?" Zoe asked, instantly.

The woman complied. "Do you know him?"

Woods stared at the image. "No, I don't think so." He glanced at Zoe. Her expression needed no explanation, so he winked at her, and rose. "I'll be five minutes." He left her and the American woman chatting. He ambled into the main entrance and over to the reception desk, where a slim, smartly dressed woman was sitting smiling at him.

"Good evening, Sir. Is everything okay in your suite?"

Woods nodded. "Everything is good."

"Excellent. So what can I do for you?"

"Err… a chap checked out this afternoon, just after we arrived. I thought I recognised him. If it's who I think it is, his first name is Devon, but I can't remember his surname."

"Ahh, you mean Mr Coleman," she laughed. "The funny thing is that he thought he recognised you; he too wanted to know your name."

Woods forced an unconvincing half smile. "Did he? Well, it would have been nice to chat with him. Do you know where he went?"

"He said he was going home to the UK."

"Okay, thanks for that." He headed back to Zoe who glanced up expectantly as he approached. "We've got a problem," he whispered, sitting down next to her.

"How can they know we're here?"

"I have no idea, but one thing is for certain; not only do they know we are here, they'll also now know we're using McLean and his daughter's passports. Consequently, they'll know we're booked in at the Jumby Bay Resort. We need to change plans, Zoe, and fast, otherwise if we do find Maria we'll be leading them straight to her."

Friday 18th September

Luthi stared through blurry eyes at her watch. "Jesus Christ," she said, to herself. She picked up her mobile and answered it. "Is it your intention to awaken me every single night with an update?"

"You told me to ring you as soon as they set foot on the island. Besides, it's only 10.30," Coleman protested.

"Yes, well, as no doubt you realise, it's 3.30 a.m. here."

"Okay, I'll ring back in the morning."

"I'm awake now," she snapped. "I take it they've arrived."

"Yes, this afternoon. They are using passports Woods borrowed from Detective Inspector Pete McLean and his daughter Sofia. They are currently staying at the hotel on Hermitage Bay and have reservations at Jumby Bay from Sunday."

"How come you've been able to work this out so quickly?"

"Because I have exceptional talents; you should know that!"

Luthi groaned loudly, and cringed when she thought about the people in the next room.

Coleman nevertheless continued. "I have a friend who's a pilot out here; he regularly flies light aircraft from Antigua to Puerto Rico. I asked him to keep an eye out for the yacht. He rang me the other day, and then I chartered a helicopter. I flew out over the ocean, claiming to be whale watching. I spotted the yacht, realised it was them, and that they'd reach Antigua today. So I checked all today's new British reservations and narrowed it down to one father and his daughter staying at Hermitage Bay. They arrived at 2.45 p.m. Are you impressed?"

She ignored the question. "And they have no idea we are on to them?"

"Absolutely not."

"Good. Keep it that way." She terminated the call, imagining Coleman full of self-gratification. She instantly felt unwell.

Woods smiled politely as he gave his order for breakfast to the waitress, who then disappeared off. He glanced up and spotted Zoe giving him that look again. He knew what was coming. He tried to divert it. "I'm fine," he said, defiantly. "It was yesterday's stress that caused it."

"I didn't realise the headaches were that debilitating. I was worried, and on the point of calling for a doctor."

"As I've said, I'm okay now."

"You need proper sleep to recover from something as severe as that."

"I'm fine on the sun lounger. I slept quite well." He watched her eyes roll.

"You need to sleep in the bed, under the mosquito net, with me."

"No, I do not."

"I promise not to do anything."

He couldn't help chuckling. "It's usually the man who says that."

"What are you frightened of?"

"Nothing. I'm old fashioned. I don't believe it is right for a fifty-three-year-old man to be sleeping with a twenty-four-year-old woman."

"Why is that not right?"

"Because it isn't."

"Don't you find me attractive?"

"What has that got to do with it?"

"So, you do find me attractive!"

Thankfully the waitress arrived and he watched enviously as the spinach and goat's cheese omelette was placed in front of Zoe.

"I wish I had ordered that instead of the scrambled eggs," he said, attempting to move on.

"Maybe tomorrow… After we've slept together."

Now he sensed she was teasing, so he played along. "Maybe. But then again, think what kind of a headache that would cause."

She flicked up an eyebrow and looked seductively at him. "I can be extremely gentle," she said, tucking into the food.

He laughed. "Yes, I'm sure you can."

She winked at him and smiled. The toast, and goat's cheese and spinach omelette in her mouth prevented her from speaking, so he poured some tea. "Can we move on to more pressing matters?" he said.

She nodded. "So what's the plan?"

"We need to fly over the Jumby Bay Resort, or Long Island as it's called on the map. I've had a word at reception and they're checking the availability of a helicopter today. I've told them we won't share."

"How much is that going to cost?"

"1,250 US dollars, for a forty-five minute flight."

"That's expensive."

He shrugged and nibbled at some toast. "It's not a problem," he said, swallowing. "Anyway, I couldn't stand having any loud-mouthed Americans sitting in the helicopter with us."

"You've taken a shine to our American cousins, haven't you?"

"Especially if they come with a spare set of car defenders that I can use."

She laughed. "I really like you," she said. "You're alright."

He felt his cheeks warm and he didn't quite know where to look. "I like you too. I… I just wish you would wear something, well, something with a bit more material to it, and not so revealing."

The apologetic look set her laughing. "You are like my father. And besides, it is thirty-two degrees here. Are you expecting me to wear thermals?"

He shook his head; she sounded exactly the same as Holly and Laura. Then he wondered what his daughters were doing right at this moment in time. What would they make of Zoe? What would they make of him being in Antigua with her?

"What are you thinking?" she asked, bringing him back into focus.

"Nothing," he lied. "Anyway, the problem we now have is that we need to check the Jumby Bay Resort and the mansion houses, and even if we do see Maria from the helicopter, we have to make it appear that this has been a wasted trip and that we're heading home. But we also have to get a message to her."

"I've been thinking about what happened yesterday. I ran Coleman's image through my software, and, surprise surprise, I couldn't find any matches. Which supports your assumption that he is an agent. But there isn't anything on Vauxhall Cross' systems to suggest that he's reported back. Therefore, perhaps it was pure coincidence that he's on the island…"

"No, it was not. Let's be clear on that. He was on the island waiting for us. Perhaps the coincidence lay with him staying here. I mean, why check out as soon as we show up?"

Her nod conceded the point. "Because his true intention is to keep tabs on us and he doesn't want to be recognised when he's following us."

"Exactly. So we play double-bluff: we keep an eye out for him and we continue to look for Maria."

"What if we don't see her from the helicopter?"

"Then tomorrow we charter a boat and sail around the island looking for her again."

"And if that fails?"

"We go to the resort on Sunday as planned, and we spend a few days there. It's the only way to access the private island."

"And if we find her?"

"We explain what's going on and then we head back to the UK, making out it was a wasted trip."

She shook her head. "I have a better idea."

"Go on."

"We find out how he's communicating, and with whom, and we intercept the communications and turn them into an advantage. Put simply, we feed them misinformation."

He grinned. "I like your style, Miss Field."

"Maybe we will sleep together after all."

At 10.30 a.m. local time Woods and Zoe arrived on the outskirts of St John's at the heliport. They completed the necessary registration forms and underwent the pre-flight safety briefing. Then they went outside, onto the veranda overlooking the two helipads, to await the arrival of their private helicopter.

The hotel had arranged for a personal driver, Carol, who would be available for them all day, to collect and take them to the heliport. Carol had agreed that after the flight she would drive them to the hotel and spa at Galley Bay, which was just up the coast from Hermitage Bay. They'd explained that they would like to have lunch there. In actual fact, the previous evening, while Woods lay incapacitated with the headache, Zoe had discovered that Devon Coleman was now staying at that particular hotel. She'd found this out by telephoning the hotels in the area, asking if a Mr Devon Coleman had checked in, claiming she was from Hermitage Bay and that he'd left some personal belonging behind, which they would like to return to him. After five calls she'd struck lucky. What action they intended taking at Galley Bay today, would be dependent on the success of the helicopter flight.

Just after 11.00 a.m. Woods grinned when he spotted the helicopter. He pointed skywards. "Very nice," he said, as the ground crew, comprising of a lady and gentleman, prepared to meet the pilot, who Woods had been told was Canadian. They waited patiently, while the helicopter, with its engine still running and blades spinning, was refuelled. Then they were beckoned by the lady and guided into the aircraft, where they donned the David Clark headsets and strapped themselves in, Zoe sitting up in the front with the pilot — who introduced himself as Patrick — while Woods settled behind them in the back.

"Are you okay in the back, Sir?" Patrick checked, in his cool, calm and authoritative voice.

Woods gave the thumbs-up, pressed the black button on his headset's microphone and answered in the affirmative.

"Good," said Patrick. "Right, I understand that you would like to see as much of this beautiful island as possible, but that you have a particular interest in Long Island and the Jumby Bay Resort. Is that correct?"

"Yes," replied Zoe, pressing the button on her microphone. "We have a friend who lives in one of the houses. I'll point it out to you. We'd like to take some photographs. We can show them to her when we visit on Sunday; we're staying at the resort there for a few days."

"Very nice. Okay, well what I'm proposing to do is take you out over St John's Harbour, and fly around the northern coast to Long Island. Then we will fly anti-clockwise around the tiny island, allowing you to get the photographs you need. After that, and because I have plenty of fuel and no further flights until this afternoon, I will fly you down the eastern coast to English Harbour, then head across to Montserrat, where you can take a look at the volcano. Then we'll make our way back here, flying up the western coast. How does that sound?"

Zoe spun round to look at Woods, her expression an indication that it was fine by her. "What do you think?" she asked, expectantly.

Woods nodded and gave another thumbs-up.

"Excellent," said Patrick, as the helicopter began lifting off and became airborne. He spoke briefly to air traffic control giving details of his initial route, and within seconds they were at 500 feet and traveling at 135 ground-miles per hour.

Woods held tightly on to his digital camera and prepared to focus the telephoto lens. He knew it would only take a few minutes to reach Long Island. He could see Zoe setting her iPhone to video mode, ready to film the island and, in particular, the property owned by Iveta Dubova.

Patrick's voice came over the coms, "This is Long Island," he said, "straight ahead. Which property does your friend live in?"

Zoe pointed. "It's on the south side of the island, going up towards the eastern tip. That one, there!"

"Okay, that looks very nice. Perhaps you could put in a good word for me."

"I'll see what I can do."

The helicopter started to swoop. "I'll swing down and around. Try and get you in as close as I dare. Some of the residents don't like us going too low." He must have seen Zoe bracing herself because he added, "Don't worry, you won't fall out, you're securely strapped in."

Woods looked down at the house and spotted a tall, blonde young woman on the sun terrace, with a toddler at her side; she'd pointed up at the helicopter and the child waved enthusiastically. He focused in and took several photographs. He noticed Zoe waving at the youngster, while attempting to film him.

"Is that your friend down there?" Patrick checked.

Zoe nodded. "Can you go around again?"

"Roger that."

They flew twice around the tiny island and then headed away, off down the east coast of Antigua towards English Harbour. Woods looked on the camera's display and noted he had taken forty-five photographs. He felt an adrenaline rush as he hurriedly flicked through them, looking for the young boy. He leaned forwards, tapped Zoe on the shoulder and offered her the camera. "What do you think?" he said, remembering to press the button.

She looked at the picture. "Bingo," is all she said.

Woods already knew the toddler was the same one Barnes used in her messages. The question now remained: who was the tall, blonde young woman?

Chapter 5

Friday 18th September – Saturday 19th September

Cody stared at Zen when the fluorescent tubes flickered on. "They're here," he said. "Let's see what they have to say. And remember, don't rock the boat."

Zen didn't say anything and the door opened. The three masked men entered. "Good afternoon, Gentlemen," the tall one said, glaring at them huddled together on the mattress. "Do we have two willing helpers?"

"Do we have a choice?" Zen said.

The tall man looked at Cody. "Haven't you explained the protocol to your assistant? Do I need the machete?"

"No. And yes, you have two willing helpers," Cody managed to say, surprising himself that his voice wasn't quavering.

"I ask the questions!" the tall man reiterated to Zen. "Not you! Do you understand?"

Zen nodded.

"Good. I need a list of the equipment you'll need."

Cody looked at Zen and shook his head. "I'll answer," he said. "Everything that is in my flat; if you bring it here we can use that."

"I'm afraid that won't be possible. There is a chance it could be traced through the IPN."

"We can hide it. We have the know-how. That's what we do."

"Yes, and that's what I want you to do, but with new equipment that we provide. Now, write down what you need."

Cody was handed a notepad and a pencil. "Some of this is specialist; it's not available on the high street."

"Write it down. We'll provide it, no matter where it comes from."

With his hand shaking, Cody scribbled away. After several minutes he handed the list back to the tall man. "If you are supposing that we can use it down here, could I point out that it is way too damp and cold? We need to be somewhere warm, dry and with good ventilation. It has to run twenty-four/seven."

The tall one turned to the other two masked men. "We need to make one of the bedrooms secure. Can you sort that?"

"No problem, Boss," one said, looking at the other, who nodded.

"We can use the metal shutters from the shop. And we can strengthen the doors," the other one added.

"How long will that take?"

"A few days."

The tall man turned back to Cody and Zen. "Right, Gentlemen, I'll source this." He waved the notepad in his hand. "Then we'll relocate you upstairs. A word of warning though, if either of you attempts to contact someone via the equipment, or tries to escape, you'll both be running around like headless chickens. Have I made myself clear?"

They nodded.

"Good. Now you can eat. Fetch the food," he instructed the other two, who went back out of the room and thundered up the stone steps.

"When you are working on the computers you will be continually watched, and when you have finished you will be shackled out of reach of them, so forget any idea of double crossing us," he said.

Cody and Zen nodded again, only this time Cody's nod was more pronounced, because he'd already formulated a plan, to do exactly that.

The food arrived and was set down in front of them.

"A treat for you, for being compliant," the tall one said, as the three masked men left the room.

Zen looked through the various containers and bags. "Chinese," he observed. "My favourite."

"Enjoy it while you can," Cody said. Then he stared at Zen. "Did you ever have contact with Hawkeye?"

"No, I saw some posts, but never actually communicated with him."

"He assisted me with access to GCHQ's mainframe. I think he knows someone who works there."

"And?"

"It's him we need, and either MI5 or MI6 on our side."

"But you've just heard what Johnny Jihadi said."

"Stop calling him that. It isn't funny."

Zen's apologetic face appeased him. "Anyhow, it doesn't matter if they stand looking over my shoulder. I can type quicker than their eyes can focus, and I have a way to secretly contact Hawkeye. All I need is a little bit of a distraction from you. Not everything is yet lost. Now get that down you. We're relocating upstairs out of this godforsaken place and away from the constant reminder of what happened to Thomas Shaffer."

Woods and Zoe landed back on the helipad at 12.23 p.m. Total flight time seventy-four minutes. As Woods walked along the path back to the veranda he paused and turned to see Zoe waving Patrick off as he headed back to his base at VC Bird International Airport. They found Carol waiting for them in the reception area. "Good flight?" she asked.

"Brilliant," Zoe replied. "I loved every second of it. Montserrat was out of this world. The power and the devastation caused by a volcano is quite humbling. We as humans think that we control what happens on the earth - I think we're deluded."

Woods nodded. It had been an emotional trip, and she was right.

"Okay," Carol said. "If you're ready I'll drive you to Galley Bay and lunch."

They exited the building and hopped into the car.

"How long will it take to reach the hotel?" Woods checked.

"Ten minutes. Have you made a reservation?"

"Yes," Zoe said, winking at Woods, who was sitting alongside her in the back.

When they arrived Carol dropped them off outside the main entrance. It was grand, luxurious and surrounded by lush vegetation. The décor was white and crisp, yet colonial and welcoming. They entered and spoke to the receptionist, confirming their luncheon engagement. Then they were guided through the entrance lobby and introduced to the restaurant manager, who enquired where they would like to be seated.

"Is it alright if we sit over here, looking at the beach?" Zoe said, already heading to an empty table she clearly liked the look of.

"Of course. Be my guest," the manager replied politely.

Zoe spun round. "Is this one okay?" she checked. Unfortunately her eagerness to reach the table had got the better of her and, because she wasn't looking where she was going, her foot clipped one of the chairs at an adjacent table and she stumbled against it, spilling the drink of the man sitting there. "Oh, I'm terribly sorry," she said, covered in embarrassment. "Please forgive me. I wasn't looking where I was going."

The man, clearly taken aback, smiled. "It's not a problem, no harm done. It was only water."

A waiter appeared, to clean up the mess, and by now Woods was beside the man. "I do apologise. My daughter's a trifle giddy today. We have just been touring the island in the helicopter. You may have seen us, about twenty minutes ago." He pointed up at the sky.

"Ahh, so that was you?"

"Yes, it's a great way to see the island." Woods smiled. He held out his hand. "Greg, he said. "It's nice to meet a fellow Brit."

The man stood up. "Devon," he replied. "Nice to meet you too."

Woods moved on and settled at the adjacent table in the seat facing away from the beach and looking back towards the restaurant kitchen, whereas Zoe had deliberately chosen to sit with her back to Devon Coleman, in the seat nearest to him. She'd placed her rucksack carefully down on the floor next to her. Obviously he couldn't see her beaming face, but Woods could, and was having trouble keeping focused. His eyes were firmly planted on Coleman, who gave the impression he was decidedly uncomfortable by their presence.

The waiter appeared with menus. He took their drinks order and enquired if they were enjoying their stay on the island.

"We love Antigua," Zoe responded, rather loudly. "Don't we, Dad?"

Woods nodded. He could sense Coleman trying desperately to look uninterested.

"Where are you staying?" the waiter enquired.

Zoe gave the answer and the waiter made a comment on how peaceful it was there. Then he disappeared off to sort out the drinks. Five minute later the Margareta and Vodka Martini arrived and the waiter took their order for food, just as Coleman's lunch was being served to him.

"Hang on a sec," Woods said, pointing at Coleman. "I like the look of that. Can I be a pest and change my order to the fish?" He felt a sharp kick to his heel, but he was enjoying this. "And I'll have another Vodka Martini, but this time shaken not stirred," he emphasised. Then he winced as yet another more forceful kick landed on his shin. He looked sheepishly at Zoe, but she was grinning.

"I just need to use the ladies' room," she said, rising and heading out with her rucksack.

She returned ten minutes later. "Got it," she whispered. She placed the rucksack carefully back down on the floor next to her.

Perhaps the alcohol and medication were affecting his mood, but Woods couldn't help smiling.

Coleman finished his meal and didn't have a desert. He stood and prepared to leave.

"Have a nice day, Devon," Woods called across. "Maybe we'll see you around the island."

"Yes, maybe you will." Coleman started to leave and then, almost as an afterthought, he turned and said, "Have a good day, Greg."

Woods didn't respond; his concentration lay elsewhere. "Well?" he said, once Coleman had disappeared out of earshot.

"I have his mobile number and the one he's been calling. The next time he rings it, this will pick up the call." She held up the phone they'd purchased in St John's on the way to the heliport.

"That's a good piece of kit you have in your bag."

"Yes, it is. It searches for nearby phone signals and downloads the data stored on them." She looked over her shoulder, presumably to make sure no-one was listening. "I've got all the texts he's been sending and the pictures he's taken. And I've been able to reprogram his phone so it will also ring us when he calls that number."

"I would suggest that he'll be making a call to it later today. It'll be interesting to see what he says, and who he's saying it to."

Zoe produced a wry smile.

"By the way, you'd make a good actor. I loved the way you accidentally-on-purpose crashed into his table. You should have seen his face. He hadn't noticed us arrive."

"So now he has a problem. He thinks we don't know exactly who he is, but the dilemma facing him is that he can no longer blend into the background. He knows we'll recognise him if we see him again."

"Round one to us. But we too have a problem. We know that the toddler used in the messages Maria sends lives in Iveta Dubova's house, but we don't know if Maria is there, or who the tall, blonde young woman is, and without going to the island we never will."

Now the look she gave him was tinged with coyness. "Perhaps we know more than you think," she whispered. "I've got a surprise for you." She pulled out her iPhone. "Maria does live in that house. Look at this!"

His eyes widened so fast that they involuntary blinked. "Jesus Christ, Zoe! It's her. But how. . ."

"When we flew over the house I noticed that the catamaran wasn't moored to the jetty. Obviously someone was out sailing. I know it's called 'Alaina Bri', so I kept a look out for it."

"Alaina and Brian are her parents' names," he managed to utter, his heart racing. "How did you know it was called that?"

"From the satellite imagery I'd viewed back in the UK, and after a great deal of digging around on social-media sites and TripAdvisor."

"What?"

"Basically, I looked at people's holiday snaps taken in Antigua. Anyway, we actually flew over the cat on the way to Montserrat, so I filmed it. I didn't say anything at the time because I didn't want to raise your hopes, but just now, when I enlarged the pictures in the loos, you can plainly see it is Maria at the helm."

"You are a star, Zoe."

"You can reward me tonight, in bed."

He shook his head. The tears fell from his cheeks. "Three years I've been searching for her," his voice croaked, "and we've finally tracked her down."

"So what do we do now?"

"Let's go back to Hermitage Bay, wait and see what Coleman does, and if he reports back. Then we'll decide."

When they arrived back at the hotel they went straight up to their suite and, while Woods grabbed a couple of beers from the minibar, Zoe changed into her swimsuit, intending to make good use of their private plunge-pool. "Why don't you join me?" she asked, gingerly stepping in. "It's lovely, it'll cool you down."

Woods shook his head, and was about to give his response when the phone they were expecting to ring started bleeping.

"Wait until the bleeps stop, then press the answer button," Zoe ordered. "You can put the call on speakerphone."

Woods followed the instructions and came to sit by the pool. As soon as he heard the female voice he knew who it was.

Luthi glanced at her watch before answering the mobile. At least today's call arrived at 9.15 p.m. and not in the middle of the night. She knew it would be 4.15 p.m. in Antigua. "Yes, Coleman," she snapped. "What is the latest?"

"They've toured the island in a helicopter this morning. Now they are back at their hotel."

"Did they fly over Long Island?"

"How are you expecting me to know the answer to that? I presume they did, but I can hardly follow them in another helicopter, can I?"

"How are you managing not to be seen? They're smart and they'll be watching out, looking for anything, or anyone, suspicious."

"Yes, well you know how good I am. That's why you sent me here."

"The reason I sent you there is because you are expendable."

"I still think you have desires on me."

"Yes, seeing you in a mortuary does sound appealing."

"You and I, in a mortuary together, sounds good."

"For God's sake. I've better things to do than listen to your fantasies. Now, how are you planning to keep an eye on them when they reach the Jumby Bay resort?"

"I have two options: charter a yacht and keep watch from the sea, or, if there are any vacancies, I could go to the resort and keep a low profile."

"I like the sound of the second option."

"Then you'd better organise a cancellation. Hold someone up at Gatwick on a trumped-up charge. I've met someone who I just might be able to persuade to go with me. She's a travel writer, good cover for me if the two of us are together on the island."

"I'll sort it. By tomorrow evening they should have a vacancy and you can be on the island from Sunday. I want to know exactly what Woods and the Field girl are interested in. If Barnes is there, then we move to the second part of the plan."

"Okay."

She finished the call and stayed seated, pondering what Coleman had divulged. Despite her distain for the man, he was actually doing quite well.

Woods noticed Zoe looking pensive. "I suppose this means we have to head back to the UK," she said, sounding subdued.

"Absolutely not! Get dressed. We need to go down to the bar and find Gina. If she's up for it, she can contact the Jumby Bay Resort and explain that she understands there's going to be a cancellation tomorrow. She can ask to be placed on the reserve list. I'll pay for her to have a suite to herself. We'll get in before Coleman has chance. He'll have to make do with watching us from a distance in a boat. Remember, there is always more than one way to skin a cat."

"A particularly annoying cat," she replied.

Saturday 19th September

Rather than waiting for his call, which recently always appeared to come at the most inopportune moment, Luthi had decided to be proactive and ring Coleman. She keyed in his number, pressed the green button, and waited. After several seconds it tripped through to his mailbox. "Hello, it's me," she said, peeved that he was not able to take the call. "Please ring me back when it is convenient for *you*." She placed the phone on the worktop and her focus returned to the beef bourguignon and how it was coming along. She opened the oven door and using her well-worn oven gloves she carefully took the pot dish out. It was piping hot and the gloves weren't as insulated against the heat as they once were. She moved quickly; it was burning her hands and she attempted to place it on the worktop, but in her haste it slipped and crashed onto the stone-tiled kitchen floor. "Damn it!" she cursed, as she leaped backwards to stop the splashing contents burning her legs. She had been looking forward to eating it. Now she would have to clean it up. She bent down and then her phone started buzzing. She looked up and snatched hold of it. The screen informed her it was Coleman. "Why do you always ring at the wrong time?"

"Having a good day, are we?"

"No, I'm definitely not having a good day! I'm hoping against hope that you are about to give me the news that will change that."

"Oh dear."

She sighed. "What has gone wrong this time?"

"I couldn't get a reservation at the Jumby Bay Resort. It was re-let as soon as it became available; apparently they have people on standby, ready to take any cancellation. It's that popular."

"Great, so I orchestrated some poor soul having contraband discovered in their luggage and being detained for nothing?"

"You win some, you lose some."

"Aptly put. Now, what are you proposing to do?"

"I'll charter a yacht and watch from that. It will definitely keep my expenses down."

Luthi smiled inwardly. "I assume the travel writer was unimpressed with your failure to whisk her off to the most exclusive resort in Antigua."

"I wasn't able to contact her, so she's none the wiser."

"Are you absolutely sure that everything is under control?"

"Yes."

"Has it not crossed your mind — for at least one second — that on the yacht you will stick out like the irksome sore thumb you are? Please tell me you are not proposing to drop anchor in the bay and stay there all week?"

"Of course not."

"Well?"

"I've looked at the list of people who have properties on the island and there is one that is owned by an Iveta Dubova. She's the only single female there. I suspect that's Barnes' new identity, because I can't find out anything else about her. She lives on the south-eastern side of the island; therefore that's where I'll be from lunchtime tomorrow. I'll stay there until sundown and I'll keep watch on that particular property. I'm assuming once Woods arrives at the resort, he won't hang around; he'll go searching for Barnes straight away. He's due to arrive there around 2.00 p.m."

"How are you going to know if they find her? I understand those properties are purposefully built for seclusion."

"Yes, but they also make the most of the sea views; that's why watching from a boat is the best option. As for knowing if they find her, I'm arranging for listening devices to be planted in their luggage."

"They're smart; they might spot them."

"No they won't. After dark tonight, their suite is being entered, probably while they are having dinner, and the devices are being placed either on, or in, their clothing. Possibly in Field's bag if it's available. I've got it covered."

Luthi wasn't convinced. "I'm going to send you an assistant."

"I don't need any assistance."

She didn't listen. "They should be with you mid-afternoon tomorrow. Text me the name of the yacht you'll be on, and I'll let them know."

"I work better on my own."

"And I work better when I don't have doubts."

"Who is it likely to be?"

"Paula Hobbs."

Coleman remained silent.

"Surely you and her don't have history?"

"No, she will be fine."

"Good. I'll make sure she's on the morning flight out of Gatwick." The call ended and Luthi glanced down at the bourguignon. She would need to clear up, but she felt better knowing that Coleman would have a partner, someone quite capable of keeping an eye on him.

Cody nudged Zen, who had fallen asleep earlier. "What is it?" Zen asked.

"It doesn't look like they're coming. It must be nearly ten o'clock. Where are they?"

"They'll be having difficulty getting some of the equipment."

"I deliberately picked the most expensive gear. I'd been looking at the latest upgrades and drooling over them last week. We might as well have the best."

"What if they smell a rat?"

"I'll claim I thought they wanted top quality."

"What if they can't afford it?"

"I get the impression that if they can't afford it, then they'll nick it." Noises from above ceased the discussion. "They're here," he said, quietly.

They listened to an array of footsteps entering and leaving the building; it lasted almost ten minutes. Finally, the lights came on. "Brace yourself," Zen said. "They're coming down the steps."

The door unlocked and opened. The three masked men entered. One carried a take-away meal and two thermos flasks.

"We've managed to source the items you wanted," the tall one said, sounding rather pleased.

"Thank you," Cody responded, thinking he ought to show some appreciation.

"When we've prepared the bedroom we'll need your help to set the equipment up."

"Okay," Cody said, nodding his agreement, and reminding himself not to ask questions, even though he had several burning issues he would like resolving.

One of the other two men collected the buckets and disappeared off up the cellar steps, while the second one gave them the food and flasks.

"You'll realise that what we want you to do will have dire consequences, and that discretion is the key to how we'll expect you to operate."

Cody nodded; everything he did on his PC at home was shrouded in discretion. It wouldn't be a problem.

Zen held up a single finger.

The tall man shook his head. "No!" he snapped. "I ask the questions."

"I didn't intend asking a question. I wanted to say that we'll need a really fast broadband connection."

Cody momentarily wished the floor would open up and swallow him. Was this going to be a step too far?

The tall guy ignored Zen and spoke to Cody. "What do you have at home?" he queried.

"BT," Cody replied.

"That's crap. We need something faster," Zen insisted.

Cody started shaking; he tried desperately to calm himself down.

"What about Plusnet?" the other masked men suggested.

The tall one shook his head, clearly annoyed at him. "Keep your mouth closed," he ordered. "I do the talking, not you!"

"I have Virgin," Zen offered up. "I don't have any problem with that."

This wasn't doing Cody any good at all. "W... why don't you see what's available and we'll decide then?" he proposed, his voice filled with fear.

"Leave it with me," the tall man said, heading to the door.

Cody breathed a large, silent sigh of relief, but Zen wasn't finished.

"If you expect us to work on one meal per day, you'll need to know that simply isn't sufficient to maintain our brainpower. We need at least two meals."

Cody screwed his eyes closed. He hated violence, and the thought of what might happen next made him nauseous. The buckets had not reappeared and he couldn't possibly throw up on the floor; he dared not contemplate the consequences of that.

The tall one spun round. "Enjoy this meal, because the next time you'll feast will be when the equipment is up and running. See how not having anything in your bellies for a few days feels. Then you might reconsider making demands. I'm running this show, I decide what and when you eat."

The two buckets were returned and the tall guy took them from his accomplice and threw them across the room, they clattered to the floor. He stepped forward towards Zen and stood on his bare foot for several seconds. Zen cringed. Then the men left, slamming and locking the door behind them.

Cody turned to Zen. "You stupid idiot! Why did you do that?"

"I'm sorry. I thought it was about time we started being proactive."

"PROACTIVE!"

"Yes."

"Jesus Christ, these guys are terrorists! Don't you understand? Our lives are meaningless to them."

"I'm sorry, what more can I say? I made a mistake. It won't happen again."

Cody shook his head in disbelief. "As if things aren't bad enough," he said.

"I didn't know he'd react like that."

"Well, you do now!" The hopelessness of their situation became blatantly obvious to Cody. His mind spun in turmoil; he couldn't think straight any more.

"Let's eat this before it gets cold," Zen proposed.

Cody's blank expression indicated he wasn't listening; he could feel a panic attack starting. Now things were really going downhill.

Chapter 6

Sunday 20th September – Monday 21st September

Woods flicked his wrist and checked the time. It was approaching 6.00 p.m. Daylight had all but faded away. He noticed Zoe watching him. "Come on then," he said. "There's no time like the present."

She came across and squeezed his hand. "It'll be okay. Maria's still the same person she was three years ago, just a little bit older."

Rather puzzled, he thought he ought to comment. "Aren't we all?" he said. He appreciated the sentiment, but the strange choice of words didn't quite fit. Nevertheless, now he had to do what he'd thought about hundreds of times over the past three years. What would he say to her? He'd rehearsed it over and over in his mind, which at this moment in time had developed amnesia. That didn't bother him; yet his nerves were on edge. Abruptly he strode over to the veranda and flopped onto one of the sun lounges. "I don't think I've ever been frightened of anything in my life, and all of a sudden I doubt if I can go through with this. Perhaps it's better if you go alone."

"She'll be expecting you. She'll know we are on the island. All the residents here have shares in the resort. She will have noted the names of arriving guests and she will have put two and two together."

"What if. . ."

"You haven't waited all this time to be put off with what ifs. It's about the here and now! We're here, and we have to do this *now!* Come on, I'll be right at your side."

He struggled up onto his feet and shrugged. "You're right. Coleman should have disappeared by now."

They walked out of the complex and headed off down the pathway that would eventually lead to the residence of Iveta Dubova. Neither of them spoke, which suited Woods, because as the screeching tree frogs echoed in his ears the trepidation spiralled up inside him. When they reached the tall imposing gates to the property he knew this was the point of no return: Vee-one, rotate or crash, he would be airborne in seconds. "And rotate," he said, out loud.

Zoe obviously understood his analogy. "Gear up," she replied, smiling.

He smiled back. "Could you press the intercom for me?"

She obeyed, and five seconds later it was answered. "Hello, Stranger."

The emotions overwhelmed him and he brought his hand up to hide part of his face. He fought back the tears and, his voice breaking, managed to say, "Hello, Maria."

"I always knew you would find me."

"May we come in?" he asked, regaining a little of his composure.

"Of course."

The electronic gate motors whirred and they opened slowly. The two visitors stepped through and into the grounds, which were, even in the darkness, impressive, lit by sporadic low-level halogen lighting that guided them to the house. As they approached, the door opened and Barnes appeared. Woods looked her over, the same slight, slender figure, the same high cheekbones, freckled complexion, deep, dark brown eyes, and curly flowing locks. "You look well," he said.

She stared at him, her expression serious and solemn. "How are the headaches?"

"You know?! How do you know?"

"You would be surprised what I know."

"This is Zoe," he said, gesticulating at her. "She helped me find you."

Barnes smiled and offered out her hand. "Hi, Zoe."

"Nice to meet you, Maria." The two women didn't exactly shake hands; it was more or less a fleeting touch, which you would have missed if you were to blink. "And, by the way," Zoe added, "the headaches are horrible, aren't they?"

Woods frowned. He looked first at Barnes and then deep into Zoe's eyes. Something troubled him.

"Come inside and meet Ben," Barnes said, hastily.

They followed her, and the little boy they'd photographed from the helicopter came running up to them. In his tiny hand he held a large plastic killer whale. "What's this, Ben?" Zoe said, bending down and pointing at the toy.

"This is Orcinus Orca. He lives in the ocean and eats spaghetti," he replied, giggling.

"No, Ben, he doesn't eat spaghetti," Barnes corrected.

"Yes, he does. Aliona said he would eat all my spaghetti if I didn't finish it."

"Get out of that one," Zoe said, smiling up at Barnes.

"Well your Orcinus Orca is a special kind of killer whale," Woods chipped in, "which lives in the swimming pool here, and, unlike all the other killer whales, he's not an apex predator, because when he was small he developed a liking for Italian food."

Barnes' smile and appreciative nod showed his contrived explanation was acceptable. "Whoever said raising children was easy?" she replied.

"Someone who'd never had any," Woods responded. Then he frowned. "Is, err?" His awkwardness indicated he didn't quite know how to put this.

"Yes, he's my son," Barnes admitted, picking him up. "Ben, meet Greg and Zoe."

Woods' smile exuded warmth. "Hello Ben," he said. "What have you and Orcinus Orca been doing today?"

"Swimming in the ocean, chasing speedboats and pelicans."

"Did you catch any?" he asked quickly, guessing Barnes might curtail the conversation, due to the child's imaginary escapades.

Ben looked at his mother and made a sad face. "No, we don't chase speedboats or pelicans, do we?"

Barnes shook her head. "No, Benjamin, we do not." Then she added, "Zoe and Greg were in the helicopter. Do you remember waving to them on Friday?"

Ben nodded and moved the killer whale around, as though it was an aeroplane. He made the noises of a helicopter. "Orcinus Orca lives in the ocean and he can fly like a frigate-bird."

Woods laughed out loud, his humour hiding his rather puzzled thoughts.

"Now you are just being silly, Ben," Barnes said.

"Shall I take Benjamin to the nursery with me?" the tall, blonde young woman, whom they had seen on the sun terrace with him, asked, appearing from a side room.

"Yes please," said Barnes, handing the youngster over.

"You must be Iveta Dubova," Woods declared, smiling at the young woman.

"I'm Iveta," Barnes stated. "It's my new identity. This is Aliona Vetrova, Ben's nanny. I suppose you spotted her Russian accent?"

"Oh, I see." This was probably one of the most ridiculous things he could have said, because his mind was trying frantically to unravel what had just been revealed. He spotted Zoe giving Aliona a knowing look.

"Hi Zoe," Aliona said.

Woods scowled.

"We'll go through to the ocean room," Barnes suggested.

He followed both her and Zoe, who now appeared to have become relatively subdued. He chose to sit away from the women, on a gigantic sofa chair looking out of the triple glazed full-height sliding windows. For several seconds no-one spoke.

"Would you two like a non-alcohol rainbow cocktail? Or, I could make you my speciality: English garden pond!" Barnes sounded somewhat pensive.

Zoe nodded, "I'll give the garden pond a try. It sounds interesting."

"What about you?"

Woods wasn't paying attention. "I'm fifty-four in a few weeks' time," he said, out of the blue. "And until this moment I've never felt the need to strike a woman. Yet now, I find myself wrestling with the problem of who I should punch first. You or her?" His eyes flicked from Barnes to Zoe, "It's a close run thing, but you're just in the lead by a whisker."

She looked down, avoiding eye contact. "I'm sorry," was all she said.

"At which particular moment in time, was either of you contemplating telling me the truth?"

"We had to do it this way, otherwise you would never have come, and you would have stayed in my flat, wallowing in your own self-pity," Barnes said.

Zoe gasped, her exasperated expression making it clear she didn't like the tone of Barnes' observation.

Woods' annoyance grew. "I suppose Coleman's on the team as well?"

Their sheepish glance to one another gave the answer.

"I thought so. It was way too easy getting access to his calls. You and he are both good actors. You ought to go on the stage, young lady. *It searches for nearby phone signals and downloads the data stored on them*," he mimicked. "Yes, sure it does!"

"Sorry." Zoe still wouldn't give him eye contact.

"You're sorry!" Woods' exasperation grew. "'*They're using a different code this time. It's impossible to crack!*'" he mimicked again. "There is no code. They're just messages about Ben! And you knew that!"

"I didn't enjoy lying to you."

Woods' blood pressure was rising. "I assume Luthi is also in on this?!"

"No, absolutely not!" Zoe replied, rather too eagerly.

He glared at her. "Oh, I see? Well what about good old Faulkner-Brown?"

"I can explain, can't we?" she retorted, clearly looking for support from Barnes.

"Let me make you a drink, and then I'll explain everything."

"I'm not thirsty," Woods said, squinting and rubbing at his head.

"Is it the headache?" Zoe wanted to know.

He sighed and fiddled in his pockets, trying to find the tablets. When he'd finally taken the small packet out of his trouser pocket he said, "It's the stress; it's not good for me."

"I'll fetch you some water," Barnes said.

"What, so I can wallow about in my own self-pity?"

"I'm sorry, I shouldn't have said that."

"No, you shouldn't," Zoe barked back. "Perhaps when you've witnessed them first hand you may think differently."

Monday 21st September

Luthi could hear the phone ringing, but for a few seconds she thought she was dreaming. Then she awoke and fumbled around on the bedside cabinet. "Hello," she answered, yawning.

"Are we disturbing your beauty sleep again?" Coleman scoffed.

"Is Paula Hobbs with you?"

"Yes, I've put you on speaker phone."

"Hi," Hobbs called out.

"Hello Paula. So have we found Barnes?"

"Not yet," Coleman answered.

"What are Woods and the Field girl up to?"

"Hard to say."

"What? I thought you were placing listening devices on their clothing."

"Apparently things didn't go to plan," Hobbs shouted. "When the guy arrived at their suite it was empty. He thought they had checked out, so he left the hotel. In actual fact they had been relocated to a beachside suite, supposedly because of a leaking pipe."

"Oh, how convenient for them," Luthi said, sarcastically.

"My sentiments exactly," Hobbs echoed.

"So, what's the plan now?" Luthi wanted to know.

"We try again tomorrow morning in the bay," Coleman said. "This time from a motor boat. I'll use the cover of diving, while Paula keeps watch from within the boat."

"There is another option," Hobbs added. "One of the mansion houses, Great Exuma, as in the island, has just come onto the market. If we could have the financial proof, for the real estate company, that we were serious buyers, we could be shown around the property, the resort and the island."

"I can organise that," Luthi said, becoming interested.

"Hang on a second," Coleman threw into the mix. "Why don't we try the motor boat first and then if. . ."

"NO!" Luthi interrupted. "I like Paula's suggestion better." She looked at her watch; it was 12.45 a.m., 7.45 p.m. in Antigua. "I'll sort out the financial details and have my secretary contact the real estate company tonight. I'll get her to organise for you to meet someone from the company on the island tomorrow. Whatever you do, don't leave without finding out if Barnes is on that island. If necessary, go knock on some damn doors."

"Kneejerk reactions produce mistakes," Coleman announced, clearly not keen on the proposal.

"You are paid not to make mistakes. I'll wait to hear some good news tomorrow evening." She finished the call, immediately placing another one to her secretary.

When Woods came round, he found himself lying on a bed, in a faintly illuminated room, with Aliona sitting in a chair alongside, watching over him. "Feeling better?" she asked.

This time he could recognise the accent. Her English was good, but she still retained that slight burr. He started to sit up.

"Stay down, rest," she said, placing her hand firmly on his chest and gently pushing him back. "Here, sip water." She held a glass containing a straw close to his face.

He took some. "What time is it?"

"11.30 p.m. You have been sleep."

He rubbed his eyes. "Where are the others?"

"Ben's in bed. Iveta, or Maria as you say, and Zoe are in pool."

"I'm washed out, and I'm not usually asleep that long."

"I gave you something. You need rest. Stress no good."

"I know."

"Listen, I doctor. Anxiety, stress, no good for you."

He sighed. "Then why are you employed as a nanny? I don't understand."

She smiled. "The person who employs me chose me specifically for role."

His eyes narrowed. "Just who is the person who employed you?"

"You ask Iveta. Now, get rest. I inform her you wake, feel sleepy. I think better you stay here, where I keep eye on you." She hopped up out of the chair and made for the door. "You like drink - tea?"

"That would be nice. Milk, no sugar."

She left the room and he struggled, propping himself up with the pillows. His head felt woozy and he wondered what she had given him. He looked around the room and considered going outside and confronting Zoe and Barnes, but what about the stress of that? He couldn't face it right now, maybe later, when he felt stronger. There was a knock on the door. "Come in," he said, feebly.

Barnes and Zoe entered; both wore sarongs on top of swimwear, and both looked relaxed. "How are you feeling?" Zoe asked, softly.

Woods scowled. "How do you think I feel? Foolish, used, or simply naive!"

"It was never our intention to make you feel like that," Barnes responded.

"Well, sorry I disappointed you." He glared at her. "Maybe I should just go home. I found what I was looking for. I needed to know you were alright, and the answer is obvious."

"I'm sorry. I don't want you to go home. I totally misjudged the situation. Don't let my mistakes spoil things." She perched on the bed close to him.

As he stared at her, he noticed her eyes were watering. It shocked him. "Emotion; something you try to hide, Maria."

"It's not often I mess things up. Please can we start again?"

"What is it that you want from me?"

"Friendship, mutual trust and respect, and, above all, we need your help."

"What kind of help can I offer you? Look at me! I'm finished."

"No, you are not!" Now the tears came. She looked distraught. "Don't you *ever* say that! You are not finished. There's still a chance. . ."

The knock on the door curtailed the discussion, and this time Zoe answered. "Come in," she said, quietly.

Aliona appeared with the tea. "Is bad timing?"

"No," Woods said. "Come here, Aliona. I'd like to ask you a few questions."

She brought the drink over, handed it to him, and looked thoughtfully into his eyes.

He sipped the tea, it tasted good and it gave him a moment or two to frame his words. "How long have you been here, working as Ben's nanny?" he asked.

"Six months."

"And when you said you were a doctor, just exactly what is your specialism?"

She looked at Barnes.

"Don't look at her," he said. "I'm asking the questions. Look at me!"

"Errm... I not sure should tell you. Sorry." She looked at Barnes again.

"It's alright, Aliona, he's probably worked it out," Barnes conceded. She sighed. "Aliona is a neuro-oncologist. She can't cure you, yet, but she's in regular contact with a team of neurosurgeons and consultants who specialise in palliative care. She can help you. And advances are being made all the time. She can slow down the progress."

"Errm… I can attempt slow down progress," Aliona made clear. "I need do tests first, before know for certain."

Unsure how to react, he said, "I suppose you'll have access to all my medical records." He winked at Zoe, who made a silly attempt at a smile.

"Yes," Aliona admitted.

He stared at Zoe. "Was anything you told me the truth?"

Barnes looked towards Aliona. "Could you leave us alone for a few minutes, please?"

Aliona smiled politely and left the room.

"Yes," Barnes said, when the door had closed. "Most of what Zoe told you was the truth, except a few white lies. It's Luthi we're going after. Faulkner-Brown, Zoe and I, with help from Coleman, have created an intricate spider's web that Luthi is about to become entangled in."

"Is Coleman a double agent?"

"Yes, he is, and don't be fooled by his flirtatious, cocky persona; it's an act. He's good at what he does."

"So, Kozlov is behind this?"

"I said the main players are Faulkner-Brown, Zoe and I, plus you, if you'll agree to help. Kozlov is supporting us and that's why we've been provided with Coleman."

Woods pondered and there was an awkward silence, then he asked something that had been bothering him for some time. "How does Ben's father fit in with all this?"

"He doesn't. He has no part to play in either my life, or Ben's."

"Oh."

"I wanted a child, and obviously the easiest way was to have sex with a man."

"You see, we do have some uses."

"Yes, but not many," she snapped back.

Now he grinned; this was the Maria he knew best.

"Anyway, we get a lot of young, wealthy, virile American men staying on the island, so I monitored my body clock and when the time was right, I chose a suitable candidate. He never knew I became pregnant, and he never will. It was not about love; it was a necessity, that's all. And I'll look after Ben."

He tried so desperately to hold back the smile, but he failed. "Do you know, somehow I knew you were going to say exactly that."

"Well, somehow I know you'll agree to work with us."

"I still don't see how I can help."

"What?" Zoe snapped. "You amaze me! When I first started taking an interest in you I thought you were a prat. A washed-up, useless old has-been. But you are far from that. You have a lightning-quick brain, which focuses in on detail, you have the ability to spot any minute discrepancy, be it in the vocabulary people use or their body language. Anything that doesn't quite add up, you immediately note it. You are brilliant. And I really like you; I mean that." She paused and looked at him.

"Carry on, I like this," he said, smirking. "It's quite good for my ego. Now I understand why you wanted me in bed with you."

Barnes formed a weird look. "The thought of you two in bed together conjures up a strange image," she said.

"It was never going to happen," Zoe conceded. "I was teasing him. He's a nice guy, straight, honest and honourable."

Woods laughed. "I think I'll have that as my epitaph - Greg Woods, nice guy, straight, honest and honourable. You need to write it down, Maria."

She scrunched up her nose. "How about: Greg Woods, a right arsehole!"

"It has a certain ring to it. Make sure you spell arsehole correctly though."

She laughed. "Does this mean you'll consider helping us?"

"Well, other than wallowing around in my own self-pity, I'm pretty free at the moment. So, maybe I will. I disliked Luthi. She manipulated and used everyone around her. I never trusted a word she said. I can't think of a more despicable person, other than Faulkner-Brown. You'll certainly have some difficulty convincing me to help him."

"Keep your friends close and your enemies closer," Zoe said, winking at him.

"So what's the plan?"

"Before I explain that, we have a more pressing matter to deal with," Barnes announced.

"Go on."

"Coleman and Paula Hobbs are visiting the island tomorrow afternoon. They are posing as potential purchasers - Great Exuma has just come on the market."

"So? I thought Coleman was on our side. Can't he deal with it?"

"It's not as straightforward as that. They intend knocking on doors. If Coleman tries to prevent it, his position could be compromised."

Woods grinned. "Right, we'd better organise a little welcoming surprise for them."

Chapter 7

Monday 21st September

Woods and Zoe left Barnes' house quite early and headed to the resort's restaurant for breakfast. The morning sun warmed them as they settled at a table overlooking the beach. They ordered, and while they waited Woods decided to clear the air. It was obvious that Zoe was being guarded in everything she said. Things had changed, and, although he felt slightly miffed by both her and Barnes' actions, he held a modicum of sympathy towards them. In fact, if he was brutally honest, he warmed more towards Zoe than he did Barnes. "Can we at least agree to be honest with each other from now on?" he asked.

"Yes, I'm sorry I. . ."

He held up his hand to stop her. "I know you are, Zoe, and I understand why you did it, or at least I think I do."

She tilted her head and made a silly, lopsided grin.

"Am I right in thinking that *your* real intention is to bring Faulkner-Brown down?"

"Yes," she said, nodding, succinctly. "I didn't lie to you about that."

"But, Maria doesn't know that you are going after him?"

She looked sheepishly at the table in front of her. "Is that a problem?" she asked, quietly.

"No. It definitely isn't a problem. I despise Faulkner-Brown." The look of relief engulfing her took him by surprise. "Correct me if I'm wrong," he said, "but from what Maria disclosed to me last night after you had all gone to bed, as I understand it she wants revenge on Luthi because it was her who prevented us from arresting Williams, Plant, Kingstone and Petrauskas?"

"Yes," she confirmed.

"And the consequences of that meant several prominent people escaped being punished for the heinous crimes that they were taking part in around that time."

"Yes," she repeated. "If Luthi hadn't interfered they would all have been locked up, just as you and Maria had planned. But Luthi wanted the main protagonist dead and silenced, to protect the others and secure her own promotion. Now the only people who pose a threat to revealing what she really did are Faulkner-Brown, Maria and us."

He nodded in agreement. "Maybe Luthi realises that I'm just a washed up, useless old has-been, who poses no threat to her." He formed a sloping smile.

She smirked back, no doubt recognising the attempt at an amusing swipe at what she'd said the previous evening. "Anyhow," she muttered, "it was also Luthi who orchestrated Maria's father being starved half to death."

"I see. So Maria clearly has a motive. And if Luthi hadn't interfered maybe your mother wouldn't have been made a scapegoat."

"Precisely."

"So you share Maria's wish to see Luthi brought to justice?"

"Of course I do. That's why I agreed to work with her."

"But you failed to mention to her your desire to see Faulkner-Brown behind bars?"

"Mmm… I knew they'd escaped together. I didn't know what kind of relationship they held."

"Did she approach you?"

"Yes, Maria contacted me. She'd been told I was looking into things and that I had a vested interest in bringing down Luthi."

"Do you know who told her?"

"She wouldn't say."

"It must have been Kozlov. And no doubt he told her about your wizardry on computers?"

"I didn't lie about that either. I can access all sorts of data."

"Including my medical records!"

"Afraid so," she admitted, pulling that silly lopsided grin again.

Breakfast arrived and they waited until it had been served. Woods poured the tea and then started to tuck into the bacon strips, scrambled egg, mushrooms and toast. He noticed Zoe appeared preoccupied and not very interested in her food. "Are you not hungry?"

She sighed. "I'm worried that I've blown it with you."

"No you haven't. In some ways I have a closer association with you than I do with Maria. She can take care of herself and doesn't need any help from me! She has Kozlov to protect her. And she trusts no-one, so watch your back, especially around Faulkner-Brown."

She stared at him, eyes wide open. "Are you sorry you found her?"

He sighed and thought for a moment. "I don't think so; maybe it's what I had to see. You know, that's she's doing okay."

"Did you ever think for one second that she wouldn't be?"

He smiled. "To be honest, I don't think I did. I just needed to make sure. The reality is that now I feel rather foolish."

"Maria cares about you. She wants to give you the best medical care there is. That's why Aliona is there."

"Yes, but who's paying for this? Aliona skirted around it when I asked her last night. She dodged the question, which indicates to me that she assumes I won't like the answer."

"But does it matter who is paying, if they can save you?"

"No-one can save me."

She pushed her plate away. She had hardly touched the food. "Please don't say that. There is always hope."

"Don't let Maria hear you saying that. She says hope demonstrates weakness."

"Well she's wrong."

He noticed the emotion building. "Listen," he said. "I'd like to see both Faulkner-Brown and Luthi brought down. But, to be honest, I've other more pressing things to worry about. Like keeping breathing."

"Then please don't walk away from Aliona. She can help you, even if you decide not to get involved in Maria's plan. Don't give up on her."

He wanted to smile. "Anyone would think *you* cared about me." He winced as she kicked his leg. "Alright," he said, laughing. "Pain's no good for me."

"Stop making stupid statements. I've told you I care about you. And I meant it!"

"And I care about you too. That's why I've agreed to be involved. I'll do my very best to look after you, and to help you achieve your goals."

"Thank you."

"Right, are you okay about what we have planned for today?"

"Are you?" she checked.

"Yep, let's live dangerously. I trust you can drive a golf buggy."

"We're rather stuffed if I can't. I trust you can sabotage one."

"How hard can it be?" he said, tempting fate.

"Not as hard as obtaining your medical records."

"Well then, we'd better go and get ready. What time are they due?"

"11.30. They are viewing Great Exuma, and then taking lunch here, before they tour the island."

"Good. Let's make sure they have a memorable trip."

Coleman nodded in the direction of the swimming pool, intent on attracting Hobbs' attention to the fact that Woods and Zoe were driving out of the resort in a golf buggy. It was 12.24 p.m. local time. "We need to get after them. It looks as though they are heading north-east. Finish your lunch and we'll make an excuse about wanting a quick whizz around the island in a buggy," he said, standing up and peering out into the distance.

"They must have eaten lunch in their suite," she replied, finishing off her last mouthful of red wine and getting up from the table.

They headed out of the restaurant and into the reception area where the two estate agents were sitting waiting for them. "Enjoyed your lunch?" one enquired, as they approached.

"Delicious," Coleman responded. "Listen, Paula and I would really like to see the island. Would it be okay if we borrowed a golf buggy and had a quick scout round by ourselves? It shouldn't take us that long."

"Sure, I'll organise that for you. Then we can head back to the mainland and you can feed back your thoughts on Great Exuma."

"We absolutely love it," Hobbs emphasised.

"Great! Give me two seconds and I'll get you a buggy."

"There's one just out the front there," Coleman pointed. "We'll take that if it's available." He purposefully glanced anxiously at his watch.

The estate agents clearly got the message. They hurried to reception and one of them returned with the keys to the buggy Coleman had pointed out.

"We'll meet you back here when you've seen all you want of this beautiful island," the estate agent said, grinning broadly as the buggy sped off.

"How fast can this damn thing go?" Hobbs asked.

"We'll soon find out," Coleman replied, pushing the accelerator pedal to the floor. "Sometimes they're derestricted." He paused, while it gathered speed. "I think we're in luck... I might be able to get twenty-two out of it. Hold on tight."

He headed out of the grounds onto the smooth pathway and in the direction Woods and Zoe had taken. "Keep watching for their buggy just up here; it's got a red and blue stripe down the sides. They might be parked outside one of the properties," he said, his attention firmly fixed on the coastal path. Although wide enough for two buggies to squeeze past, the speed limit on the pathway was, supposedly, ten mph. Unfortunately most other people who were out and about were either on cycles or walking, and probably not concentrating as much as Coleman, or expecting someone to come tearing up in the opposite direction.

"I can't see it," Hobbs said. "Be careful up here," she shouted. "We don't want to kill anyone."

Coleman kept his foot planted to the floor as they approached a slight incline and a sharp, blind, left-hand bend.

"Slow down, you fool!" Hobbs yelled.

But Coleman was not listening. He swung the buggy to the left and, at the last second, spotted another buggy, with a red and blue stripe on the side, heading straight for him. He swerved violently to the right, off the pathway, clipping a large boulder with the offside front wheel. The buggy hurtled down the slope towards the headland. He hit the brake pedal hard and his foot went straight down. There was no resistance. The brakes had failed. "Brace!" he shouted, steering straight for a small tree, rather than risking going over the top of the headland.

BANG! The force of the impact sent the buggy careering into a spin, and Hobbs was immediately flung out on to the rough terrain. Coleman managed to stay inside the vehicle, assisted by his gripping onto the steering wheel with all his strength. Finally, the buggy lurched to a standstill.

He looked up to see a young woman, from the buggy they had just avoided, running towards him. It was Zoe Field. He could also see Woods standing at the side of the path watching him.

Hobbs lay on the floor groaning and holding her left ankle.

"Is everyone alright?" Zoe called out.

Coleman ignored her and made his way over to check on Hobbs. "Are you okay, Paula?"

"I think I've broken my ankle. What the hell do we do now?" she whispered, clearly seeing Woods and Zoe.

"They don't know who we are. We'll have to wing it, and not arouse suspicion."

"Are you alright?" Zoe repeated, panting, as she finally caught up with them.

"It was my fault," Coleman admitted. "I'm extremely sorry, I drove way too fast. I wasn't looking where I was going. I think my friend's broken her ankle. I need to get her back to reception, but the brakes have failed on our buggy. I must have shattered a pipe when I clipped that rock up there."

"If we help your friend to our buggy I can run you back," Zoe suggested.

"Do I need to ring for the air ambulance?" Woods hollered, from the path.

They all looked towards him. "No," Coleman shouted back. "I think we can manage."

"We're going to run them down to the hotel, Dad. Their buggy's brakes don't work," Zoe bellowed.

Coleman spotted Woods nod an acknowledgement, so he helped Hobbs up, placing her left arm around his shoulder and supporting her weight so she could keep her left foot off the ground. Zoe took the other arm around her shoulder, and together they walked with her, slowly back up to where Woods and the buggy were.

"You could have killed someone!" Woods said to Coleman when they arrived.

"It's okay, Dad. No-one was seriously hurt."

"No, it doesn't look like it!" Woods scoffed, pointing at Hobbs' ankle.

"Hopefully, it's just a sprain," Hobbs replied, apologetically.

Together they helped her into the buggy and then, while Coleman got into the back seat with her, Woods settled in the front with Zoe.

"I'll drive slowly," Zoe said.

"It's a pity that idiot didn't do the same thing," Woods grumbled.

"I'm sorry. I've admitted I was to blame."

Woods spun round and stared at him. "They shouldn't allow cretins like you on the island. It's for respectable people like us. I'll be having a word with the management when we get back."

"Dad, please don't get stressed. It's not good for you, remember!"

Luthi sipped the Chardonnay and chewed slowly on her inner lip. She glanced yet again at her watch and reconsidered, for the umpteenth time, telephoning Coleman. Why hadn't he rung with an update? She had been expecting his call from around 8.30 p.m. and it was fast approaching midnight. What could have gone wrong? Could he be doing this deliberately, to wind her up? If so, he had achieved it. She strolled over to the window and looked out of her top floor penthouse flat across the twinkling London skies towards Vauxhall Cross. What would she do if things went pear-shaped? "Stop being so damned pessimistic," she told herself. "Things are not going to go pear-shaped. And if they do, deal with them. Turn negativity into opportunity." She jumped when her phone buzzed. She sprinted over to it and glanced at the screen. "Where the hell have you been?" she snapped. "I've been waiting up for your call. Have you found her?"

"Are you sitting down?"

"Put Paula on!"

"I can't do that."

Luthi's heart sank. "Dare I ask why?"

"She's in hospital."

"What?"

"She's fractured her ankle, quite badly. She's in surgery now, having it put back together. She'll be on crutches for the next three to six months."

"What happened?"

Luthi listened with ever increasing dismay as Coleman spent the next few minutes relaying the events leading up to the "small mishap", as he put it. "So you didn't have the chance to find Barnes?" she concluded.

"No. And the problem we now have is that both Woods and Field have seen us. So we can hardly start watching from a yacht, or revisiting the island, because they'll recognise us."

She held her breath for almost twenty seconds, thinking, and then she exhaled deeply. "Turn negativity into opportunity," she said, quietly to herself.

"What was that?" Coleman asked.

"How much is that house on the island?"

"$4.5m US Dollars. Why?"

"Purchase it."

"How much have you had to drink tonight?"

"I'll get the funding authorised and our legal team to sort it out. Then, both you and Paula can be on the island twenty-four/seven, posing as the new residents."

"But we don't even know for sure that Barnes is there. It's one hell of a waste of money if she isn't!"

"She's definitely on that island. That "small mishap" as you call it was no accident. I'll wager my pension on that being a deliberate act of sabotage to prevent you finding her."

"I hope your judgement is better than my driving."

"Good night, Coleman. Don't bother me again until you are on the island and we know exactly which house Barnes is living in." She ended the call and poured herself another glassful. She would sleep soundly tonight.

"Yes!" Barnes shrieked, jumping up and punching the air. She looked across at Woods and then Zoe. "Well done, and well done Coleman. Now she definitely has the hook in her mouth."

Zoe grinned and placed the phone they had just listened to in her bag.

Meanwhile Woods frowned and stared at Barnes. Yet again something troubled him. "Did *you* place Great Exuma on the market?" he asked.

"Not personally, but it was all part of my plan."

"Who currently owns it?" Zoe asked.

"It's registered to a Mr and Mrs Hayden."

"Yes it is," Woods scoffed. "But they don't exist, do they, Maria?"

She shook her head.

"Does Kozlov own many other properties on this island?" he muttered, cynically.

"He doesn't own any," she snapped back. "The FSB own Great Exuma, if you must know."

"Do you own this?" Zoe asked. "I know it's registered to Iveta Dubova, but is it yours? There's no mortgage."

"Yes, I own it outright, under that identity."

"What about the catamaran?" Woods queried. "Who owns that?"

She held up a finger. "It's mine. I take wealthy holiday makers who stay at the resort out sailing on it, and it pays quite well. Why, what is this?"

"There must be nearly four million pounds worth of capital here."

"How very astute of you, Zoe." She scrunched up her nose and looked through the corner of her eye at Woods. "I suppose *you* are going to ask where it all came from."

"A certain London safe-deposit bank, I would guess," he offered up.

"Correct."

"I'd thought Faulkner-Brown had his grubby mitts on that," he said.

"And he thinks Luthi stole it from him," she grinned.

"Oh what a tangled web," Zoe observed.

Woods thought he had better make something crystal clear. "I don't want anything to do with stolen goods."

"And neither do I," she said, firmly. "When we've finished here I'll sell everything and then give the money to charity."

He knew that she supported "Blueberry Woods" and he was not going to challenge that. Considering his current situation, the charity was close to his heart too. "Ever the righteous one," he said.

"I try." She smiled. "How's the headache tonight?"

"I'm okay; the tablets are helping. Thank you."

"Aliona will have the results of the blood tests tomorrow and then she can organise a more appropriate course of medication."

"Why won't she tell me who's paying for this?"

She groaned and shook her head. "Why won't you leave it alone? Why do you have to know?"

"Because I think it's either Faulkner-Brown or Kozlov and if I'm right I don't want to accept it from them."

"You are so far off the mark, you silly man."

He pondered, and then it hit him like a freight train. He uttered just one word, "Pauline?!"

"I swore I wouldn't say."

"How long has she known about this?!"

"Six months. And before you start mentioning conspiring against you, all three of us agreed that if you knew the truth before we'd got you here you would never have come. Isn't that right, Zoe?"

Zoe produced the same silly lopsided grin that she'd used earlier in the day. "Pauline said you were stubborn and cantankerous."

"Two more words you can stick on my epitaph."

Barnes chuckled. "It's going to be one hell of a monument."

"We'll have it made in granite," Zoe said.

"Very funny," he replied. "Wait until I see Pauline."

"When you'll thank her and explain that you never realised she held you in such high esteem," Zoe said.

He nodded. He knew she was right. "Anyway," he said, "from this point onwards can we *all* agree that we'll be honest with each other?"

"Yes," they answered in unison.

The problem he now had was that he didn't believe either of them.

As they had finished speaking, Barnes went to check on Ben, who was sleeping in his bedroom. As she poked her head around his door he stirred, so she went in to settle him back to sleep. "Hello, Sweetheart," she whispered, as she bent down. "How is my little angel?"

"How is Mr Greg?" he asked.

"Feeling better."

"Good, I like Mr Greg." He snuggled up into the covers, stretched out, and then drifted off to sleep without saying another word.

She kissed him gently on the forehead and stroked his short fair naturally wavy hair. "Sleep safe and well," she said, quietly. She tiptoed out of his room and went back to the others.

"Is he alright?" Woods asked, as she walked in.

"He's always alright when he's sleeping. It's when he wakes that the fun starts," she replied. "Would anyone care for a nightcap?"

"Not for me," Woods said. "I think we'd better be getting back to our suite."

"You can stay here tonight with us," she offered.

She watched him look to Zoe. "What do you think?" he asked.

"Yes, let's stay," Zoe agreed. "At least you'll sleep in a bed here."

She smiled inwardly. Deep down, she knew she'd missed him; his straight-laced approach, his no-nonsense, upfront manner, his chiselled features, his tall, skinny build, and his dry sense of humour. She'd hated the thought of him suffering, and seeing him writhing in pain yesterday evening made her even more determined to encourage Aliona in her quest to discovering a cure.

Although she tried to hide it, and she definitely didn't like admitting it, she was worried sick about him. She sensed his pain and discomfort and she guessed he too wasn't exactly playing with a straight bat. The next few days might reveal why that was, but for now she would need to concentrate on other matters, not least of which was Coleman and Hobbs' imminent arrival on the island.

Chapter 8

Tuesday 22nd September

Woods stirred. He fumbled around under the pillow and eventually grasped hold of the mini- flashlight, which he had placed there before falling asleep. He flicked the torch on and simultaneously pulled at the mosquito net, locating the opening section. Finally he reached out and took his watch from the bedside cabinet. In the bright torchlight he could see it was nearly 3.20 a.m. He stepped out from the bed and went to the en-suite bathroom. After switching the light on he used the loo. Then he washed his hands, and while doing so he stared into the large oval mirror, which was fixed to the wall, over the twin wash-handbasins. He sighed; the sight made him realise how old he looked. What was he doing here, with three young women and a very young child? After several seconds of reflection he moved back into the bedroom and, feeling restless, he decided to go and make himself some tea. He pulled on a tee-shirt and a pair of shorts, and then tiptoed barefoot out onto the landing. He went quietly downstairs. The house was in darkness. Everyone appeared to be asleep, but with the aid of torchlight he made his way safely and silently to the kitchen. He bobbed on a light and filled the kettle with bottled water. Two minutes later, with the hot drink in one hand and the torch in the other, he turned off the kitchen LED ceiling spotlights, and headed into the ocean room. The grounds were, as one would expect at this time of night, unlit too, and he settled into the large sofa seat with his drink and then flicked the torch off. He preferred darkness; he could concentrate and think better when there were no distractions. He stared out into the night, considering his options. Barnes had only given him a brief outline of her plan and there were a few minor things that he did not feel totally comfortable with, but one single issue caused him great concern. He needed to discuss this in detail with her because he had come up with an alternative solution. He could not allow her to place her young son in danger. He had to voice his disquiet, and he would do it first thing in the morning.

He finished the tea and leaned forward to place the empty mug carefully on the ornate marble coffee table. Just as he settled back into the sofa chair something outside caught his eye. "What was that?" he whispered, as his heart rate quickened. He squinted into the dark, trying desperately to focus. Then he saw it again; there was definitely something moving out there. Was it one of the palm trees, caught by the wind? "Jesus Christ! There's someone snooping around," he said to himself. He froze momentarily, unsure what to do. Then he took the torch out of his pocket. The shadowy figure came close up to the large glass doors which led out onto the sun terraces and the pool area. He rose slowly and crept towards it. The figure outside took hold of the handle which gradually moved down. It wasn't locked. He prepared to pounce. The latch clicked open and the door started to move.

"What the HELL do you think you're playing at, Sunshine?" he growled, clicking the torch on and shining it at the intruder's face.

There was an ear-shattering scream, followed by, "It's me! You idiot!"

"Maria!! I'm sorry. I thought you were a burglar."

She caught her breath and then laughed as she closed the door. She pressed and twisted the switch on the wall, dimming down the lighting. "You scared the living daylights out of me," she said. "What are you doing down here in the dark?"

"What am *I* doing? What about you, snooping about at the dead of night!"

"I couldn't sleep, and I went to sit by the pool. It's my favourite spot."

"Neither could I, so I made a drink and came in here to think."

"Peas in a pod," she said.

"Don't you get eaten alive by all the bugs out there at night?"

"No, I use a special repellent I bought from the Liverpool School of Tropical Medicine."

"I should have guessed you would do something like that. Actually, my ankles are swollen and itching like there's no tomorrow."

"That's the sand fleas. The locals call them no-see-um! Because you can't. . ."

"See them?" he said, sarcastically.

She stuck her tongue out and scrunched up her face.

"I can imagine what you would say to Ben if he did that to you."

"He does it all the time, behind my back. He thinks I can't see him."

He chuckled at the image that created in his mind.

"Let's sit down," she said. "I sensed you weren't happy when I spoke to you earlier; that's partly why I couldn't sleep. Would it be better if I outlined the whole plan?"

He nodded, so they went to one of the gigantic sofas and seated themselves next to each other. He looked at her and instantly knew she was amused by something. "What's so funny?" he asked.

"You. Shorts and a tee-shirt?"

He frowned and nodded at her attire. "Well, that doesn't exactly leave anything to the imagination, does it?"

"It's what I sleep in."

"Doesn't the air conditioning work in your room?"

"It dries my throat and eyes. I don't have it on."

He understood.

"Would you care to explain what's troubling you?" she prompted.

"There's a few things, niggles I suppose you'd call them, that I think we need to iron out, but my main concern relates to using Ben as bait. I'm absolutely, totally and unreservedly against it. And it amazes me that you appear to think it's a good idea."

"He'll never be placed in danger."

"Maria, the second Luthi knows about him, he's in danger. And he always will be, while ever she's alive."

She looked out of the windows, clearly mulling over his point. He spotted her chewing at her inner lip, evidently deep in thought, so he stayed silent.

"If I don't use Ben, Luthi will organise for my mother, or father, or my brother to be abducted, and they are 4,000 miles away. I won't be able to control what's happening to them."

"I appreciate that, but to have Coleman disclose you have a son and then for him to convince her that if he kidnaps Ben and holds him to ransom you'll comply with their demands, is way too risky."

"But Ben won't be kidnapped. He'll be here with me all the time. It's a trick. Luthi will be none the wiser."

"And what about Paula Hobbs?"

"She's going to be on crutches for the next six months; she'll be going home. Then Coleman will be on the island on his own, living up on the headland in Great Exuma. He can claim Ben is held captive there and that he has someone looking after him. He's a convincing liar. Luthi will swallow it."

"What if Luthi tells Hobbs to stay, or sends a replacement?"

"We'll cross that bridge when we come to it. And if Hobbs stays on the island I might subject her to the same treatment that she put my father through."

He frowned, unsure what she meant.

"Paula Hobbs was the agent who organised my father's abduction and torture. I appreciate she acted on orders from Luthi, but nevertheless she played a significant part in him nearly being starved to death."

"Maria, don't try to kid me. The one thing I know about you is that you would never subject anyone to torture. Would you?"

She tweaked up her nose and formed a resolute pose. "Probably not."

"Probably?"

"Alright, you win. No, I wouldn't!"

"Thank you. So if Hobbs stays, your plan starts to unravel."

"We'll deal with it."

"I have a better idea."

She squinted. "Go on."

"Coleman doesn't mention anything about Ben. Instead, he claims to have uncovered that you and I have some kind of deep bond with each other, and his suggestion would be that he abducts me, rather than Luthi taking one of your family back in the UK. He could rightly claim he's discovered that you are attempting to extend my life with some new treatment, and obviously, if I'm not around to receive it, then I would die quicker. That's good leverage. I'm sure Luthi would go for it."

She frowned. "I thought we did have a special deep bond."

He glanced at her, wondering if what she had said was tongue-in-cheek, but the impression he received made him think she was deadly serious. "Well, I suppose we do have," he replied, grimacing inwardly, in case he had said the wrong thing.

"Good." She nodded and smiled warmly. "Then if Hobbs stays you could actually be held in Great Exuma by Coleman and she would be none the wiser. She'd assume everything was in order," she said slowly.

"And that would also apply if Luthi sent a replacement."

"And if neither of those two scenarios occurred you could still stay here."

"Yes."

"And if you were held by Coleman he could ensure you secretly received your medication."

He nodded succinctly.

The smile she produced took a while to form, but then out of the blue a tear fell from her cheek.

"What's the matter, Maria?"

"I'm touched that you would do something like that just to protect Ben. That means a lot."

"I like him. He's so full of energy and mischievousness. He knows exactly how to wind you up."

"Yes, he's an expert at it," she admitted. "And he likes you too."

"He knows you won't approve of what he's saying, but he says it anyway. He even knows what your response is going to be. You should be so proud of him."

"I am," she conceded. "But he has the ability to drive me up the wall."

"That's what kids do; it's how you deal with it that is important." He paused, and then said, "Nevertheless, do you accept my amendment to your plan, or not?"

"It sounds good. So what were the other things troubling you - or niggles, as you supposed I'd call them?"

"Top of the list is good old. . ."

"Faulkner-Brown?" she interrupted, before he could finish.

"Got it in one."

"What can I say?"

"That you want to see him behind bars too."

She shook her head dismissively. "We'll have to agree to disagree."

"I can't believe you just said that. Three years ago you told me you would never trust the man, you were sworn enemies, and you wanted me to arrest him. What's changed?"

"I still don't trust him, but now I understand him, much more than I did before. And you won't accept this, but under that belligerent exterior there is a really decent, intelligent, intellectual guy."

"What?"

"You heard me."

He was taken aback. For several seconds he struggled to form a response. Eventually he asked, "What exactly happened in that chateau?"

"Williams killed Petrauskas, and Faulkner-Brown killed Williams, Kingstone and Plant."

"That's what I thought. And with Williams, Kingstone, Plant and even Dudley out of the way, no-one was left to testify against him or Luthi."

"So?"

"Are we on the same planet, Maria?"

"Yes, we are. But Williams had implied that he and I would be given a new identity and a job working with Luthi; yet she had told you she wanted everyone, excluding me, arrested as they came out of the chateau, but it was her who arranged for the abduction of the librarian, hence preventing you and me communicating. So not only was she interfering with our investigation, she was also double-crossing Williams, and the first thing *he* tried to do when we reached the room was kill Kingstone. So he'd lied to me all along. And Faulkner-Brown told me that Williams had planned to kill all of us! Every single one of them was a liar!"

"Yes, I know that, and Pauline was right when she said you can never believe a liar, even when they're telling the truth."

"I'll never know if Williams intended killing me. The impression I held was that he would protect me, but he'd been a double agent, skilled in convincing people he was on their side."

"What you appear to be forgetting is that Faulkner-Brown instructed Dudley to kill me!"

"That's not how he sees it. He says it was never their intention to kill you, they just wanted you off the investigation and out of the way. He claims that if I hadn't have been in the room with you, Dudley would have rushed in and saved you. That was the plan, but of course with me being there Dudley couldn't do that. Therefore when you collapsed McLean and I came to your rescue. The poisoned coffee has a set time before it takes effect. Dudley knew exactly what he was doing."

"And you believe him?"

"Yes, I believe him, but I also appreciate the risks they took were stupid and that you could still have been killed."

"So, placing that to one side for a second, I'm assuming you are prepared to overlook the fact that Faulkner-Brown killed Dudley, Williams, Kingstone, *and* Plant."

"They were all killers."

He stared at her, his mouth agape, his bewilderment staggeringly obvious.

"I know exactly what you are thinking."

"Do you, Maria? Do you *really* know exactly what *I'm* thinking?" he could no longer hide his anger.

"You're making comparisons with what I did."

He shook his head and immediately knew he needed to calm down. He took several long, deep breaths and gradually slowed his heart rate. No doubt she saw this because she asked if he was okay. With his breathing under control he finally responded. "For once, you are completely wrong, Maria. I wasn't bloody thinking about what you did. I know why you did it, and I accepted your reasoning. As far as I'm concerned, the world is a much better place without arseholes like Peter Glendale."

"So what were you thinking?" she asked, sheepishly, pulling her fingers through her curls.

"That you are keeping something from me; that you're being economical with the truth. After all, it wouldn't be the first time, would it?! You and your high morals would never allow Faulkner-Brown to go unpunished. Never in a million years. I know you too well, Maria."

She sighed and started chewing at her inner lip again.

"Well? I'm waiting."

Her eyes narrowed to no more than tiny slits. "I know that Zoe wants both Luthi and Faulkner-Brown brought crashing down. She's never mentioned anything about him to me, but I can read between the lines. If Faulkner-Brown and Luthi are discredited then Zoe's mother might be able to get her sentence reduced." She glanced at him, but he remained stone-faced. "Anyway, Faulkner-Brown also knows what she is up to and he will deal with her."

"And the reason you are willing to overlook his past?" He was not going to let this point go unanswered.

"Because, like me, apart from the really terrible things he's done, he's also done some quite remarkable things. He's helped so many people across the world, all of whom were living in dire situations, and he's provided them with better lives, and a future."

Woods turned up his nose. "Are you absolutely sure about that?"

"Yes, absolutely. He's not the person you think he is. Trust me on that." Suddenly she appeared crestfallen. "And please try to persuade Zoe not to go after him."

He closed he eyes, and after a while he blinked them open. "I don't know what to say."

"If I'm willing to overlook his past, doesn't that prove something to you? If Little Miss Moral High Ground, as he calls me, can accept he's not a bad person, why can't you?"

"I don't know," he said, sighing yet again. "I'll tell you what I will do... I'll speak to Zoe, but don't forget, her motive is helping her mother, not forgiving Faulkner-Brown because he's done something good. I'll let her make up her own mind."

"Okay," she nodded, appreciatively. "Thank you, yet again. Now, is there anything else bothering you?"

"Can we just go over the plan, and please can you make sure you don't leave anything out?"

"Okay."

"Right, we agree that Luthi wants both you and Faulkner-Brown silenced."

"Yes. She has come up with a plan that she thinks will do just that and give her worldwide recognition."

"Yes, but little does she know that we will turn her worldwide recognition on its head. She'll be finished and totally discredited, and then both Faulkner-Brown and I can forget about her, and live out our lives in relative peace, without having to keep looking over our shoulders."

"Or so you hope." As soon as he had uttered the word hope he knew what was coming. "*Know!*" he added, quickly. "You don't hope, you *know!*"

She grinned. "You see, you do take notice of some things I say."

"I'm just not sure Luthi is going to fall for all this."

"Listen, perhaps I didn't explain it as well as I could have last night. Let me try again."

He shrugged, indicating his willingness to give her a second chance.

"You'll appreciate the majority of the entire world's intelligence agencies are currently focusing in on the jihadist fighters of IS, ISIS, ISIL, Daesh, or whatever else you prefer to call them. Every conceivable resource is being utilised in the fight to prevent terrorist attacks."

"Yes, of course."

"The problem is the jihadists are now experts in modern telecommunication networks. Not only for recruiting followers, but also in different forms of cybercrimes; in a nutshell, they have become cyberterrorists. They pose a threat to a nation's security and its financial health. The biggest fear now is cyberwarfare, where cybercrimes, such as financial and data theft, and espionage, cross international borders and pit nation against nation."

"And that's why Zoe's skills are vital."

"Exactly. Have you seen the amount of equipment she has in the computer room? It's working twenty-four/seven monitoring the Dark Web, and specific international communications."

"Did she set it up herself?"

"Yes. She's a very skilful young woman."

"So, if I understand this right, Zoe is ahead of the game."

"Yes. Six months ago the CIA were given information that there were plans for a massive, prolonged and coordinated cyberattack on the western hemisphere. The problem is they currently have no idea where this will originate, or who the perpetrators will be. Some say it'll be the Russians, others think it will come from the jihadists, some say North Korea, others say Iran."

"But we know for certain it *won't* be the Russians," Woods said, winking at her.

She nodded. "The Russians fear they will be implicated - i.e. East against West. That's why they have an interest in what we are doing, and that's why they have offered assistance. Our plan will prevent the attack, discredit Luthi and exonerate the Russians, whose image in the world is far from outstanding at the moment."

"And it will clearly show that Luthi is not the right person to be leading the British intelligence services."

"Exactly."

"So Luthi thinks Faulkner-Brown is involved with the Russians and plans to attack the British Intelligence Service's mainframe?"

"Yes. Faulkner-Brown has been drip-feeding misinformation to British spies about a supposed attack on GCHQ. That's why Luthi is in the process of spending millions tightening up security."

"And all this is being monitored and recorded by Zoe."

"Correct again."

"And Luthi's plan is to obtain control over you and get you to disclose the whereabouts of Faulkner-Brown. She'll force you to use Zoe's skills to prevent the cyberattacks on the intelligence-gathering agencies, and then she will claim responsibility for defeating the criminals, and she will dispose of you and Faulkner-Brown and probably Zoe and me."

"Bingo. Only we'll be the ones coming out on top and she'll be the one rotting away in prison."

"Err… I hate to mention this minor point now, but what if the cyberattack is being planned by the jihadists? Don't you think they'll feel rather upset and come seeking retribution if you scupper their plan?"

"No-one will know we were responsible. The Russians will take the credit for defeating the cyberterrorists. We'll slip away into the night. Don't you think it's an almost perfect plan?"

"It's the word 'almost' that I'm having difficulty with."

"Oh, ye of little faith."

"You said that to me once before, when we were having a discussion with Gerrard Crean."

"And I was right then too."

"That's not how I remember it, but anyway it doesn't matter. I suppose even the best plans have some uncertainties."

"Is anything else troubling you?"

"Only the headaches."

"As I said yesterday, Aliona will have your treatment sorted within the next few days," she reminded him, yawning and stretching her arms.

He nodded. "Look, you're tired, you'd better go back to bed," he said.

"What are you going to do?"

"I'll stay here. It'll be light soon."

"Then I'll stay with you," she replied.

"Suit yourself."

She inched closer and leaned against him, snuggling in to his side. "I'm glad you are here," she said. "I've missed you."

"I missed you too." He felt slightly uncomfortable with her being so close to him, but when he looked down at her, she was drifting off to sleep, so he remained quiet. Five minutes later he also fell asleep.

He awoke when the door to the ocean room opened. He looked down. Barnes was now snuggled into his lap, fast asleep. He turned around slowly to see who had entered. "Hi Zoe," he said, quietly. "Maria's asleep."

Zoe came closer. "Oh, so I see," she said, staring down at Barnes. "So you don't mind sleeping with a half-naked woman in your lap, but you won't go to bed with me."

"She's not half naked, and keep your voice down," he whispered.

Zoe raised an eyebrow, tilted her head and nodded at Barnes' tee-shirt. "She looks half-naked from where I'm standing."

He noticed it had ridden up and instinctively moved his hand, intending to pull it down. Then he decided against it. "Can you do it, Zoe?" he asked, anxiously.

She started chuckling. "What are you frightened of?"

Now Barnes stirred, waking up. "Hi Zoe," she said, stretching out and causing the tee-shirt to ride further up.

Woods looked the other way, much to Zoe's amusement.

Barnes tugged her attire back in place. "Sorry," she said, looking embarrassed.

"Don't apologise, he's loving every minute," Zoe said, obviously enjoying the situation.

"No I am not," he snapped. "I was asleep! I didn't even know… err… your tee-shirt was… err…"

"Showing your bits and bobs," Zoe said, finishing the sentence off for him.

Both women looked at his horrified expression.

Chapter 9

Tuesday 22nd September

Mrs Pat Middleton walked nervously up the steps and through the entrance doors into Reading Police Station, which, even with its fairly modern-looking sharp clean lines, had a sinister appearance. She went to the front desk and waited patiently while the fresh-faced young policewoman finished writing something on a form and then looked up at her.

"Good afternoon," she said, softly, not really knowing the protocol or procedure.

The policewoman no doubt noticed how unsettled she appeared, because she asked her if everything was alright.

"Yes, err, no. I mean no. I'm so sorry dear." She became flustered. "I'm a little overcome," she said, nearly in tears. "This is my first time in a police station."

Thankfully, the policewoman demonstrated some empathy by producing a friendly smile and speaking quietly, saying, "There's nothing for you to be afraid of; we're here to help… Now, what can I do for you, Mrs?"

She took a deep breath. "Mrs Middleton," she answered, adding, "My daughter's partner has disappeared and she's asked me to report him as a missing person."

"Okay, I'll need to ask you a few questions, but why hasn't your daughter come in herself to report this?"

"She's in New York, until the end of September."

"I see. What's your daughter's partner's name and how old is he?"

"He's called Harry Zen, and he's twenty-two." By concentrating on the questions, Mrs Middleton regained some of her composure.

"And where does he live?"

"In a flat on Addington Road. I have a key. I've been to check, and he's not there. I asked some of the neighbours, and they all said they'd not seen anything of him since the middle of last week. His mobile phone is switched off and we can't reach him."

"Could you tell if anything was missing from the flat, such as some of his clothes, or his travel documents, things that might indicate he's gone away for a few days?"

"I didn't go through the drawers. Should I go back and check? Am I looking for his passport? I could ask Jen where he keeps it." Then she frowned. "But he wouldn't have gone away without telling her, and he's supposed to be at the university. I've telephoned his tutor and he hasn't seen him since last Wednesday."

"Has he ever gone missing before?"

"No." But then she thought she ought to add, "I don't think so."

"Does your daughter usually live with him?"

"Yes. She works at the university. She's in New York doing research. She'll be back on the thirtieth."

"They've not been falling out recently, have they?"

"No. My daughter's really worried about him. So am I. He's a nice young man. They've been together three years."

"What about his parents? Could he have gone to stay with them?"

"His father died when he was young, and his mother lives in Cornwall. I've already telephoned her and she's not spoken to him since July. They don't have much contact."

"Any siblings he could have gone to see?"

"He's an only child."

"What about friends?"

She groaned. "I think they are mostly from the university. He uses his computer quite a lot; maybe he has friends through that. Social media, is it called? But he and Jen are very close; he would have told her if he'd intended going off somewhere, and he would have texted, or called her." Her tone became tense. She didn't feel she was getting through to the young policewoman, who appeared to have a somewhat indifferent attitude to what she was saying. "What if he's lying injured somewhere, or even worse?" she said, shaking her head and scowling.

"Please don't get upset, Mrs Middleton. Usually there's a perfectly good reason behind someone's disappearance. Most people turn up after a few days."

"Have you not listened to anything I've said?!"

"Yes, of course I have. Maybe he's gone off somewhere and lost his phone, or perhaps it isn't working. Have you telephoned the local hospitals?"

"Yes!" she snapped, but then said quietly, "I'm sorry, yes I have, and there's no record of him being admitted, or of anyone in there who they don't have an identity for."

"Okay, I'll get you some forms to fill in."

Mrs Middleton sighed. Now she would have to complete forms. Why couldn't the policewoman do that for her? It wasn't as if she appeared busy. She started to think she was wasting her time and perhaps ought to walk out, but what about Harry and what about her daughter, Jen? She had promised her she would do this. She would have to stay and complete the paperwork. Hopefully then the police might start taking the matter seriously. She stood tapping her fingers on the counter and waited while the policewoman disappeared off. Two minutes later, the forms were handed over.

"If you need any help, give me a shout," the policewoman said, leaving a biro on the counter nearby.

It took fifteen frustrating minutes to complete the paperwork and Mrs Middleton had to ring her daughter in New York twice to obtain some of the information required. Eventually she placed the biro down and held the forms in her hand, not knowing quite what to do with them.

"All done, Mrs Middleton?" the policewoman asked, obviously seeing her staid expression.

"I think so. I've answered all the questions."

"Do you have a photograph of Mr Zen?"

"Yes. Jen said you'd need one, so I brought these." She fished three pictures out of her handbag. "That one is the most recent," she pointed out.

The policewoman took them and, using a stapler she had removed from a drawer, she fastened the photos to the forms. "Right, I'll give you these," she said, passing a handful of colourful leaflets over, which she had also taken out of the drawer.

"What are they?"

"Useful information, telephone numbers, and a few websites you might like to visit. In the meantime, I'll register this," - she waved the forms in the air - "and someone will be in touch."

"Thank you," she uttered, in a tone indicating she was anything but grateful. She folded the leaflets up and crammed them into her handbag. As she left the police station she couldn't help thinking that her time would have been better spent searching for Harry on her own. She didn't really expect anyone would make contact with her, and supposed she would have to keep telephoning to chase up the matter. Nevertheless she had done what her daughter had asked her to. In the meantime she would keep visiting the flat and hoping against hope that Harry would turn up.

Cody squinted as the florescent light tubes flickered into life, and simultaneously he heard numerous footsteps descending the cellar steps. "They're here," he said to Zen, whose eyes widened in anticipation. The two men huddled together, on the filthy mattress, wrapped in the quilt and blankets, to protect themselves from the cold, damp atmosphere within the basement. The keys rattled in the lock and the door opened. The same three masked men strolled in.

"Hungry?" the tall one, the one the others called Boss, mocked, not waiting to be answered. "Well, we're going to move you up to the bedroom. One at a time, and, provided there isn't any trouble, you can have a meal later today. I assume the emptiness of your stomachs is a reminder of the consequence of making demands?"

Cody and Zen briefly nodded, although, in actual fact, they had eaten since the Boss had stormed out, late on Saturday night, saying he would starve them until the equipment was up and running in the bedroom. The masked man who came each evening to empty the slop buckets, who they had christened Sahib, had brought them the odd snack — Mars bar, packet of crisps, Snickers bar, and even a sandwich, plus the odd can of coke — which they had then devoured, under strict instructions not to mention anything about it to the Boss.

"We've set the equipment up," the Boss went on. "We've had one of our cousins sort it. He's a bit of a whiz on computers, so he'll be able to monitor what you are doing, and spot anything untoward."

Cody held back a smile. He doubted what he said was anything other than bluff. And even if it wasn't, the so called cousin would need to have exceptional observational skills to monitor what he would be doing.

The Boss pointed at Zen, saying to the other two, "We'll take him first."

Sahib moved swiftly, unlocking the chain from the cellar wall, and then he and his colleague, who they'd nicknamed Abbas, pulled Zen onto his feet and frogmarched him out of the room and up the cellar steps, while the Boss stayed staring at Cody, who, shivering, rewrapped the quilt and blankets quickly around himself.

"Your assistant needs to know when, and when not, to speak," the Boss muttered, almost to himself.

Cody nodded. He dare not say anything.

"Keep him in line and I'll reward you."

Cody nodded once more. Although he doubted Zen would speak out of turn again - following Saturday night's debacle Zen had become passive and resigned to the fact that they were dealing with fanatical terrorists, who would stop at nothing to obtain their goals.

"I'm expecting you to gain access to the Ministry of Defence's mainframe," the Boss stated, more or less as an off-the-cuff remark.

Cody swallowed, his mouth dry, the minimal amount of spittle he had produced not assisting him. He could feel himself tensing. His breathing became laboured. As much as he tried, he could not stop himself shaking.

"Are you alright?" the Boss checked.

"S... sorry, Sir, yes. I have panic attacks... when I'm stressed. I'm sorry." He bit hard on his lip, frightened the Boss would react badly to the news, and his shaking intensified.

"Do you need a paper bag?"

"No, Sir. It is best if I calm my breathing and try not to be anxious. I'm sorry." Now his voice quaked.

The Boss' stance appeared to mellow. "It's okay. Take a few deep breaths. Would a drink of tea help?"

"Yes," Cody replied, knowing it probably wouldn't, but thinking the time taken to go and fetch it would give him a break from the intimidation and possibly calm him.

"I'll make a drink and see how your assistant is behaving. They should have secured him by now. Are you sure you are going to be alright?"

"Yes, Sir, thank you."

The Boss disappeared up the stone steps, leaving the door open, and Cody refocussed on slowing his breathing. As he did this, he blocked out the fact that his abductors wanted access to the mainframe of the Ministry of Defence. Throughout his captivity, and particularly since he had learned that his computer skills were the reason he was being kept alive, he had tried to second-guess what they wanted from him. Now he knew, and one of his greatest fears had been realised. The question remained: what specifically did they need from the MOD? It must be related to the conflict in Syria, or Iraq; it had to be one or the other. But which one? The British weren't involved in the fighting in Syria - Parliament had voted against it. Maybe things had changed, or were about to. The descending, echoing footsteps curtailed his thought process, and significantly increased his anxiety. The three men returned, the Boss carrying a mug, which he passed to Cody. "Drink this, it's hot, and then we'll go upstairs."

"Thank you, Sir." While he sipped the sweet tea Cody's shaking started to diminish, and gradually he regained some control. He gave an apologetic look at the Boss. "I'm sorry, Sir."

"You can access the MOD's mainframe, yes?" the Boss asked.

Cody glanced fearfully up at him. "It's the thought of what you want me to do once I'm in there that frightens me."

"But you can get in?"

Cody nodded. "Yes, with a lot of luck and Godspeed."

"Excellent. I knew you would be able to do it. If you succeed we'll release you unharmed."

Cody sighed. "But, even if you spare my life, which I doubt you will, I suspect what you want me to do will result in me being hunted by the intelligence services. Then I'll spend the rest of my days in jail."

"Are you Christian?"

Cody grimaced and shook his head.

"What religion?"

Cody looked sheepishly down at the bloodstains from the beheading. "I don't have one," he admitted.

"Everybody should have one. You could become Muslim, study the Quran, and join us in our fight against the western states."

Yet again Cody nodded, although it wasn't in agreement to becoming a Muslim, it was an involuntary response to his fate being sealed. His only way out of this was to contact Hawkeye, get a message to MI6, and attempt to discover exactly where they were being held.

"Unlock the chain," the Boss said to Sahib, who responded accordingly.

Cody struggled to his feet, the blankets dropping to the floor. He was handed the heavy chain, and he prepared to shuffle towards the door. "There is one last thing that I have to let you know," he said quietly.

"What is that?"

"I need my reading glasses to work on a PC. I'll get headaches if I can't see properly. I have to concentrate for long periods of time to do what you want me to."

"Are they in your flat?"

"Yes, on the bedside table."

"I can get them," offered Sahib. "At this time of day it shouldn't take me much more than ninety minutes to reach his flat. I can be back by five o'clock."

"Is there anything else you'll need from there?" the Boss wanted to know.

"Some warm clothes?" Cody replied, shrugging hopefully. He held his breath, would the request be granted?

"No, you're less likely to try to escape wearing just your boxer shorts. Besides, it is much warmer upstairs."

"Okay," Cody responded, trying to appear downbeat. "It would help if I had my watch," he offered up, more as a last-ditch suggestion.

"It's not one that transmits a signal if you are lost, is it?" Sahib enquired, grinning, causing his accomplices to laugh.

Cody shook his head. "No, it's just an ordinary watch," he lied. "It should also be on the bedside table. It helps me remain calm if I know the time. I have a thing about the time."

"Get his watch. It can't do any harm, but I want to see it before you give it to him. I'll need to check it," the Boss concluded.

"Right, Boss," Sahib said sharply. "Let's get him upstairs and secure. Then I'll shoot off."

Cody shuffled out of the room, glad to see the back of it. With some difficulty, he made his way up the stone steps, the others close behind. Although he supposed that the three masked men didn't spot this, he'd been rejuvenated. He could now look forward to getting his watch back. He knew the Boss wouldn't spot anything out of the ordinary with it, and he would feel easier if he knew the time. More importantly, he could make good use of the watch's special features.

When he reached the ground floor room, disappointingly the curtains were drawn; hence it was shrouded in darkness. Nevertheless, he gingerly made his way across, towards what he thought would be the staircase up to the first floor; with no interference from the others, he pressed on. He must have been heading the right way. Unfortunately, as he shuffled past an array of cardboard boxes, presumably from the equipment's packaging, the chain he carried, which was secured to his ankle shackles, caught on one of the boxes, causing him to stumble forwards, falling into the window reveal and up against the curtains. The others rushed to his aid, unaware that, as he had gone down, he had caught a glimpse of the street and the car parked outside.

Once Cody had slowly and carefully made his way up the staircase it took the three men less than five minutes to secure him in the first floor bedroom. They then left him alone with Zen, locking the bedroom door behind them as they went out. As in the cellar, both he and Zen were tethered by their respective chains, which were now fixed to the solid internal wall by a strong metal eyelet at mid height. In addition to this, the chains had a second fixing just above skirting board level, which, unless unlocked by the men, restricted their movements to no more than a few feet around the new double mattress that lay on the pale carpeted floor below the fixing points.

Cody looked around. The bedroom walls and ceiling were freshly plastered and, although the plasterwork had dried out, it wasn't painted and gave the impression of recent refurbishment works having been undertaken in the room, which measured approximately twelve by sixteen feet. A new radiator fixed to one of the other walls provided heat, and positioned along the window wall were two separate tables with a couple of PC screens on each one. He saw four screens accompanied by a keyboard and mouse compilation. A conglomeration of IT cables, extension leads, and PC boxes festooned the area below the tables, and two grey low-backed swivel chairs were positioned centrally in front of all the equipment. Unfortunately, the way they were secured meant they couldn't access the equipment without the lower chain locks being released. So any thoughts of using it without their captors' knowledge were out of the question. In addition, and rather regrettably, the internal window frame had been completely covered with a strong metal shutter which prevented daylight from entering, and them from seeing out. Consequently, artificial light illuminated the room, and was comprised of two small wall-lights and a central single rose fitment: all with low energy lightbulbs. However, the switch on the wall next to the door was within their reach, so they could control the lighting. Cody had deduced that the conditions they now faced were far superior to those in the cellar and, since being left in there, he had spent the majority of the past three hours assessing his surroundings, while Zen had made the most of the new mattress and lay quiet and sleeping next to him on it.

Eventually, Cody decided to break the silence. "What do you think?" he asked.

"To what?" Zen mumbled, coming round.

"The room!"

"It's a shit-hole, just like the basement."

"Don't be stupid; this is much better."

"Is it? The only thing that will be better than this is death. Because that's what we are facing!"

Cody sighed. "Maybe there is a way out of here," he said, nodding towards the equipment.

"They're going to be watching everything we do."

"So what are you saying? We just obey them and await the inevitable?"

"I don't see there is any other option."

"Your girlfriend might have reported you missing?"

"I told you, Jen's in New York until the end of the month, and by that time we'll both be dead. Once they get what they want, we become surplus to requirements."

"It'll take weeks, if not months, to give them what they want. And we'll require access to the PCs twenty-four/seven."

Zen's face lit up with interest. "You know what they want?"

"The MOD's mainframe," Cody said, grimacing.

"You've got to be kidding me!"

Cody shook his head.

"When did they spill the beans?"

"The Boss informed me, while you were being brought up here. And before you ask, that's all I have been told. The worrying part is what they want us to do once we're in."

Zen's eyes narrowed. "They'll want to nuke the States." Then he laughed nervously.

Cody though, wasn't amused. "Don't even joke about that," he snapped. "It's not funny, and besides, it's impossible. The USA's defences would destroy the bombs before they got anywhere near them."

"You think?"

"I know!"

"Not if they were fired from a sub, say just off the coast in international waters."

Cody stared, eyes wide open. "No, they can't want that! You're being stupid."

"Am I?"

"Yes, you are."

"Well, don't come crying to me when they tell you to press the button."

Cody shivered. The thought filled him with dread.

"What are you thinking?" Zen asked.

The front door banging shut downstairs indicated someone had returned and Cody did not get the chance to answer. The bedroom door was unlocked and Sahib and Abbas appeared - both were wearing masks. The Boss must have been busy elsewhere. Sahib passed Cody a pair of spectacles. "Are these what you need?" he asked.

Cody nodded. "Thank you," he said, putting them on. "Yes, that's better. I can see."

"Right, here's your watch. The Boss checked it and you can have it." He handed it over to Cody. "The Boss also says you can have a feast. Is Chinese okay for you?"

Zen nodded.

"Yes, please," Cody endorsed.

"Give me your orders then, Gentlemen." Abbas asked.

"Chicken and green peppers in black bean sauce, with fried rice," Zen piped up.

Abbas looked to Cody.

"Gluten-free battered chicken in chilli plum sauce with chips, please," Cody replied.

"Does Zac do gluten-free?" Sahib asked.

Abbas shrugged. "I don't think there is a need for it round here."

"It's not a problem if they don't," Cody said, making out it wasn't important.

"Ring round a few Chinese takeaways. See if any of them can deliver gluten-free battered chicken," Sahib insisted.

"I don't want to cause any trouble," Cody managed to say, his voice stuttering.

"We'll sort it. The Boss wants you to eat well, because tomorrow you start working for us."

Cody looked at Zen who smiled at him. "I didn't know you were gluten-free, Mate," he whispered.

"Yes, I am," Cody lied, knowing the first small part of his plan had passed off without incident.

Chapter 10

Wednesday 23rd September

Luthi pulled the phone from the inside pocket of her jacket and keyed in the security code, seconds later pressing the speed dial number for Hobbs. She waited for the call's connection and then listened to the ringtone. "Hello Paula," she responded, as soon as her subordinate answered. In a quiet voice, scanning the train carriage and watching the other passengers, she asked how Hobbs was feeling.

"The painkillers help, but mobility is the problem. I need crutches to get around."

"What's Coleman doing?"

"Actually he's been really good, looking after me and dashing about trying to keep an eye on Woods and Field. He's out now, on another boat, scouring the island from the sea. He left at first light."

"Excellent," she said, delighted with the update and that he hadn't let things slip. "Well, the good news is that the Great Exuma sale is being fast-tracked. The lawyers are confident you should have the keys tomorrow. When is Woods scheduled to leave the resort?"

"Saturday, but Coleman hasn't seen much of him. He thinks he may have located Barnes and is spending his time with her."

"For once I agree with him."

"Consequently, he's arranged a second viewing of Great Exuma this afternoon, just to get us back on the island, saying we want to measure up for new furniture. He's planning to snoop around some of the other houses, while I stay with the estate agents, discussing contractual matters."

"Good; he is taking things seriously. I was starting to think I might have needed to replace him."

There was a pause. "Err, are you considering pulling me out?" Hobbs enquired, her voice shaded with an air of foreboding.

"Not unless you want me to."

"No, certainly not. It's just that I feel rather incapacitated."

"That won't be a problem. I need you on the island keeping an eye on things, particularly when we've located Barnes. Owning a property will work in our favour. I'm pleased I sanctioned it."

"I understand. Any news on... the... err. . ."

"No further news," Luthi interrupted, knowing full well Hobbs was referring to the anticipated cyber-attack. "I'll update you with an encrypted message when I hear anything."

"I understand," Hobbs repeated.

"Right, good luck this afternoon. Let me know what happens."

"I will."

Luthi ended the call and slid the phone back in her jacket pocket. She checked her watch; it was 12.05 p.m.

A bespectacled Cody fidgeted around on the grey swivel chair, trying desperately to find a more comfortable position. The problem: the ankle shackle and the heavy chain securing it to the wall. Because of the chain's length, even with its lower fixing point unleashed, which allowed him to reach the desk and equipment, his seating position was restricted. Had it been half a metre longer things would have been bearable, but that was not the case, and, due to the pressure placed on the ankles, he was now sitting hunched over the keyboard, suffering severe pains in his lower back and legs. Zen too had complained to him about the constricted position and suggested they might ask for it to be rectified but, on second thoughts, both decided not to risk the wrath of the Boss.

When first allowed to operate the equipment, yesterday evening, after their promised Chinese meal, Cody spent the first hour and a half tidying up the wiring below the desks. No-one else, including Zen, appeared to understand that, without the wires being neatly tied together and perfectly aligned, he could not concentrate on his work. Nevertheless he had used cable-ties that Sahib had provided, to achieve the desired effect. Since then, he and Zen had only moved away from the desks when needing to use the buckets. They had spent the full eighteen hours setting the data-monitoring and decrypting systems in motion, and then fine-tuning and testing all the equipment. The cousin whom the Boss claimed to be a bit of a whizz on computers, had been there all the time, watching closely as they worked, and Cody quickly surmised his wizardry amounted to nothing more than a basic knowledge - something that most people, who regularly used systems, could self-develop. The parody was that they had christened him Bill Gates, which he had taken as a compliment; yet another indication of his intellect.

Now Cody stretched out his arms, grimaced and contorted his back, letting out a prolonged yawn.

"Are you alright, Man?" Bill Gates asked.

"I could do with a break. I need to sleep."

"I think we all could," Zen said. "I'm knackered."

"Zen and I will have to take two-hour alternate shifts from now on. The systems need constant monitoring. We have to act the second we're in, because access and security codes are constantly checked. Once we're there we need to authorise and validate our access, otherwise we'll lose it."

"So you'll be working round the clock?" Bill Gates checked.

"Absolutely." Cody produced the slightest of winks to Zen.

"Until we have access, we can't risk leaving the screens," Zen reinforced.

"What am I supposed to do?" Bill Gates grumbled. "The Boss said I'd to keep watching you, whenever you were on the computers. He didn't say anything about twenty-four/seven cover!"

"Maybe he thought you'd realise," Zen said, his voice tinged with sarcasm.

"I'll ring him."

Cody nodded at Zen. "You take the first break, Harry; you look shattered."

Zen struggled up out of his chair and shuffled across to the bucket. While he urinated, Cody watched Bill Gates, busy pressing some buttons on his mobile phone. "Hello, Haziq. It's Kaleem," he said. "I need someone to come to the house while I go home and get some sleep. It's been eighteen hours and they are still at it."

There was a short pause, presumably while Haziq spoke. Then Kaleem explained the need for the twenty-four hour working. "They're proposing to do alternate two-hour on and off rotas, so they can watch for a connection."

Another short pause. "It might it take days," Kaleem said, looking at Cody, who nodded quickly, in agreement.

A third and much longer pause. "Right. Thanks, Haziq. I'll see you later." The call ended. "Okay, this is what he wants," Kaleem said, apparently oblivious to the fact that, unless he was using false names, Cody and Zen now knew what he was called and suspected the Boss to be Haziq. "Zen can have his break now, while you monitor the systems. I'll secure him to the wall and then I'll leave. Someone will be here in a couple of hours to feed and swap you over. They'll stay with you until I get back later this evening. I'll be doing the night shift from now on, and the others will split the day shift around their work in the shop and the taxis."

Cody nodded, amazed at how much information he was gleaning. He would use it later.

"The Boss trusts you more than him," Kaleem said to Cody, pointing at Zen, who by now was at the mattress. "And I'll check what you've been doing. If I discover you've tried to contact anyone, he loses his head and you lose a leg."

"I'm not going to do anything stupid," Cody said, trying desperately to sound sincere. "I know you'd find it. All I want to do is help you and then get out of here. The Boss said I could become Muslim."

"That's good to hear, Man. Islam is the only way, for all of us, and Allah is the all-powerful and all-knowing creator and judge of everything in existence," Kaleem replied, as he secured Zen's chain to the lower fixing point. "You need to become Muslim too, Man," he said.

"I will," Zen responded, sounding sceptical.

"Okay, get some sleep," Kaleem replied nonchalantly, as he went towards the door. "I'll see you tonight," he shouted, locking it behind him.

Cody turned around and looked at Zen. "Now the fun starts."

"Just remember, it's my neck which is literally on the line."

"I know, along with my leg. But they'll never discover what I've been doing. If I can hide my communications from the security services, I'm sure I can fool four dumb terrorists."

"Please be careful."

"I will. Now go to sleep. I'm contacting Hawkeye."

Barnes wandered out onto the sun terrace, wearing a bikini under a cover-up sarong. She found Woods and Aliona sitting together, playing with Ben by the pool. As soon as he saw her, the child came running across. "Mr Greg's headaches are better," he shouted.

"That is good news. How come you know?"

"Aliona asked him. She's pleased, and wants him to keep taking his medicine."

"So do I," Barnes replied, smiling across at Woods, who, she could see, was eaves-dropping on the conversation.

"Me too," said Ben, darting back to him. "Keep taking your medicine, Mr Greg. It's better than Calpol, which is no use whatsoever."

Woods frowned and laughed.

"Benjamin! Who told you Calpol is no use whatsoever?" Barnes enquired.

"You said it to Aliona, the last time I had a fever."

"Oh, maybe I did. Well, it's good for some things."

"But not fevers," he said, giggling. "Can I go in the pool?" he asked.

"Yes, but be careful."

The little boy, already leaping through the air as Barnes' words faded away, crashed into the water causing a large splash which soaked her.

"Benjamin!" she hollered.

"Sorry," he spluttered, resurfacing. He grinned and drew back his hand as though he was going to splash more water on her.

"Benjamin!"

"Go on, Ben," cheered Woods, laughing.

"No!" She spun to face him. "He doesn't need any encouragement from you, thank you very much! It's hard enough keeping him in check as it is."

Woods shook his head dismissively. "It's good to have some fun, Maria. Loosen up."

She jumped out of the way as more water came towards her. Before she could say anything, Ben dived down and surfaced at the far side of the pool. "Sorry," he yelled, spluttering, then he tweaked up his nose and laughed.

She looked at his cheeky grin. Normally she would have chastised him, and made him leave the pool, but Woods was right. He was always right. She needed to be more considerate and heed his advice. She meandered across to where he and Aliona were sitting. "Perhaps I should let Coleman take him, and then at least I'd get some peace."

Woods tut-tutted. "Don't even joke about it."

"I know…" she responded. "I love him to pieces. I just wish he would calm down. It's like having a whirling dervish. If only I had his energy."

"Me too," said Woods, waving across to him, and giving him the thumbs-up.

"Come in the pool, Mr Greg." he shouted.

"Maybe tomorrow."

"Maybe now?" Ben obviously wasn't taking no for an answer.

"We'll see." He turned to Barnes. "So what do we have to do today?"

"Nothing, Coleman has everything in hand. You and Zoe can stay here and keep out of the way. That fits with his plans."

"Where Zoe is?" Aliona questioned.

"As usual, working on the computers. She said she would be ten minutes, and that was an hour and a half ago."

"Zoe and the intelligence services are searching for the same thing. Why can't she let them find it?" Woods queried. "She has access to their systems. She could pick it up there."

"She also has contacts on the Dark Web," Barnes answered. "She stands a better chance of finding it than Luthi and her chums."

"Okay, I appreciate that, but she told me that several of her friends have not been online recently. She was concerned about their lack of activity."

"Jump in the pool, Zoe," Ben called out.

The others looked up to see her heading towards them. "I'll be in later, I need to have a word with your mother first."

"Be quick," he bellowed, hurling a tennis ball into the water near to where she walked.

She skipped out of the way to dodge being splashed. "I'll get you back for that," she shouted, bending down, snatching the ball out of the water and throwing it in his direction. He dived down, avoiding it.

"Ah, ha, ha," he shouted, when he resurfaced.

She arrived where the others were sitting and joined them.

"Sorry," Barnes said, thinking she ought to apologise for his behaviour. "He's being a monster today."

"It's okay," Zoe acknowledged, waving the issue aside.

Barnes though thought she looked troubled. "What's wrong?" she asked.

"I think I've found what we are looking for. I'll have to check a few facts, but I'm definitely on to something."

"That's fantastic news!" Barnes exclaimed.

"And at least I now know why Fish and Buzz have not been online recently."

The look of bewilderment on Woods' face demanded more of an explanation, and Zoe continued. "Fish and Buzz are my contacts from the web. They're hackers too. I didn't know their identities, or even what gender they were. We all keep a low profile. It is better that way, less chance of being exposed. Anyhow, Fish contacted me this morning, claiming to have been kidnapped by an Islamic terrorist cell, possibly based in the north of England, somewhere ninety minutes' drive from West Bridgford where he lived. He's given me his real identity; his name is Mike Cody and Buzz is Harry Zen. They are being held by four masked terrorists, all Asian, with what he suspects are Yorkshire accents. They are led by a man, possibly in his late forties and possibly called Haziq. One of his three subordinates is in his early twenties and could be named Kaleem. The other two are most likely in their mid-thirties. They all have a connection to some kind of shop, and appear to run taxis."

"That's a lot of possibilities," Barnes observed.

"What do they want?" Woods asked, frowning.

"Access to the MOD's mainframe."

"Do they?" he huffed.

Barnes wanted clarification. "Why?"

Zoe shrugged. "Good question, which they don't yet have an answer to."

"Why have they contacted you?" Woods queried.

"I once assisted Cody with accessing GCHQ's systems. He assumed I had a contact on the inside, possibly a relative. Quite perceptive, don't you think?"

Barnes nodded. "And?" she said.

"They want me to contact MI5, so the terrorists can be arrested."

Barnes' mind suddenly went into overdrive. "I wonder if this is a trap... set by Luthi."

"That's what I need to check," Zoe said. "I'll go through her systems and telecommunications - see if there is any indication."

"How long will that take?" Woods wanted to know.

"All day."

"Is there any more information on where they might be held?" he asked, clearly going into detective mode.

"Cody says they're in what appears to be a traditional small terraced property. The house is undergoing, or has recently undergone, internal refurbishment works. When he arrived, another chap called Thomas Shaffer was already held there, down in the basement cellar, but he wouldn't cooperate, and as a result Haziq beheaded him. Cody said it was the most horrific thing he has ever witnessed. Then a few days later Zen arrived, and now they are chained up in the first floor front bedroom, where the windows have been boarded over. They're monitored whenever they are on the machines."

"Then how come he could contact you?" Barnes asked.

"He uses a special code, basically sets of four numbers. I can decode it. To the person monitoring him it will just look like he's entering pin numbers, the sort of thing you do when you are attempting to break down codes."

"We'll need to find out where they are," Woods said. "If it's in Yorkshire I can use McLean and Jacobs. But unfortunately there's not much to go on."

"There is something else, but it's a long shot."

"Go on," Barnes encouraged.

"On Tuesday evening, around six-fifteen, one of the terrorists ordered a Chinese take-away for them, which was delivered forty minutes later. Zen asked for chicken and green peppers in black bean sauce, with fried rice, and Cody ordered gluten-free battered chicken in chilli plum sauce with chips."

Woods looked exasperated. "Is that it?"

Zoe's apologetic nod sufficed. "The gluten-free battered chicken may give you a lead."

"Okay," Woods muttered.

"Oh, I nearly forgot. One of the terrorists most likely drives a grey BMW X1."

Woods showed signs of frustration. "Anything else?!" he barked.

"Sorry, that's it."

"I'll ring McLean. He's going to love me for this."

"Hang on a second," Barnes said, thinking this was ill-advised. "If it is a trap, Luthi will be monitoring his phone."

"What was it you said to me? Oh ye of little faith! He has an unregistered mobile. I'll leave a message and he'll call back."

She scrunched up her nose. "He'll be searching for a needle in a haystack."

"Possibly so. However, if he concentrates on the Asian areas of West Yorkshire first he might get lucky."

"And while he's doing that, I'll ask him to have Jacobs look at where Cody, Zen and Shaffer were living," Zoe added. "You might get a lead from there."

Barnes nodded. It was beginning to sound promising. She looked across at Woods, instantly noticing he was displaying some purpose, something she hadn't seen in him in a long time.

At 9.25 p.m. Luthi received the call from Hobbs. "How did it go on the island?" she asked.

"You were right. Coleman discovered Barnes is living in one of the houses on the North-East coast."

"I knew it. How did he manage that?"

"He went to the resort's manager, claiming he wanted to thank Woods, or McLean as he's known there, for his help when we crashed golf buggies. The manager explained that McLean and his daughter had just checked out of the hotel and were intending to stay with a friend on the island: Miss Iveta Dubova. That's Barnes' new identity. Coleman drove past the house and spotted both Woods and Field with her."

"Excellent. Pass on my congratulations to him. In the meantime I'll organise the abduction of her brother. Then we'll move to the second phase."

"Coleman would like a word. He's uncovered something that you might find interesting. You may want to change your mind about the abduction."

Intrigued, Luthi said, "Well you'd better give him the phone."

A few seconds later Coleman said, "Hello. I trust you are impressed?"

"I wouldn't have expected anything else." She allowed him a few seconds of self-gratification. "Now tell what you've uncovered."

"There's another woman staying with Barnes. Dr Aliona Vetrova. Believe it or not, she is a highly regarded neuro-oncologist."

"Is she?" Luthi sniggered.

"Yes! The signs are that Barnes orchestrated Woods being there. I assume the intention is to try and save his life. Dr Vetrova researched and studied his particular cancer; she's become quite an expert in its treatment. Apparently various specialised prescription medicines have already been shipped to the island."

"That is interesting. And I suppose you're thinking that abducting him would be better leverage."

"We all know that he and Barnes had a *special* relationship. Think how much it must be costing her to have the doctor there. And what is the treatment going to cost?"

"So what are you proposing?"

"I kidnap him and hold him at Great Exuma. The gymnasium would make an excellent prison. Paula could keep an eye on him while I monitor Barnes and Field."

"When?"

"He always takes an early morning stroll around the island. I could strike then, and when you contact Barnes with your demands, you could claim he was being held offshore, somewhere like Anguilla."

"I'm beginning to like you. I especially like your thought process."

"Why don't you give me a day or so to sort it, and then pay us a visit? It's beautiful here, and no doubt you'll take great pleasure in speaking face to face with Barnes."

"I might just do that," she replied, surprising herself.

"So the plan's revised."

"Yes. Let me know when you have Woods. I'll enjoy breaking the news to Barnes. Give my regards to Paula." Luthi ended the call and leaned back on the sofa. Today had been a very good day. She needed to make a quick call and reserve a first class seat on a flight to Antigua.

*

"You see," Woods said, as Zoe closed down the equipment used to listen into the call. "I knew she would take the bait."

"She couldn't resist," Barnes added. "And it couldn't have gone better for us. She's walking straight into the web."

He laughed. "If we discover that Cody and Zen are being held by Islamic terrorists, then we most certainly will have the upper hand."

She nodded. "We'll have her believing that Faulkner-Brown is behind the cyber-attack and is intending to reveal GCHQ and all the other leading intelligence-gathering countries' secrets. Meanwhile we'll stop the terrorist attack, free Cody and Zen, and we, along with the Russians, can claim the credit, while she'll be discredited."

Woods glanced at Zoe. He noticed hadn't said much; he raised an eyebrow in her direction.

"So what's this *special* relationship?" she asked.

"No idea," he replied, grimacing.

"I suppose they mean special *working* relationship," Barnes put forward.

Zoe rolled her eyes. "I'm sure they did," she observed, in a tone no doubt intended to indicate her disbelief. "Why don't you two stop arsing about and move in together? It's obvious you have feelings for each other. You'd be good together."

Woods instantly felt uncomfortable. He looked away, hoping Barnes would respond, but she didn't. He preferred not to make eye contact either with her or with Zoe. Eventually he managed a quick glance at Zoe, who had that enquiring little smirk planted across her face. "I'm not sure," he said.

"You're not sure about what?" she asked.

He finally plucked up enough courage to look across at Barnes, who surprisingly was smiling at him.

"Maybe one day we will," she said, appearing calm and sincere. "When this is over and he's recovered."

Woods' shock must have been clear to the others. He managed a shallow nod. "Did you just say what I thought you did?"

"Why? Don't you like the thought of living with me?"

He wasn't expecting such a direct question. "Err... Yes, I suppose I do. I just..."

"Good." She interrupted.

He half expected to awaken at any moment, but it all seemed perfectly normal, and Zoe's grin was real enough. "Oh," he said, not sure what to add.

Chapter 11

Thursday 24th September

Woods stared up at the mosquito net, which, illuminated by the moonlight shining through the window, looked strangely alluring tonight. Slumber so far had proved impossible, as he lay under the bedsheet, his mind awash with thoughts surrounding Barnes, and what she had said earlier about the two of them cohabiting. Had she been testing him? Well, she'd appeared deadly serious, and completely sincere. Was it a game? He doubted she would stoop that low. Surely she wasn't messing about. He hoped not, no, he definitely knew she wouldn't do that. But did she have feelings for him? "That's a stupid question," he told himself. Obviously she held feelings for him, but what kind? As always with her, he was never quite sure of the answer, and second-guessing wasn't his strong point at the moment. What did *he* think about living together? He kept asking himself, but he couldn't answer. Each time he tried, he ended up questioning her motives. It was almost as if he dare not commit until he was absolutely sure of her intent. It was driving him crazy. Maybe the medication was affecting his judgment. He decided to ask Aliona in the morning, check if it was normal to feel insecure and confused.

He blinked, thinking he had heard a quiet tap on the bedroom door. Was he now hearing things? He peered through the haze of the net and stared at the door handle, which appeared to be moving. Was he hallucinating? Then a shard of light appeared around the jamb. Someone was there.

"Hello," whispered Barnes, poking her head into the room. "Have I woken you?"

"No, I couldn't sleep," he replied, somewhat surprised to see her.

"May I come in and talk to you?"

"Err, yes, of course."

She stepped inside, closing the door silently behind her. "Jesus, it's cold in here," she said, shivering.

He noticed her attire: another loose-fitting, baggy tee-shirt, similar to the one she'd worn when she'd fallen asleep in his lap. "It's the air con," he replied, knowing he was stating the obvious.

"I don't have it on in my room."

"I know, Maria. We've already had that conversation: it's because it dries your throat and eyes." He started looking for the parting in the mosquito net, intending to step out, find the remote and turn the temperature up.

"Do you mind if I get in with you?" she asked, as he located the opening, pulling it aside.

"No... not if you don't," he said, then he worried she would think his intention had been to lure her into bed. "I was going to turn the fan off," he added, pointing at the ceiling, thinking he ought to clarify.

She wasn't taking any notice. She hopped through the gap onto the bed and slid under the sheet. "It's okay, you can warm me up," she said, snuggling into him.

When he felt her bare legs touching his, the awkwardness heightened. Thankfully he had shorts on, but nothing else.

"So why weren't you asleep?" she asked.

"I was thinking."

"About?"

He relaxed a little. "All sorts of stupid things."

"Like what?"

"The first time we met. Do you remember?" He knew she would.

"You kept me waiting for over an hour, sitting outside your office. I could feel everyone's eyes burning into me. I suppose you did that on purpose, to make me feel uncomfortable and emphasise that you were in charge."

"No, I did not, and I apologised for being late."

"And made some lame excuse about being held up in a meeting."

"I'll have you know it wasn't an excuse. I'd been with Foster, in his office, being lectured on the importance of keeping an eye on you, not letting you take liberties, and being wary of your every move. I think he half expected me to be accused of molesting you on the first day. Your besmirched reputation preceded you."

She smiled. "But you were, as always, the perfect gentleman."

He frowned.

"You didn't do what most men do."

He frowned again.

"Mentally undress me. You kept eye contact. In fact I've never caught you looking at my tight skirt, or trying to peer down my blouse."

"That's because I'm good at hiding it."

"And you are rubbish at lying," she laughed.

Now the tension left him. "What had you been told about me?" He'd wondered this many times, but never asked her.

"Like me, your reputation preceded you. I knew you didn't suffer fools, but guessed that wouldn't be a problem. I'd been told you were ill tempered, grumpy and unforgiving. That you were a perfectionist, attentive and fixated by detail, the great Greg Woods, the best detective in the force." She smiled again. "The reality was I thought you'd be like the rest of them. But my luck was in and you weren't. You were decent with me from the start, and you always have been. You gave me the benefit of the doubt. Do you remember telling me that you weren't interested in what had happened, you would only focus on that day forward, and if I knuckled down, worked hard and followed your direction, we'd make a great team?"

He laughed out loud; he couldn't help it. He had forgotten those few words of wisdom. "Little did I know that I would be following your direction!"

She snuggled in closer still. "What were your first impressions of me?" she asked.

He felt her right calf fall between his legs and she raised her knee slightly, no doubt finding a more comfortable position. As she did this she placed her right arm on his chest. Her smooth delicate skin had warmed and its gentle touch felt sensual. He became aroused, and his breathing shallow. She nuzzled her curls into his upper arm. The tension returned, but he focused in on answering her. "To be honest, I'd been so hacked off by Foster banging on about your over active imagination, and what he called your false allegations, that I was determined to give you a chance. Everyone deserves a chance, and I wanted it to work, to prove the others wrong. And you certainly didn't disappoint."

"You brought out the best in me. You believed in me." She leaned up and kissed him lightly on the cheek. Thank you," she whispered.

Now he threw caution to the wind. "I was so proud of you, that night, on *Crimewatch*. That was the first time I was attracted to you. You were absolutely stunning, confident, cool, and calm, relaxed, and in complete charge of the situation. You were better than the presenter. Everyone in the Incident Room agreed. And from that point onwards Foster held you in the highest regard."

She propped herself up onto her left elbow and looked into his eyes. "I never knew you'd felt like that."

He shrugged. "I'm good at hiding my feelings."

"Sometimes."

"What do you mean?"

"You were emotional when I told you about Glendale."

"Yes, I was. And at that moment in time, if he had still been alive I would have hunted him down and torn him to pieces. You didn't deserve that. Your intentions just didn't go to plan, and you were left with few options, other than to clear up the mess and destroy the evidence. I had no doubts about that. I didn't want to see you punished further. I just wanted to put my arms around you, and hold you close. I would have never let you go."

She leaned forwards and kissed him again, and, as she did, he felt a tear fall on his chest. "I'm sorry," he said, "for bringing up unpleasantness."

There was an uncomfortable silent pause, and then she whispered softly in his ear, "I want to make love with you," she said. "I can't think of anybody more special than you."

He took a deep breath and hesitated. "Are you absolutely sure, Maria?"

"Yes, I'm *absolutely* sure. Please don't say anything else." She shuffled slightly out to the side of him, sat up and pulled her tee-shirt off. Now she was naked.

"I don't have a condom." He felt embarrassed.

"Don't worry, you don't need one."

He watched as she tugged his shorts down, throwing them off the bed, and then climbed astride him, her form arching as she bent down and lay on top of him.

"The occasional groan of pleasure is acceptable though," she said, quietly in his ear, as she nibbled hard on his lobe.

"Ouch," he complained. But her hand was already on his groin and any thought of discomfort had instantly diminished. He placed his long spindly arms around her slender frame and gently pulled her in. Then he ran his hands very slowly down her back, but as he felt the scarring he pulled them away. "Sorry," he said, instinctively. He had forgotten about the burns and skin grafts.

"You don't have to apologise. I adored it, please don't stop. The wounds don't hurt; they just feel strange."

He resumed where he had left off and as his hands reached her pert buttocks he paused, momentarily caressing them. She kissed him passionately on the lips and her tongue ventured into his mouth. He absolutely loved it. Fleetingly and sensually their tongues touched and then intertwined. He couldn't remember the last time he'd been so turned on. He dug his fingers into the soft flesh around her thighs and picked her up, moving and positioning her exactly where she needed to be. Then he lowered her, ever so slowly on to him. She inhaled deeply and then groaned a pleasurable tender moan, matching the rhythmic movement of her thighs.

"This is good," she whispered, panting heavily.

He nodded and didn't speak, because he didn't want to ruin the moment. His heart pounded against his chest as his mind filled with pleasure. She was right: it was good; in fact it was better than good. He didn't want it to end.

"Oh my God," she shouted out loud. Then she sank her teeth into his chest and bit hard.

"Maria!" he growled, but the pain was overwhelmed by the desire to climax. He fought against it, desperately trying to prolong the euphoria. Her body writhed and he felt her warm tender skin, now covered in small droplets of moisture. He tensed. This was it; he'd gone way past Vee-one, forgetting any thoughts of rotate or bringing gear up. His breathing quickened as his body thrust into her. He shuddered, gasped and exhaled, slowly relaxing. Then he bent his neck forward, kissed the top of her head, and gently caressed her back.

She loosened her bite, looked up at him and tweaked her nose. "So when can we do it again?" she asked, seductively positioning herself across his abdomen.

He rolled his eyes. "You'll have to give me time to recover, Maria. I'm not as young as I used to be."

*

As the morning sun flickered in through the bedroom window he stirred. He opened his eyes and turned his head to see her lying at his side, facing him and smiling. "Good morning," he said. "Did you sleep well?"

"Not as well as you."

"You wore me out!"

She laughed, leaned across and kissed him. "Thank you," she said.

"It should be me thanking you."

She raised an eyebrow. "You know exactly what I'm talking about."

He scowled and pretended he didn't.

"Stop teasing. What you did means a great deal to me."

He nodded diminutively. "I didn't want you to feel uncomfortable or threatened. I thought it best to let you take the lead."

"Thank you. When I'm ready, I'll let you know. Then we can switch."

"Does this mean there will be more opportunities for you to sink your teeth into me?"

She pulled the sheet and looked at his chest. "I got a bit carried away. Sorry. I'll ask Aliona to look at them."

"They'll be fine. Besides, how are we going to explain three bite marks?"

"We don't have to explain anything. We're adults, this is my house and what we do is up to us. Anyway, I'll tell her the truth; she won't be bothered."

"Okay, I'll leave that one with you. You can explain it to Zoe too."

She stuck her tongue out. "You'd better do that!"

He shrugged; he'd no intention of doing anything of the sort. "Can I ask you a question?" he said, moving on.

She gave him a withering look, and he wondered if she'd guessed what it would be about.

"Yes," she said, after a short pause.

"Are you taking any form of contraception?"

At first she appeared pensive. "No, but don't worry, I won't be pregnant. I know my body clock."

"Maria! It's not an exact science."

"So... is it a problem if I become pregnant?"

He scowled. His immediate thought was that he wouldn't be around to see the child grow up, but then he remembered what she had said about Ben's father. "Maria! You're not using me, are you?"

"In what way?"

"To get pregnant knowing I haven't got long to live."

"NO! Absolutely not! And stop saying that! Aliona is going to save you! She's told me about a new treatment where they genetically engineer stem cells which produce pseudomonas exotoxin to target specific brain cancers; they're resistant to the poison themselves. The stem cells are able to kill it!"

"Are you sure?"

"What? You think I made that up?!"

"No, but Aliona hasn't mentioned anything."

"She's worried because it hasn't been tested on humans yet. In other words, it's not a licensed treatment. She wanted me to broach the subject with you."

Now he frowned. "So we don't know if it will work?"

"No, but the option of sitting around and waiting five years until the tests are complete isn't viable. We need to take risks. She's willing to do that, but the final decision comes down to us."

"You mean me."

She took hold of his hand. "I mean us! I want us to decide together. And I want you to beat this."

"I need to think about it."

She nodded in agreement. "Speak to Aliona. She'll explain in much more detail. Then we can decide what's best for you. I can't bear to think of you not being around."

He became angst-ridden, and she must have noticed because she added, "I know this is a big decision, that's why I don't want you to have to make it on your own."

He appreciated the sentiment. The trouble now was that he worried the whole thing had been contrived: with her coming to his room, getting into bed with him, making love without using contraception, and then the final bombshell of the available unlicensed treatment. "I think I need to go for a walk to clear my head," he said.

"May I come?"

"I need to be alone."

"Okay," she replied.

He stared into those big brown eyes. "Last night was really special, Maria. You said some really nice things."

"I meant every one of them. Don't start doubting me again."

He smiled. "You have a habit of making me do just that."

"Then I need to break it. Listen, you are one of the best things that has ever happened in my life – you, and having Ben. And if, by some miracle, I'm pregnant, then having a little brother or sister for Ben would be brilliant, but having you there as its father, and Ben's stepfather, would be the icing on the cake. I can't put it any simpler than that."

He watched a tear dribble down her cheek. He leaned over and gently nudged it away with his forefinger. Then he kissed her slowly and tenderly on the lips. "I'm sorry. I should never have doubted you."

"No, you shouldn't. Now, shall we go for that walk before breakfast?"

"Either that, or we could make love again."

"As long as I don't bite you."

He nodded. "Some people like pain because it heightens their senses. For others, the simple act of erotic sensual love is enough."

"I'm sorry, I'm not experienced in any of this. I've read a few books and I watched a film."

"Yes, and I'd wager I could guess which one."

"Charlie Tango."

He nodded. "I thought so. Look, forget the film. Do you remember David Kolb? His book was in your flat. I read it."

She laughed and nodded. "Experiential learning," she replied.

"Learning by doing. Let's try that instead. Starting now!"

By the time they arrived in the kitchen, Zoe, Aliona and Ben were already sitting outside, around the breakfast table on the sun terrace, eating. "I'll make eggs benedict," Barnes said.

"Okay, I'll go and have a quick word with Aliona," he replied.

"Are you absolutely sure you want to go ahead with the treatment?"

"Yes, I'm sure. Are you?"

She nodded. "I'll be at you side. We'll do it together."

He feigned a smile and she must have known what he was feeling because she said, "Are you scared?"

He nodded. "Scared the stem cells won't work."

"They will. Be positive. We'll beat this."

"Fingers crossed," he said, on purpose, knowing it would wind her up.

"You know I dislike that!"

He laughed. That had made him feel better.

"I'll bring breakfast," she said.

He wandered outside to where the others were sitting. "Good morning," he said.

Zoe raised an eyebrow and didn't return the greeting. She looked tired, whereas Aliona smiled and said good morning. Then she asked how he was feeling.

"I'm fine. I slept quite well, thank you," he replied, sitting down next to her.

"I'm surprised you got any sleep, judging by the noises coming from your room," Zoe chuntered.

He scowled at her.

"Good morning, Mr Greg," Ben chirped up. "Are we going in the pool today?"

"Maybe later on, after I've spoken with Aliona."

"What about?" Ben wanted to know.

"Benjamin! Is rude to ask," Aliona told him.

"Sorry," he replied, making a sad face.

"It's okay, Ben," Woods reassured him. "I need to discuss my treatment, something that might make my headaches go away."

The little boy nodded as though he'd understood. "Please may I have some more toast?" he asked Aliona.

"Certainly. You come with me and I make some." She turned to Woods. "We talk after breakfast," she said, disappearing off with Ben, who tagged along behind her.

"Are you okay, Zoe?" he asked, when the others were out of earshot.

"Yes, I didn't get much sleep. What the hell were you and Maria doing?"

He looked sheepishly down at the table. "We slept together."

"I know. I heard most of it."

"Sorry." He cringed. "Are you alright about it?"

"Why shouldn't I be?"

"I don't know. You look a bit peeved."

"Like I said, I'm tired, and what you and her get up to has nothing to do with me. I just don't want to see you get hurt."

"I'm sorry we kept you awake."

"Actually, I worked through the night. It wasn't your cavorting that kept me from sleeping. I've checked all Luthi's telecommunications and there's no indication that this is a trap. I think Cody is telling the truth, and that we are definitely on to something. We need to find where they are being held. If you agree, can you ring McLean and get him on to it?"

"I'll do it now." He started to get up.

"Sit down. You can do it after breakfast."

He frowned, but acquiesced.

"It sounds like she's convinced you to go with the stem cell treatment."

"I'd be stupid not to try it."

"I agree. I hope it's as successful as Aliona claims it will be."

He nodded, although Zoe's look unnerved him. "I'm trying to remain positive," he said.

"Good. That's what you need to do."

"It's not easy though."

"I can appreciate it isn't."

Her empathy helped.

"You do realise that you'll have to travel to Moscow for the treatment?"

"Yes, but I understand it is going to take Aliona two to three months to organise things. Therefore we should have more than enough time to complete the plan."

"And if we don't?"

"Then we revise it."

"Coleman is getting the keys to Great Exuma today and no doubt he and Hobbs will be moving straight onto the island."

"I know. Maria says he's planning to…" he held up his fingers in speech mark style, "…*abduct me,* tomorrow morning. He's expecting Luthi to arrive within a day or two and he wants me captive before she does."

"We really need Hobbs out of the way."

"I agree. I too want her off the island. Then I'd have some flexibility; I could even stay here after Luthi has left."

"I've been giving that some thought."

"And?"

"I wonder if Maria would organise for Kozlov to kidnap her."

"But Luthi would just send another agent to replace her."

"Not if Coleman convinced her that he could manage better if he was left alone."

"Okay, but Kozlov would need a reason to justify the kidnapping."

"Hobbs tried to starve Maria's father to death, and it could be revenge for that. Her father saved Kozlov's daughter, remember?"

"Good point. It might work."

"We'll have to make it work. I want you here with me, not stuck across there in Great Exuma with them. Maria listens to you, whereas she takes little notice of what I say. And I want Faulkner-Brown, remember? That's why I'm here."

"I know, and Maria wanted me to persuade you that he's an angel."

"So why haven't you?"

"Because I share your view, and I'd like to see him behind bars."

"So we work together with that aim."

"Agreed."

"Excellent. So, is she any good in bed?"

"Zoe! I'm not discussing it."

"I see she's into biting."

He looked down and realising that one of his shirt buttons had popped open. He quickly refastened it.

"Is she into kinky stuff, or is it you?"

"Stop it!" He didn't know what else to say. Thankfully Barnes, Aliona and Ben were on their way to the table.

"We'll go to bed and then I'll show you what I can do," Zoe said quietly, as Barnes arrived.

"What are you two whispering about?" she asked, placing the plate of food in front of him.

"Nothing," he answered quickly.

"We were discussing. . ."

"Kozlov," he interrupted Zoe. "We were discussing Kozlov. He might be able to. . ."

"Bite us!" Now Zoe had interrupted him and she was smirking.

"What?" Barnes said, frowning.

"Help us," Woods said, kicking Zoe's shin. "How Kozlov might be able to help us. Zoe has a suggestion. Don't you?!"

"Yes, I have a suggestion. I'm just not sure *he'll* go along with it." Zoe smiled sweetly at him, flicking her eyebrows at him.

"Let's hear it then," Barnes said, appearing none the wiser to what was actually going on.

He decided to clarify. Zoe was sailing way to close to the wind. He therefore spent a couple of minutes explaining the idea.

"I'll speak to Kozlov and see what he says."

He breathed a silent sigh of relief. He picked up a piece of toast and gave Zoe a disapproving contemptuous look. He would speak to her later. She'd gone too far.

"Are you going to take a *bite* out of that? she asked, grinning.

Chapter 12

Thursday 24th September – Saturday 26th September

Cody waited until the door locked and he heard the footsteps descending on the staircase, then he spun round and looked at Zen, who was snoozing on the mattress. "Harry! Harry! Are you awake?"

Zen stirred. "W… what is it?"

"Sahib has gone to get something to eat. He's usually no more than ten minutes."

"A… are we in?" Zen asked, looking around confused.

"No! But I've had confirmation back. They're trying to locate where we are! They need more information."

"Who are they?"

"Hawkeye's actually a young woman. Her name is Zoe Field. Her mother used to work for MI5; that much she's revealed. I'm assuming she's alerted the anti-terrorist police and probably the Secret Service. They'll all be searching for us now."

"That's brilliant news. I can't believe it."

Cody nodded, but he was desperate for more information. "Can you think of anything that might give a clue to who these idiots are, or where we are being held?"

Zen scratched his head frantically, the anxiety plastered across his face indicating how hard he was trying to help. "I… I don't know."

"Anything at all, no matter how insignificant," Cody said, calmly attempting to highlight the importance. "It might help."

"I think I told you everything I know." Zen quietened and looked to be deep in thought. There was a long drawn-out pause. Had he recalled something? Cody remained silent and pensive.

"Last night, when you were sleeping, Kaleem received a phone call," Zen said.

"Go on," Cody encouraged, hoping this might be the lead they were looking for.

"I don't know who telephoned, but the conversation sounded to be about a fuse tripping out in a consumer unit. Kaleem said he would nip out of work today and go and check it."

"So Kaleem has a job?"

Zen nodded. "It sounds like it. How he manages to stay awake all night watching us and then work during the day is beyond me."

"What kind of job would he do? IT, do you think?"

"He's rubbish at that."

"I know, but what else might he do?" Cody concurred.

"Perhaps he's an electrician," Zen offered up. "He might have done the rewiring of this dump. Why else would he know about consumer units?"

"*I* could find out which fuse had tripped and then go searching to see what had caused it. You don't need to be a qualified electrician to do that."

"I agree, but he'd said he'd check it. You couldn't check a circuit. Could you?"

Cody shook his head. But that had set him thinking. He stared at the wall, the fear intensifying on his face. "Oh my God," he said to himself, and then he started shaking, and his breathing became laboured.

"Are you alright, Mate?" Zen called across.

Cody battled for air. His hands gripped tightly onto the table top and in his mind he counted, trying to breathe long deep slow breaths.

"Are you alright, Mate?" Zen repeated.

Cody nodded, still focusing on his breathing. He was fighting the attack. He must stay calm. He just needed a minute or two to come round. He held up his hand, attempting to let Zen know he was alright. "Just give me a sec," he coughed.

Zen complied and after several minutes Cody regained control of some of his faculties. He managed to turn around and speak. "I… I think I might know who he is?"

"Kaleem?"

"Yes." He still fought to control his breathing. "I've been so stupid; why didn't I realise?"

"Who is he?"

"I think he was at Sheffield Hallam Uni with me. That's how they must know me."

"What's his name?"

"I don't know, but he studied something related to buildings."

"Electrical Engineering?"

"Possibly. Look, I'm not one hundred per cent sure, but if it is him, I'd seen him in the canteen. He was always banging on about Islam. Some of his mannerisms look familiar. Although I kept my distance; I didn't want to become involved with him. He tended to knock around with the building surveyors. He did a part-time course, if I remember correctly, presumably funded by work."

"It must be him. It can't be a coincidence. There are too many similarities."

Cody wasn't sure.

"So did he know you were into computers?"

"I repaired them; it generated a bit of money. I rebuilt one of the surveyor's PCs. I suppose word gets around. I had a reputation for fixing anything related to IT."

"They should be able to find him from that. When were you there?"

"2008 to 2012."

"That's why he wears a mask, Mate. He knows you'll recognise him. It has to be him."

"I could be wrong." Cody was having doubts. "And all the others wear masks."

"Listen, even if you are mistaken, it's the only good lead we've got. All they need to do is find the students named Kaleem who did a building-related course at Sheffield between those years."

"I don't want to send them on a wild goose chase."

The sound of footsteps ascending the stairs curtailed the discussion. "He's back," Cody said, refocusing on the screen.

"Tell Zoe," Zen whispered. "Let her decide." He stopped speaking as the door was unlocked.

Friday 25th September

Barnes dutifully watched through binoculars, from the sun terrace on the roof, while Woods was abducted. In truth, the whole operation was quite civilised. Coleman had decided to carry it out on this side of the island, near to Barnes' house, and out of sight of Hobbs, who was confined to Great Exuma due to her limited mobility. Woods simply hopped into the back of the buggy, allowing Coleman to first handcuff him, then secure his ankles with electrical ties and gag him. He then lay down, let Coleman inject him, and cover him up with a tarpaulin. Coleman then drove slowly off in the direction of Great Exuma. Now that the first part of the plan was out of the way she needed to prepare for Luthi's arrival on the island later today. She turned around and shouted for Ben. "Come here, Sweetheart. You're going for a ride in the boat this morning. Aliona's taking you shopping and then you are going with her to a hotel in Antigua for a few days."

He came running up to her. "I don't want to go. And where's Mr Greg gone?"

"He's staying at the house over there for a few days. He needs a rest."

"Can I go see him?"

"No, Sweetheart, you'll see him when he gets back."

"I want to see him now!"

So do I, she thought. "You like him, don't you?"

"He's fun," he said, smiling and fidgeting around on his feet.

She smiled and nodded in agreement. "So why don't you want to go? Aliona said she would take you in to St John's first and buy you something special."

"What?" He stood stock still now.

"You can decide."

"Okay, I'll go. What are you doing while I'm staying with Aliona?"

"Acting."

"Are you going to be in a film?"

She laughed. "No, Sweetheart, but I'll be pretending, like they do in films."

"Can I stay and watch?"

"I thought you'd agreed to go with Aliona to the hotel. Remember, she's going to buy you something special."

He nodded. "I'll go with her."

"Good, you can choose something nice, and when you return I'll tell you all about the acting."

He nodded again and appeared placated. "Is Zoe acting too?"

"Yes. Now come on, you'll miss the boat." She gathered some of his toys up and walked with him back down to the pool area where Aliona was sitting waiting.

"Mother's going to be acting for a few days, and Zoe is too. Can we stay and watch?" he asked her.

"Ben, we've already agreed you are going with Aliona. Now hurry or you'll miss the boat-taxi."

As Aliona walked off with him, Barnes quickly tidied away all the toys. She didn't want any evidence that a child was living in the property. Once she'd done this she went inside to find Zoe, who she understood to be working in the computer room. She knocked on the door and went in. "Luthi's due to be on the island around lunchtime. We need to have everything in order," she said.

"I know. I'm sorting it. Has Aliona taken Ben?"

"Yes, we're on our own. Are the cameras and recording equipment set up in the ocean room?"

"They are. Look." Zoe clicked the mouse and the screen filled with four images, each covering the various seating positions in the room. "The cameras and microphones are concealed; she'll never spot them."

"Good, we'd better get ready. We've only got a few hours. This is going to be fun."

"Before you go, take a look at this," Zoe said, opening up another screenshot.

Barnes stooped and spent a few moments reading the words on the screen. "I'll ring McLean and leave him a message."

"If I get chance I'll let Coleman know," Zoe said. "Then he can update Woods."

"Okay, but be careful. Luthi doesn't miss much."

Luthi stepped gingerly from the small boat and was helped up onto the quayside by Coleman, whose grip she considered to be way too firm. "Welcome to Long Island," he said, grinning. He took hold of her travel bag. "Nice flight?"

"No. BA doesn't do a first class service to Antigua. I had to settle for business class. It was almost as dire as cattle-class."

"You always insist we fly economy. It will have been useful for you to experience how the other half travel."

"Peasants," she scoffed.

"If that's what you think of the populace, why didn't you charter a personal jet?"

She ignored him. She was not in the best of moods, and she had more pressing matters. "Have you achieved your goal?" she asked, tetchily, as they walked slowly towards the golf buggy.

"Yes, he's at the house. He's far from happy though. Paula is keeping an eye on him."

"Did you make it appear as though he'd been taken from the island?" she asked, as they climbed in the buggy.

Coleman nodded. "I organised for a high-powered speedboat to hurriedly leave and coincide with his disappearance. Will that suffice?"

She could tell he'd been annoyed by the question. "Just checking," she said, smirking. "Which house does *she* live in?"

"That one." He pointed towards the headland. "The one with the gigantic satellite dish, and the solar panels on the roof."

She peered over the top of her spectacles. "Very nice. Is Great Exuma as impressive?"

"I'll let you decide," he replied, starting the buggy and moving off. "Hold tight," he laughed. "I'm not the safest driver on the island."

"Can we go past Barnes'?"

"Sure. Do you want to call in there now?"

"No. I'll freshen up, speak with Paula, see how Woods is, and then you and I can go and speak to her and the Field girl. Have they called the police yet?"

"No, I assume they probably think he's gone fishing, or to the mainland shopping."

"That's good. We need to get to them before they make that call."

"I'll put my foot down then," he said, forcing the accelerator pedal to the floor.

As Coleman drove past her house he slowed, and Barnes ducked down behind the parapet on the roof. She had seen them approach and, now they were rounding the bend, she popped her head up and focused the binoculars in on the buggy. She smiled inwardly. "Softly, softly, catchee monkey," she said to herself. She watched them disappear into the distance and then she hurried down to Zoe who was reading by the pool. "Luthi's arrived. She didn't look very happy; they've just driven past. They'll be here shortly."

Zoe placed her book on the table. "Would you like a drink before they come?"

"I'm tempted to open the champagne, but we'll do that after they've gone."

"I'll make some tea then," Zoe said.

"While you do that I'll have one last look around the house and grounds, check I haven't missed anything."

"Maria, you've done nothing else all morning except check around the house and grounds. Everything's fine. Relax, we've got it covered. Stay here and I'll make the tea."

As soon as Zoe disappeared inside she was on her feet and scurrying around the shrubs and boarders searching for discarded or misplaced toys. She didn't like to admit this to Zoe, but she was nervous, very nervous. It was not like her at all; she knew she needed to be calm and relaxed. Maybe she would open the champagne after all.

Two hours later Barnes deliberately waited longer than normal before answering the intercom. "Good afternoon," she said, calmly. "I suppose I'll have to invite you in."

"Hello, Maria. It's been a while."

She stared at the footage from the camera on the gate, and quickly enlarged the image. Luthi hadn't changed that much. She decided to get straight to the point. "What have you done with Woods?"

"If you let me in I'll explain. I'm pleased you haven't involved the police. I knew you'd work it out."

"The idiot standing next to you, and his so-called girlfriend, suddenly buying a property on the island kind of gave it away."

"Are you going to let us in?"

She pressed the button on the intercom receiver, allowing the gates to open.

"Stay calm," Zoe said.

"Don't worry; I'm going to enjoy this." She went over to the entrance and opened the doors. "Would you like some coffee?" she asked, as they entered.

"No thank you," Luthi responded.

"Do you have Cartwright and Butler?" Coleman enquired, in an incredibly posh voice.

Barnes glared at him. "No I do not!" she snapped.

"Oh," he said, appearing perturbed. "I understand it's quite chic. I thought you'd have it. Perhaps you ought to get some, for our next visit."

Luthi gave him a dirty look. "Ignore him," she said. "You were right, he's an idiot. I can't get the staff. You should work for me."

"I doubt I would have this kind of lifestyle if I did that."

"No, you appear to be doing surprisingly well."

"Come through to the ocean room. We can talk there." She pointed them in the right direction and they obligingly settled on the sofa near the windows. Zoe was perched on one of the sofa chairs nearby and Barnes deliberately chose the sofa facing her guests.

"Who's this?" Luthi enquired, nodding at Zoe.

"You know very well who she is. Stop playing games and tell me what you've done with Woods," she demanded, attempting to assert her authority.

"He's perfectly fine. He's being looked after."

"He needs medication."

"Yes, where is his personal oncologist?"

"In Antigua. She's meeting a few colleagues, they're here on business. Not that it's any of your concern."

"Well, give me his medication and I'll make sure he takes it. Nothing is going to happen to him, provided you do exactly as I say."

Barnes' eyes narrowed. "What do you want?"

"Firstly, I'd like to know where Faulkner-Brown is."

"I don't know his exact whereabouts. I can't help you on that."

"Then I can't give Woods his medication."

Her breathing became noticeably louder. "Something very terrible will happen to you one day."

"Yes, it probably will. But, before that day arrives, Woods will be long gone."

Barnes made a point of swallowing before she spoke, attempting to demonstrate how difficult this supposedly was for her. "Faulkner-Brown is in the Americas," she said. "He moves around. He doesn't stay in the same place very long; he knows you are after him. He'll know you are here."

Luthi smiled. "Okay. For now I'll believe you."

"It's the truth," she stressed.

"We'll see. Now, tell me what he's planning?"

She glanced at Zoe, looking worried. Zoe's expression was perfect. Now she turned back to Luthi. "If I tell you, he'll have me killed."

"And if you don't, Woods dies a slow and painful death. The choice is yours. If you assist me and help capture Faulkner-Brown I'll provide you with protection, so he can't have you killed."

She got up off the sofa and walked slowly across to the windows. She stared out over the ocean. "How do I know you'll keep your word?"

"You don't; you'll have to take that risk. I hold the aces. Your half-brother was a good teacher."

"What do you think, Zoe?"

Zoe shrugged. "You're damned if you do and you're damned if you don't."

She strolled around the room, making out she was deep in thought. "Alright," she said. "I'll tell you what his plan is."

"Good girl."

"I'm a woman, not a girl!" she snapped back.

Luthi sneered. "Well, let me tell you my thoughts on what Faulkner-Brown is preparing to do. I suspect he's planning an intensive and prolonged attack on the world's intelligence-gathering agencies. His aim is to disclose their sensitive documentation and data, causing absolute mayhem and disorder."

Barnes intentionally flicked up an eyebrow and nodded, giving the impression Luthi was correct in her assumption. In actual fact all this misinformation had been fed to her by Coleman and his associates over the past few months. It was all part of the plan and had clearly worked.

"And I suspect that you have assisted him in some way, or that you are intending to assist him." Luthi looked over the top of her glasses at Zoe. "*You* think that Faulkner-Brown's antics will help your mother."

Zoe smirked. "Do I?"

"Yes. Otherwise why would you be here?"

"I fancied a holiday."

"The only way to help your mother is to do exactly what I tell you. If you comply, I'll put the wheels in motion and have her sentence reduced."

"Will you?" Zoe asked, flippantly.

"Yes."

"So, what exactly do you want us to do?" Barnes questioned.

"Come on, Maria. You're smart; surely you've worked it out. We want you to be instrumental in stopping Faulkner-Brown's attacks. You and Miss Field can do things we can't."

"Like giving you him on a plate, along with the worldwide recognition that you personally prevented the biggest cyber-attack ever planned."

"Ten out of ten."

"The trouble is we don't trust you."

"And I don't trust you either. But I've got Woods, and, apart from your father and Kozlov, I think he's the only other man you've ever trusted. Am I right?"

"Drop dead."

"Maria, don't be so churlish. If you help, I'll allow you to stay here, with Woods if that's what you want. And I'll forget everything I know about the disappearance of Peter Glendale. And Miss Field's mother will be released early. Everyone wins."

Barnes looked at Zoe who nodded back at her. "We don't have much choice," Zoe said.

"For now, we have a deal," Barnes stated. "But if Woods' condition deteriorates I want his oncologist to have immediate access. Otherwise the deal's off."

Luthi looked to Coleman. "Access for the oncologist might be difficult. But if it were absolutely necessary we could sedate her, so she didn't know where he was being held."

"We'll be able to overcome that problem," Coleman insisted.

"Right, I think that will suffice for now. I'm pleased you'll be working with me again, Maria. Oh and by the way, Coleman is going to be keeping a close eye on everything you two do."

"I'll keep popping in. After all, we're neighbours now. Don't forget to purchase some Cartwright and Butler coffee. I love it; you will too. I'm sure we'll become really good friends."

"Get lost, creep. I think it's time you left."

"Okay," Luthi said, getting up off the sofa. "We'll be in touch within the next day or two. I'll instruct you on how we want this to proceed."

"Please? I need to use the loo before we go." Coleman said, rubbing his abdomen.

Barnes sighed. "If you must, it's down the hallway, first door on the left."

"Err, that one's blocked, Maria. We need a plumber. I forgot to mention it earlier," Zoe announced.

"Oh," she said, surprised by the news. "Well, he can use the bathroom upstairs."

"I'll show him where it is," Zoe said, heading towards the staircase. "Follow me," she called to him.

Coleman went with her, leaving Luthi and Barnes alone in the hallway. "I'll fetch Woods' medication," she said, disappearing off. A few moments later she returned, handing Luthi a small brown paper bag. "Make sure he takes these," she emphasised.

Luthi peered in the bag, and then placed it in her pocket. "Maria, I know you'll be doing everything within your power to double-cross me."

"Likewise."

"That's why I'm having Coleman keep a close eye on you."

She scrunched up her nose.

"Why don't we let bygones be bygones? It's easier that way," Luthi said.

"I'm becoming tired of this conversation," she responded, Luthi's exasperated look pleasing her.

"I'm finding it hard to understand why you chose to side with Faulkner-Brown," Luthi went on. "You loathed the man. I had to stop the two of you tearing each other apart."

"It was all an act. I've been on his side from day one."

Coleman descending the stairs curtailed the discussion.

Barnes opened the entrance. "We'll be in touch," Luthi said, as they walked up the path.

"The gate will close automatically when you've gone," she shouted, slamming the door shut. She turned to see Zoe's smug face grinning at her. "The toilet isn't blocked, is it?"

"No, of course not. I needed to update him."

"How did he know to ask for the loo?"

"I told him to."

"I was there all the time. I didn't notice anything."

"You're not as sharp as you used to be. I caught his eye and then tapped the message out silently in Morse code with my finger on the chair arm."

"Luthi could have seen it!"

"No, like you, she didn't lose eye contact with her prey. Apart from the time she spoke to me, her stare was transfixed on you."

"I see," she said, impressed.

"Coleman said Woods is absolutely fine. Luthi spoke with him and made threats that if he attempted to escape, you and I would be killed."

"Such a delightful woman, don't you think?"

"She's going to get what she deserves."

"She certainly is. How do *you* think it went?"

"Perfect. I think we pitched it just right. It'll be interesting to see what Coleman has to say when he's spoken to Luthi. He said she is flying back to the UK on Sunday morning."

"That's good. Ben's safe and off the island until she's left. I'll organise for Kozlov to abduct Hobbs on Monday. Woods can then return."

"Has McLean rung you?"

"No, I'm not expecting him to call until late this evening. Just a thought though, and to try to pre-empt things, can you access the university database and download a list of all students named Kaleem who were there when Cody attended?"

"I've already done that. There aren't any. It looks like it's a dead end."

She tapped her tongue on the roof of her mouth. "Maybe Kaleem isn't his real name. Maybe he is smarter than Cody realises. Never mind, we'll see what progress McLean has made with the other information we've given him."

Saturday 26th September

Cody waited patiently through most of his two-hour night sessions for Kaleem to need a toilet break. Finally at 4.30 a.m. he obliged. As soon as the door had been locked Cody attracted Zen's attention by clicking his fingers.

"What is it?" Zen whispered.

"There wasn't anyone called Kaleem doing a building-related course at Sheffield Uni while I was there. They've checked the records. I must have been mistaken," Cody whispered.

"You seemed so sure, Mate, and it all appeared to fit."

"Sorry."

"It's not your fault. You want to get out of here as much as I do."

"The funny thing is, the more I looked at his mannerisms and his stance tonight, the more I was convinced it was him. I'm going to test something out when he gets back from the loo," he said quietly.

There was no time to explain further, because the door unlocked and Kaleem strolled in.

"Kaleem," Cody said, anxiously. "It gets so cold at night, and my feet start aching: do you think it might be possible to run an electric heater in here?"

"It all depends on the wattage of the heater and the other items drawing off the circuit. I could check it out for you, but I'd have to ask Haziq first. I rewired this place for him earlier this year; it meets the 2015 electrical regs, but you've already got a heavy load - look at all this." He pointed at the equipment on the desks. "It's running twenty-four/seven. Haziq will go into anaphylactic shock when he gets the bill."

Cody shuddered. "It's alright, don't ask him. I don't want to upset him anymore. I'll put up with cold feet."

"I could get you some socks, Man. Will that do?"

"Thank you. So long as it doesn't get you or me in trouble."

"No problem. I'll bring them tonight."

"Thank you," Cody repeated, as he hunkered over the keyboard and typed like fury. He guessed Zen would know exactly who he was contacting and why. His message was simple. Check all the Asian young men undertaking electrical engineering courses during the same period. Concentrate on those living in Yorkshire and the surrounding areas. He knew time, luck and hope were all diminishing by the second. He still hadn't utilised his watch; he needed Zen to work with him to create a diversion. It would be an enormous risk, but if they managed it, the chances of identifying Haziq would be significantly increased.

Chapter 13

Saturday 26th September – Sunday 27th September

"They're here," Barnes informed Zoe, watching the gate's CCTV footage displaying on her laptop. As Luthi and Coleman approached, she pressed the button on the small handheld fob, enabling the solid mahogany gates to swing open. She closed the laptop and slid it under the sun lounger.

"I'll get Coleman to help me with the drinks, and leave you two alone. Then he can update me on what her thoughts were after yesterday's little soirée," Zoe said, stretching out on the lounger, looking chilled, calm, and in control.

"Hello! We're round the front," Barnes shouted, knowing her visitors would be nearing the entrance doors.

They appeared and were invited to sit with them around the pool. Both Barnes and Zoe wore stylish Christian Dior sunglasses and designer coveralls, over swimwear, deliberately trying to give the impression of elegance and wealth.

"Good morning, Ladies," Coleman said, smiling. "I could get used to this lifestyle. Couldn't you?" he asked Luthi.

She obviously wasn't impressed. "We need to get down to business."

"How's Woods?" Barnes asked, as her opening gambit.

"The last update I received stated that he was reading and resting. Like I said yesterday, he's fine. You can be assured he's being well looked after."

"Would anyone like some fresh fruit juice?" Zoe piped up.

"Yes please," Barnes replied.

"Certainly would," Coleman said, rubbing his hands together. "I don't suppose you have fresh mangos?"

Barnes shook her head. "Should I buy some, for your next visit?"

"Ignore him, Maria. He'll drink whatever you've got," Luthi insisted.

"What about you, Miss Luthi?" Zoe asked, politely. "Would you like some?"

"Okay, that would be nice, and now that we'll be working together you can call me Beth."

Zoe produced the falsest smile Barnes had ever seen.

"You can help me," Zoe said to Coleman. "That's if you can manage to carry a drink without spilling it!"

"It would be my pleasure, Miss Field," he replied, jumping to his feet.

As Zoe and he wandered off towards the house, Barnes pulled her sunglasses down to the end of her nose and tilted her head forward. She looked at Luthi. "How come you have a creep like him working for you?" she enquired.

"It's a long story. However, he does have some uses."

"Like what?"

"I don't know." Luthi clearly didn't want to go any further.

"So, what do you want us to do?" Barnes asked, moving things on.

Luthi leant forward. Keeping her knees tightly together, she straightened her back, her tight, short skirt clearly not suited to the low level sun loungers. "Firstly, I need to know exactly which countries Faulkner-Brown is planning to attack. Do you know how many, in what order, and where from?"

"This isn't going to be as easy as you appear to think it will be. Faulkner-Brown has scores of people working for him, spread across the globe. It's a multi-million pound operation. He has some of the finest hackers in the world on his payroll. Only he knows where each cell is based and only he knows how to communicate with them."

"That doesn't answer my question."

Barnes produced the longest of prolonged sighs, and then said, "I know he's going for all the big guns, the main players, the ones with the most to lose. Oh, and of course *you*, and backward-thinking Britain."

Luthi's eyes were now no more than slits. "What about the Russians?" she snarled.

Barnes couldn't help snorting. "No, of course not, he's working with them! They are helping him. I thought you knew that!"

Luthi's response was indicative of her refusal to rise to the bait. "When is he planning to start the attacks?" she said.

"I know they are currently undertaking preliminary testing, hitting large corporations, telecommunications networks, TV stations, banks and the likes. You'll no doubt be aware of some of the attacks."

"Yes."

Luthi was clearly bluffing. Barnes presumed all she really knew was the misinformation passed to her by Coleman, the Russians and Faulkner-Brown's associates.

"I'd like you to contact him. Make an excuse about needing to see him and arrange to meet up. You can then ask him about the specifics."

"You really don't get it, do you? He still has numerous contacts within your department. My God, he used to run the whole operation. Are you so far from reality? They're feeding him information all the time. He's way ahead of the game. He'll know exactly what your plan is. He's not stupid, he knows you are already investing millions to increase the security on the systems at GCHQ. He knows everything! He'll already have something sorted to scupper you. If I ask to see him, and then start questioning him, he'll see straight through it."

"I removed his allies; they're gone from the service. Besides, only a select few, who I trust, know anything about this."

Barnes laughed and scrunched up her nose. "Delusion is a dangerous bedfellow."

Luthi appeared rattled. Barnes could sense she'd been drawn in. Her strategy was working. Now she needed to go for the kill. "You'll need to have another purge. Rid yourself of those who hold alliances with him. Otherwise none of this will work."

Luthi perched on the lounger, scratching at her top lip with the immaculately manicured fingers of her left hand. Barnes assumed she was mulling over ideas.

"Then you'll have to sort it. Get me evidence of the ones that need removing and I'll do the rest."

Bingo! Barnes removed the sunglasses, placed them carefully down on the table beside her and then stared straight into Luthi's eyes. "How, in the name of all that's holy, are you expecting me to do that? It's not as though I can just ring him and ask him where he's getting his information!"

"That's your problem."

"You'll have to cut me some slack and provide help."

"You can have Coleman and Hobbs. They can work with you, and they can draw on my other resources to identify the leaks. Field can use her skills to track Faulkner-Brown's communications network. That's what she's good at, isn't it?"

"You've totally underestimated the operation. You are expecting me, Zoe, Coleman and Hobbs to go up against Faulkner-Brown, his multi-millions, his dedicated team of ruthless hackers, and of course, the Russians!"

"Stop the attacks and give me Faulkner-Brown, or Woods dies."

Barnes made out she was speechless. She stared down at the crystal blue water lapping against the pool side, shaking her head slowly and attempting to give the impression of utter bewilderment.

"Maria, you are the most intelligent, resourceful and capable woman I have ever had the misfortune to meet. You, above anyone else, are equipped to complete this mission. All I ask is that you do that. Then you, Woods and the Field girl are free to go."

"She's a woman, not a girl," she barked. That kind of language infuriated her.

"Whatever."

Zoe and Coleman's return cooled the waters.

"Here we are, Ladies," Coleman said, offering first Luthi, and then Barnes, their drinks.

"I think we're done," Luthi said, abruptly standing and placing the glass on the nearby table.

Coleman's look of displeasure met with Barnes' approval. "Aren't we going to finish the fruit juice?" he asked.

"We don't have time," was Luthi's curt response. "We've a great deal of work to do!" She looked down at Barnes who was nonchalantly sipping the juice. "You have five days to get me the names of the informants, and then an additional five days to provide me with the details of Faulkner-Brown's plan and deliver his head on a platter. I have every confidence you'll achieve both targets. Have a nice day, Maria. We'll show ourselves out."

As Luthi strode off, with Coleman following, Barnes winked at Zoe. "I'll open the gates," she shouted, pressing the fob. She didn't think Luthi had heard, but that was not a problem.

"How did it go?" Zoe asked, flipping open the laptop and checking the CCTV to make sure they had exited through the gates. She gave a thumbs-up sign to Barnes, who then pressed the fob for a second time to close them.

"Sweet," Barnes answered. "What did Coleman say?"

"That we're on the money, whatever that means. I know it's only an act, but I really don't like him."

"He's fine. As I said, we're supposed to react as though we detest him. Does he think Luthi has swallowed the bait?"

"Hook, line and sinker."

"Excellent. I need to use the satellite phone to call Faulkner-Brown. He'll be impressed. She wants a list of those supposedly leaking information to him. It's his chance to settle a few old scores. Once he gives me their names, you'll need to plant the evidence that will incriminate them. Will that be a problem?"

Zoe shook her head.

"Great."

"I've received another message from Cody. He's still convinced Kaleem was at university with him - studying some kind of part-time electrical course. So I've compiled a list of Asian men doing exactly that. There were fifteen during the years Cody was there. I have their names and addresses and I'm sending them to McLean's daughter Sofia and asking her to pass them to her father. I can do it via e-mail and keep below the radar."

"Ask that McLean checks them out on the quiet. We don't want any of this getting out too early."

"Will do."

Sunday 27th September

Cody's attention switched as the bedroom door opened and Haziq strolled in. His anxiety levels instantly increased; this was the moment he'd been waiting for. He pulled himself up into a sitting position on the mattress, allowing the blanket to drop to his waist. Now he fought to control his trembling hands as he made out he was resetting the time on his watch.

Sahib jumped to his feet. He had been watching Zen, who in his turn was busily working away on the keyboards. "Hi, Boss," Sahib said. "What's up?"

"I thought I'd see how thing are going." Haziq came over to Cody, who still fiddled frantically with his watch. "What are you doing?"

"I forgot to wind it and I've lost track of the time. I get anxious if I can't see the exact time. Sorry."

Haziq looked at his own watch. "It's nearly two o'clock," he said, frowning over at Sahib, clearly looking for some confirmation.

Sahib checked his phone. "It's 1.57 to be exact," he confirmed.

"Thank you," Cody responded, setting the watch.

"So how are we doing?" Haziq asked Cody.

"Harry, have we made any progress over the past two hours?" Cody deliberately involved Zen, because he needed Haziq's attention to be focused elsewhere.

Zen spun round. "No, we're still struggling to break through the initial level of security. We're doing our best. We're working nonstop."

"I know. I get regular updates. Is there anything else that might help you?" Haziq said, turning to Cody, but Zen answered quickly, so Haziq switched back to him.

"There's a high grade multi-function decoder that might speed things up. The problem is that they're only available on the net, and they're really expensive. You can't buy them on the high street."

"We could have it delivered here," Sahib suggested.

Haziq sighed, obviously annoyed. "Give me the details," he insisted.

Zen scribbled away on some paper. It took him several seconds before he handed it over.

"How much does it cost?" Haziq wanted to know.

Zen immediately answered. "It's about eleven hundred pounds, Sir," he said,

Cody tried to swallow but his mouth was dry. He held his left arm and elbow high across his chest, intentionally scratching his back over his right shoulder.

Haziq looked angry. He turned to face Cody, shook his head and pointed his finger at him. "I'll buy you this, but I'm expecting results. You'd better not let me down."

"No, Sir. It'll help speed things up," he replied, trembling.

"Right," Haziq muttered. "I'll let you know when it arrives."

Cody slowly lowered his arm, praying that what he had just done would be sufficient to save them. If he had successfully completed the initial phase of his plan, the second phase would come later tonight, when Zen could undertake a more daring and dangerous task.

Barnes smiled as the taxi-boat bobbed slowly up to the jetty. Aliona and Ben were sitting in the rear seat and as soon as the child saw his mother he waved eagerly, jumping up and down. "Where's Mr Greg?" he shouted.

"He'll be back tomorrow, Sweetheart. Have you had a nice time?" she asked, as the boat was moored and the passengers prepared to disembark.

He rummaged around excitedly in Aliona's bag, pulling out a pirate's hat, eye patch and a large plastic sword. He quickly donned the hat and eye patch and turned to face his mother. "Ahoy, Captain!" he called, waving the sword around. "I'm a swashbuckling pirate!" he concluded, much to the amusement of the other passengers who were now leaving the boat.

Aliona shrugged. "He insisted," she said. "Sorry." She lifted him up and passed him to his mother, who kissed and hugged him.

On this occasion Barnes decided not to raise concerns. She didn't approve of him having anything resembling a weapon, but she knew how persuasive he could be. It took steely determination on her part — whenever he wanted something she didn't favour — to resist that cheeky little grin and those big blue sparkling eyes. In truth she had missed him. Even though he and Aliona had only been away two nights it had not been easy for her. She initially thought she would enjoy the rest, but in reality she had been desperate to see him and cuddle him. If anything, the separation had reinforced how special their bond was. She was so pleased to see him back home.

Luthi had left the island earlier that morning. Coleman drove her to the airport and she was now presumably at thirty-eight thousand feet, on her way to the UK. Hobbs was at Great Exuma, keeping watch over Woods. Her abduction was scheduled for tomorrow morning. Once she was out of the way, there would be no need to keep Ben indoors. Woods could return to the house, and on the face of it things would have returned to normal.

But Barnes knew things were going to be anything but normal. The next ten days would be fraught both with intrigue and danger. She had spoken to Faulkner-Brown, updating him on Luthi's plans, and the situation surrounding the terrorists in the north of England and outlining their demands. She had been surprised by his reaction: he said he would speak to Kozlov and if the two of them agreed they would both come to the island and coordinate the operation from there. An hour later he had called back to confirm the two of them would be arriving tomorrow afternoon. He'd said Kozlov and himself would stay at Great Exuma with Coleman, because they'd realised the speed at which things were developing and wanted to keep a closer eye on events.

Now Barnes worried about the kind of reaction Faulkner-Brown's presence would produce from Woods and Zoe. Maybe Kozlov and Coleman could assist her to calm the situation. She knew Faulkner-Brown enjoyed riling people and getting under their skin, particularly if he sensed, or knew, that they were a threat to him, which no doubt he would have already worked out. Likewise, Woods' reputation for hiding his feelings was, at best, non-existent. She would need both him and Zoe to behave; she didn't want either of them jeopardising the operation. There was no doubt; it would be an interesting few days.

Zen struggled up and attempted to move away from the desk. Unfortunately the chain fastening the ankle shackles to the wall behind him became entangled around the chair leg and he ended up jolting the seat from the desk, the motion of which caused him to trip and fall head first, crashing into the wall. "Shit!" he yelled, feeling straight for his forehead. He pulled his hand away and stared in dismay at his blood-covered fingers. "Shit, I'm bleeding!"

Cody, who had been standing to the side, awaiting the changeover, looked on in horror. "Are you alright, Harry?" he asked, concerned.

Kaleem ran over and checked Zen. Cody could see a two centimetre gash oozing blood from his forehead. He immediately felt nauseous.

"Are you alright, Man?" Kaleem checked.

Zen shook his head. "I don't know." He looked shocked and pale.

"We've got to stop the bleeding. He needs to go to A&E!" Cody shouted.

"He can't go to A&E. I'll have to help him. There's a towel downstairs; I'll fetch that. You'll have to press it firmly on the wound for fifteen minutes, while I'll go and fetch some Steri-strips. They should fix it."

"W… what if he's got concussion?" Cody stuttered, freaking out.

"Keep an eye on him," Kaleem barked, clearly flustered. "I'll get the towel." He ran out of the room and down the staircase.

Cody bent down beside Zen. "Fucking hell, Harry! I didn't expect you to nearly knock yourself out," he whispered.

"I'm okay. It looks worse than it is."

Kaleem ran back into the room, towel in hand. He threw it at Cody. "I'll be as quick as I can. Keep the pressure on it. He ran back out, this time locking the door behind him.

Cody passed the towel to Zen. "Can you hold it to your head, Harry, while I download the footage from my watch?"

"Yes! Get on with it. I didn't do this for the fun of it. We don't know how long he's going to be."

Cody picked up the discarded chair and moved it away from the desk. He got down on all fours and reached under the table, grabbing hold of the Wi-Fi hub. He turned it upside down, noting the WEP key. He struggled to his feet, pulled the chair in and settled in front of the PCs. He then carefully prised the watch face open with his thumbnail, revealing the tiny keyboard. He touched the required buttons with the tip of the pencil they'd been using, and attempted to connect to the network by entering the WEP key. He prayed it hadn't been changed.

"How long will it take?" Zen asked.

"Seconds, once I can get the link set up. Come on!" he hissed.

"Hurry up!"

It took a moment or two, but his luck held. "Okay, okay, we're connected." He pressed the send button and watched as the media loaded to the PC.

Zen got on his feet, holding the towel to his head and watched as the footage played out. "Is that all we have? Is it enough for them?" he asked.

"I think so. We'll just have to hope there's a recording of his voice somewhere else on the web, so the voice recognition software can pick up on it."

"I didn't even know of its existence," Zen said, moving the towel away from the wound and squinting at the red mass on it. "How does it look?" he asked.

Cody squirmed. "Keep the pressure on."

Zen did as instructed.

"It's what they used to identify the British terrorist who beheaded the hostages," Cody clarified, addressing Zen's earlier statement. Then he quickly sent the footage, along with a short message, to Zoe. "Now I'll have to remove all traces of this from the PC," he mumbled, working as quickly as he could. He heard the door downstairs bang closed. "He's back. Quick, get on the mattress." He shuffled across to where Zen was sitting and took hold of the towel, just as Kaleem was unlocking the door.

"How is he?" Kaleem wanted to know, the second he entered the room.

"The bleeding has all but stopped. Take a look," Cody answered, moving the towel and intentionally not looking at the wound.

"Right, let me clean that up and use these," Kaleem said, taking over.

Cody shuffled back to the PCs. His eyes widened as he stared in disbelief at the screen. He whirled round. "We're in!" he hollered. "Harry we've done it! We're in!"

Kaleem rushed to his side. "What do you need to do now?"

"Work like fury to authorise the access, otherwise we'll lose it."

"Well done, Man. You'd better get on with it. Haziq will be over the moon."

"I need to sort it, now!" Cody said, fingers blasting across the keyboard as though they were possessed.

As Cody was working away on the computer, Barnes was pressing the button on the intercom receiver allowing Coleman to enter the grounds. She went to meet him. "Come on in," she said.

He wandered through the doors and glanced around. "Where is everyone?" he asked.

Zoe's in the computer room, Ben's in bed and Aliona is in the hot tub."

"Is she?" he said, his eyes widening. "Does she need any company?"

"Not from you!"

"Oh yes, I was forgetting. She prefers females."

"So what do you want? And how's Woods?"

"That's why I'm here, to reassure you he's okay. Hobbs is keeping him company. She's loaned him her Kindle. He's enjoying reading it. I think she's taken a shine to him."

"Has she?! Well what a pity she'll be leaving tomorrow."

"I'll be glad to see the back of her, and, as planned, our little chat with Luthi has made my task — of convincing her that I can better handle things here on my own — much easier. She's paranoid that someone's going to spill the beans and uncover her plot. She's gone back with plans to root out the traitors."

"Good. The more stress we can keep her under, the better."

"Exactly."

"Would you like a drink? Aliona's brought you some Cartwright and Butler from the mainland. I telephoned her and asked her to look out for it. She couldn't buy it in the shops, but the hotel had some, which they gave her, so she's brought that."

He laughed out loud. "Thank you. Have you tried it?"

"Not yet."

"Then we'll both have one. I'll give you a hand making it and we'll sit outside under the moonlight. How does that sound?"

The noise of Zoe clearing her throat at the top of the stairs drew their attention. "I have some breaking news," she said, running down the steps. "Firstly I've got footage of two of the terrorists: Haziq, and the one Cody calls Sahib. They're both masked, but I'm using voice recognition software to try to find a match."

"Great, I'll come up and take a look at that. What's the other news?" Barnes asked.

"Cody's broken into the MOD's mainframe."

"Wow." Coleman whistled, clearly impressed. "Cody is a clever boy."

"He's a young man!" Barnes scolded.

"Yes he is," Zoe endorsed, "and we'll soon know what the terrorists are planning."

"The pressure just went up several notches!" Barnes exclaimed. "Now it's imperative that we find out where they are being held!"

Chapter 14

Monday 28th September

Woods strolled up to the gates and pressed the button on the intercom. The call wasn't answered, but the gates slowly opened, allowing him to enter. He wandered in to the house, through the open doors, and started searching for the others. "Hello," he called out.

"We're up in the computer room," shouted Barnes.

Before he had a chance to reach the stairs Ben came running into the hallway to greet him. "Mr Greg, Mr Greg! Can we play pirates?"

He chuckled. "Yes we can. I like the sword, and the hat. And what have you done to your eye?"

Ben pulled the patch up and grinned. "Nothing. Look Mr Greg, it's fine! It's a pirate's patch."

"Oh, I see. I thought you'd had an accident," he fibbed.

Aliona appeared. "How you are today?"

"Fine, thank you. I'm pleased to be back."

"We pleased have you back, aren't we, Ben?"

Ben's attention lay elsewhere. "What's that?" he asked, pointing at Woods' hand.

"It's a Kindle. There are lots and lots of books on it."

"On there?!"

"Yes, they're e-books." He thought he'd better explain. "Electronic books. It can store them in its memory."

"How many?"

"Hundreds."

"Have you read them?"

"No, not all of them, not yet."

"Will you read to me?"

"Yes, if your mother will allow me to. I'm sure I can find an appropriate one."

Then he had a thought, but Ben ran off up the stairs, shouting excitedly, "I'll ask her."

Ben being out of the way gave Aliona a chance to have a word. "I spoke with colleagues in Moscow," she said. "I get okay. Now get ball rolling, as you say. I need take full blood count and other samples too. You be pin cushion."

He laughed. "Any idea of timescales?"

"A month or so."

He nodded, immediately worrying that the treatment would be starting too soon.

"Hello, you," Barnes said, from the landing. "I understand you're going to read to Ben." The little boy rushed past his mother and ran back down the stairs.

"Yes he is! Aren't you, Mr Greg? A story about pirates."

"Benjamin, what have I told you about running down the stairs?" she said, stern-faced.

"That it's dangerous."

"Exactly! So why did you do it?"

"I've seen *you* run down the stairs, and Zoe, and Aliona."

Woods looked across at Aliona. He could see she too was struggling to keep a straight face.

Barnes sighed. "Well, we are careful."

"Well, so am I. I didn't fall."

"Aliona, please take Ben outside so he can let off some steam." She looked at Woods. "I presume Miss Hobbs has gone?"

He nodded. "About an hour ago."

Barnes beckoned him. "You need to see this. We've received footage of the terrorists."

"Okay. Ben, you go and get some fresh air and we'll play pirates later. Then I'll read you a story about an aardvark called Pendleton." As he made his way up the stairs he could hear Aliona trying to explain, in broken English, exactly what an aardvark was. He reached the landing and Barnes immediately hugged him. "It's great to have you back," she said.

He smiled. He'd missed her too. "How come you've allowed him to dress in a pirate costume and carry a sword? I would have thought you'd disapprove."

"I do, and it's a long story. Basically I told him he could choose something from the shops, and, despite Aliona's best efforts to persuade him otherwise, he insisted on that. He even slept in the hat last night. I'm trying not to make a fuss, so that he'll lose interest in it."

"The important thing is that he said *play* pirates, clearly recognising it's a game."

"I suppose so," she replied, seeming tired. "Anyway, how did the abduction go?"

"Pretty smooth, I think. I didn't see or hear much. A guy came down to the gymnasium, unlocked the door, and told me to wait an hour before going out. Coleman wasn't there. The house was empty."

"He needed to be out of the way. In actual fact he'll be back shortly, although he'll explain to Luthi that he went across to the mainland with Zoe and me, to buy new equipment in readiness for what she has asked us to do. He'll claim we'd been out all day and that it was dark when he supposedly discovered Hobbs had been abducted. By the time he rings Luthi, she will be half way to Russia."

"Good," he said, noticing she'd spotted what he held.

"I see you've stolen her Kindle."

"She loaned it to me. Besides, she won't need it now. Anyhow, I'm reading Peter Best's *The Burden of Truth*. It's an amazing book; you'd love it."

"I promise I'll read it. Now come and have a look at this."

He followed her into the adjacent room and found Zoe working on three PCs simultaneously. "Hi," she called out, not taking her eyes off the screens.

He moved closer so he could see. "What do I need to look at, Zoe?"

"Just give me a minute," she replied.

"Did Coleman tell you Faulkner-Brown and Kozlov are arriving today?" Barnes asked.

He spun round. "No, he didn't."

"They're staying with him."

"Oh, I suppose that's better than having them with us. How long are they here for?"

"Until we've reached a successful outcome."

"Right," Zoe said, positioning one of the screens so Woods could see it.

He stared at the footage. "They definitely sound like they have a Yorkshire twang in their Asian accents."

"Zoe's using voice recognition software to identify them," Barnes clarified.

"Any luck?"

Zoe shook her head. "Not yet."

"Okay. I'll ring McLean and see if he's made any progress," he said.

"Before you do that, something important has just arrived from Cody. Maria, you also need to see this." Zoe opened up another tab. She moved to the side, on the swivel chair, so they could read the post.

Woods' hoot gave an indication of how nervous he was. "So now we know exactly what Haziq wants. Although that's impossible, isn't it?" He was grasping at straws. "Surely there's God knows how many levels of security to get through before you could do that."

"Four levels, to be exact," Zoe confirmed calmly. "And yes, Cody and Zen can't do it alone, and they know that. However, with some expert assistance from me, they might be able to."

The anxiety set in. "I trust you're not suggesting that we get involved?"

"That's exactly what I am suggesting." Zoe looked at Barnes. "Until we know where they are being held, and we can free them, we'll have to play along. If Haziq can't achieve his goal, Cody and Zen are as good as dead."

Barnes nodded in agreement. "Zoe's right. We can't allow that to happen."

He stared at her in disbelief. "No, we can't! But neither can we launch a bloody nuclear attack on the States!"

"I know we can't! And we won't need to, provided we find out where they are being held."

"And what if we don't?!"

"Even if we did launch an attack, the USA's defence systems would blow the missile out of the skies before it got anywhere near them," Zoe muttered, as though the thought had already crossed her mind.

"Whoa! This is getting out of hand. We can't be seen to be assisting them."

"Don't you think I know that?" Zoe snapped. "But right now I can't come up with an alternative."

Woods stood scowling, desperately trying to find another option.

"Well?" Zoe said. "I'm waiting!"

Barnes looked to Woods. "We need to chase up McLean and ask him what's happening. He might be on the brink of finding them, and if that's the case we're worrying over nothing. Don't forget, our aim is to prevent the attack and save Cody and Zen. Then we'll be the heroes - the ones, along with the Russians, who prevented a catastrophe."

He knew that; it was blatantly obvious to him. That wasn't what was troubling him.

"Meanwhile," Barnes went on, "Luthi will be focusing in on a fictitious cyber-attack. We'll make sure she doesn't know anything about Cody, Zen, or the terrorists, even though it will have been happening under her nose. She'll be discredited."

"I can see that, but what if she has support from those inside Government? If that's the case, she'll keep her job."

"Listen!" Barnes said firmly. "The Civil Service is under increasing pressure to cut budgets, and there's a view held in Government that Luthi's department should share in the austerity. Remember, we're all in this together? Nevertheless, the terrorist attacks are increasing and the atrocities mounting. Luthi's expected to be ahead of the game, yet her resources are diminishing and her budgets are being slashed. Put simply, she doesn't have the staff. She's caught between a rock and a hard place!"

Woods nodded. He knew she was right about that too.

"Luthi was grilled by the Intelligence and Security Select Committee recently," Barnes continued, "when she argued that, without a significant increase in her resources, the country's security would be compromised. Now there's talk of her being replaced; after three years her standing is at its lowest. She knows she's in serious danger of losing her job and her £750,000 salary."

"And that's partly why she's swallowed our ruse," Zoe chipped in, supporting Barnes' argument. "She needs to increase her own credibility. The recognition of preventing cyber-attacks on the intelligence-gathering agencies across the world will do just that."

"Whereas when she has been discredited, we'll be right there with the evidence, proving that she interfered in a police investigation, turned a blind eye to several murders, and consequently saved numerous prominent people from going to jail, hence furthering her own career. This time she'll be the one in jail!"

Woods nodded again. "I understand that," he said, scratching his head. "But how many other people, within her inner circle, know about the cyber-attacks — supposedly organised by Faulkner-Brown — and the fact she's blackmailing you to prevent them? The very people who, if she needed them to, could support her when she says she'd been deliberately mislead?"

"That's the beauty of our little scam. She's kept those in the know to a minimum. She's hardly likely to broadcast the fact that she's resorted to blackmail, is she?"

"No, I don't suppose so," Woods had to conclude.

"According to Coleman, she's only involved four people: him, Hobbs, Jacob Hartley — one of her senior group commanders who is under strict instructions to keep it to himself — and finally, Cuthbert Fisher, the Deputy Foreign Secretary."

"And that's it?"

This time Barnes nodded. "Coleman's on our side, Hobbs is incommunicado, and would you like to guess which two people are going to be identified as leaking information to Faulkner-Brown?"

Woods sniggered. "Jacob Hartley and Cuthbert Fisher."

"Correct."

As soon as Luthi discovers that, they'll be history," he said.

"Consequently, no-one will be there to back her claims," Zoe concluded, staring at the screens.

Woods didn't feel he had much choice other than to acquiesce. "Okay, Zoe, so you need to inform Cody that, in order to keep him and Zen alive, you'll help. However, you need to emphasise that we're doing everything within our power to locate where they are being held, and as soon as we've done that, they'll be set free and the attack aborted."

She sighed. "I've already done that! You need to ring McLean."

"Yes I do." He looked at his watch. It was 11.30 a.m. local time – 4.30 p.m. in the UK. "I'll use the unregistered phone and call him from my room," he said, going out of the door.

"Do you need any help?" Barnes shouted.

"No! I'll do this on my own."

*

Woods' fingers tapped apprehensively along the dresser as he waited for the call to McLean to connect. "Come on, Pete," he uttered, sitting on the stool as the ring tone sounded in his ear. A few moments later he heard the unmistakable sound of his former colleague's voice.

"Aye, you bugger. You don't make things easy for me."

He smiled. "Hello, Pete. Are you okay to talk?"

"Aye. I suppose you want an update?"

"Please, things are starting to spiral out of control. You've got to find Cody and Zen."

"You'll appreciate that Foster's absolutely crapping himself. He's given me and Chris Jacobs until close of play on Wednesday, and then he's calling in SO15, that's the Met's new anti-terror team."

"Okay, I understand. I suppose I should be grateful that he's sanctioned time for you and Chris to look into this."

"Aye. Well he too wants Luthi and Faulkner-Brown brought before the courts. And the fact that Kozlov is involved has impressed him."

"Good, so where are we?"

"Jacobs has been to Reading, to Zen's flat, knocking on doors, but no-one remembers seeing anything out of the ordinary. On the way back he called at Cody's flat in West Bridgford. A woman there, who lives in the flat below, remembers seeing an Asian guy going up the stairs on the afternoon of Tuesday 22nd September."

"That will be when they collected Cody's glasses and watch. Do we have a description?"

"Yes, but I doubt it will lead anywhere. It's too generic."

Woods sighed. "What about the Asian young men who undertook electrical courses when Cody was at University?"

"Aye, I've made good progress on that."

"You can narrow it down somewhat now. I've listened to their accents: there's definitely a Yorkshire twang, and, in fact, I'd wager they are from West Yorkshire." He listened to papers rustling, while he presumed McLean checked the list.

"Aye, well that restricts it to three. One in Agbrigg, here in Wakefield, one in Ravensthorpe, and finally, one in Bradford."

"Excellent. What about the gluten-free Chinese take-away?"

"Sharron's sorting through this for me. She hasn't had any luck yet, but I'll tell her to concentrate on these three areas."

"How is she?" Woods asked, feeling ashamed that he'd never bothered to contact her or check how the treatment was going.

"Aye, she's doing okay. She's not as quick-minded as she once was, because the chemo affected her. Chemo-brain, she calls it. But it's good to have her back."

"Give her my regards," he said, disgusted with himself.

"Aye, I will. She's always asking about you."

His feeling of self-remorse instantly turned to utter revulsion at how he treated people. "Tell her I'm sorry, I'm an arsehole and I don't deserve friends."

"Aye, don't worry about it. We all know you, and what you're like."

This only made him feel worse. "I don't know why you put up with me."

"Because we all have long memories and don't forget how bloody good you once were."

He nodded to himself. "What about the special multi-function decoder that was ordered yesterday. Have you sourced that?"

"Our IT guys are chasing it up. I should have an answer by the end of today. I'm presuming that's our best lead."

"Okay, Pete. Thank you. Ring me the minute you have anything. From now on this mobile won't be switched off."

"Aye!"

The call ended with Woods staring into the dresser mirror. He sighed. "Two days to find Cody and Zen," he said quietly. Was that going to be enough? "We're screwed if it isn't," he said. Now his fate lay in McLean, Jacobs, Sharron West and the IT guy's hands; the majority, in fact the core, of his former murder investigation team. They wouldn't let him down. Would they? He doubted they would. He knew he owed them. When this was over, and he'd finished the treatment, provided the outcome was successful, he would take them out for a meal. No he wouldn't; he'd treat them to an all-expenses paid day at the races. McLean would love that; so would the others, even Foster. It would be time to mend a few fences and make amends for his unforgivable actions.

Barnes smiled wryly, focusing the binoculars in on Faulkner-Brown as he waddled off the jetty and squeezed his large frame into Coleman's golf buggy. It was a tight fit, but he managed without any mishaps. Meanwhile, Kozlov hopped in the rear. "They're here," she called across to Woods, who pulled a disgruntled face.

"What a pity he didn't drown in the bay," he responded.

She yawned, intentionally indicating her displeasure at his comment. "I trust you will behave."

"Of course. Where's Zoe?"

"I'm here," she said, appearing at the top of the steps, which opened out onto the baking hot roof terrace. "Has he arrived?" she asked Woods.

"Yes," answered Barnes. "They'll be here in a couple of minutes. They want an update."

"Won't Faulkner-Brown need something to eat?" Woods asked.

"Like a suckling pig?" Zoe suggested.

"Stop it, the pair of you!" She wasn't going to put up with this. "We need his help."

Woods smiled. "We'll be as nice as pie with him, Maria, wont we, Zoe?"

"No, we'll treat him with the same animosity that he shows to everyone else."

"Right, if you're going to do that, you two can stay up here and I'll deal with him on my own," she said, walking briskly off towards the steps.

"Hang on a sec," Woods said. "We'll behave; you don't need to do this alone. Come on, Zoe."

They walked down the steps together and as the intercom sounded Barnes hit the button on the fob in her hand and opened the gates. Coleman, Kozlov and Faulkner-Brown strolled in and met them by the entrance doors. "Hello," Barnes said. "Would you care for a drink? We could sit by the pool."

"That would be nice, Maria," Kozlov replied. He looked at Woods. "How are you?"

"Still breathing."

"I can see that. I understand that you are to undergo a new kind of treatment. I trust it will be as successful as my daughter's treatment that Maria's father organised twenty-five years ago."

"Thank you."

"I'll help Zoe with the drinks," Coleman suggested. "Maria, you can show everyone else to the pool. Where are Ben and Aliona?"

"Playing pirates, on the catamaran."

"I'd like to meet him," Faulkner-Brown said, sounding sincere. "I've heard so much about the young rascal."

"I'll take you," Woods offered, much to Barnes' surprise. "The cat's moored to the private jetty; we just need to go down the path. Follow me."

She watched as they wandered off together. She couldn't help wondering what kind of conversation they would be having. She'd ask Woods later. "We'll sit by the pool while they make the drinks," she said to Kozlov, seeing Zoe and Coleman go inside.

As they settled in the shade Kozlov gave her a knowing look. "So they want to launch a Trident missile at Capitol Hill."

She frowned.

"My people are closely monitoring Zoe's activities."

"How?"

"She gave us access to her computers." Then he smiled. "Well, to be truthful, she doesn't know she's given us access, but she has. We too have very talented hackers. And let me say now that she's a very skilful young woman. My people are suitably impressed, particularly with how she and the other hacker, Cody, communicate. The four digit number system is quite good. I appreciate she uses a programme that she developed to decipher his messages and create her responses, whereas he's doing it while being watched, without the aid of the programme. He must have a phenomenal brain."

"Maybe Asperger's?" she put forward.

"Possibly."

She nodded, spending a moment pondering the observation. "So what are your thoughts about the nuclear strike?" she asked, moving on.

"Even if Zoe could orchestrate its launch, which I doubt, the Americans would know the second it left the sub. It would be shot down."

"But the terrorists don't realise that."

"No they don't. In fact, from what I can see, they are nothing more than a bunch of amateurs."

"I agree. However, all that proves is that a bunch of amateurs stand a far better chance of staying below the radar than the professional."

He nodded. "That's very true."

"Have you made any progress locating where they are being held?"

"I have an address for you." He rummaged in his jacket pocket and passed a slip of paper over. "That's the address where the multi-function decoder is being delivered tomorrow. I've had it checked out. It's a corner shop, owned and run by the Ahmed family. As you'll see, it's in Agbrigg, Wakefield, about two miles out from the city centre. It's unlikely that Cody and Zen are being held at the shop, but it will lead us to where they are. I have it and the family under surveillance. We're monitoring all their calls and internet usage. The father, Mustafa Ahmed owns a grey BMW X1, his four sons help him with the shop and with running a small taxi firm."

"That must be Haziq. Maybe they are not as amateurish as we think, if they are smart enough to use false names."

"Yes, but why?"

She chewed on her lower lip. "We need to be careful. I smell a rat."

"One of my people will deliver the decoder. It will have a tracker in it, but we need Cody to make an excuse for requiring it at the house. Now that they have access to the MOD's systems, the terrorists may decide to return it and get their money back."

"I'll ask Zoe to message him."

"Could you do it right now, please? It's important we don't lose the initiative."

"Yes, consider it done. If Cody makes the request tonight, then by tomorrow afternoon we should have them within our grasp."

Kozlov smiled. "Yes, we should."

She stepped up out of the chair, intending to go inside and instruct Zoe accordingly, but out of the corner of her eye she caught sight of

Faulkner-Brown, down by the catamaran, falling off from the jetty into the water. "Oh my God," she said, thinking Woods had just tried to kill his old adversary.

Chapter 15

Tuesday 29th September

Luthi switched the bedside light on and snatched up the buzzing mobile. "Hello Coleman," she responded, with an air of foreboding, noting the time as 3.15 a.m.

"Hobbs has been taken. I've been out all day and when I arrived back this evening there were signs of a break-in, and an almighty struggle. She must have put up a fight."

"What about Woods?" Luthi asked, quickly trying to process the facts and how this could have happened.

"He's still locked in the gymnasium. He says he heard shouting and what he thought was some kind of scuffle. Then silence."

"What time was this?"

"Around 7.30 a.m. He's been on his own since. They must have been watching the house and pounced as soon as I left."

"And where have you been?"

"With Barnes and Zoe Field in Antigua. We left at 7.20 this morning. We've been buying the equipment they needed to entrap Faulkner-Brown and discover who is feeding him information."

She sighed. "How come you went with them?"

"They asked me. You'd said we should assist."

"Barnes must be behind this! She's enticed you away, then organised for Hobbs to be kidnapped in retaliation for Woods. She'll probably want an exchange."

"No she won't. She's smart, and she'll know you couldn't give a damn about your staff. Ten a penny, wasn't that what you said during your last purge?"

She sucked in her cheeks. Coleman was correct. If Barnes tried to bargain Hobbs off, it wouldn't work. "What has she been saying to you today?"

"Nothing really. She obviously doesn't like me, but they needed a hand with all the equipment."

"Don't you find that odd? Why didn't she have it delivered?"

"She said she couldn't wait; your deadline has placed them under intense pressure, or at least that's what she claims."

"Thankfully they didn't get Woods," she observed, thinking Coleman had been too easily led away from the house. "I'll trace Hobbs," she said, confidently. "And in the meantime I'll send someone to replace her."

"Do you really think that's a good idea? I can manage on my own. The more people you involve, the more chance there is of this leaking out. We need to keep a tight lid on things."

She gave his words the briefest consideration. "Alright, I haven't got time to argue. I need to ring Hartley and have him trace Hobbs. When I've found her I'll decide whether or not you need assistance."

"Okay, I'll get off the line."

"Good. Don't let Woods, Barnes or the Field girl out of your sight from now on. I'd like daily updates on progress. Understood?"

"Yes."

Immediately the call ended, she hit the speed dial button for Jacob Hartley. "Hi, it's me. We have a small problem: Paula Hobbs has been abducted." She heard a slight sigh.

"Where from and when?"

"Great Exuma, yesterday morning, around 7.30 a.m. local time. Find her for me?"

"Give me half an hour. Is Coleman alright?"

"Yes. He was out."

"What about Woods?"

"Whoever took Hobbs appears to have overlooked him. Which I'm having difficulty understanding. But let's get her back and then we can determine exactly what happened."

"Will do." The line went dead and she tossed the phone aside. She knew the implant in Hobbs' left thigh transmitted twenty-four/seven. All Hartley needed to do was press a few buttons and he would instantly have her location, and with a bit more time he would know the route she'd taken to it. Luthi just needed to bide her time. She decided to get dressed and head into work. She could better coordinate things from there.

Thirty-four minutes later she strode into her office at Vauxhall Cross and, as she hung her immaculately pressed jacket on the coat stand, her phone buzzed. She looked at the display and, as expected, it was Hartley. "Hello," she said. "Where is she?"

"This isn't looking too good. According to the current signal she is outside the Post Office on Hockerill Street in Bishop's Stortford. She's been there for the past three and a half hours."

Luthi cringed. "Go on."

"I suspect the implant has been surgically removed and then placed in an envelope, presumably addressed to you, and posted in the box outside the Post Office. I'm arranging to have it opened shortly and that's what I'm expecting to find."

She shook her head. "Let me guess, she was flown into Stanstead on a private jet, which refuelled and then flew on to Moscow."

"That's how it's looking."

"Damn it! E-mail me the details and a link to the programme? I'm actually in my office."

"I'll do it right now. You'll have the current live feed and if you rewind you'll see the journey. Give me a couple of minutes and I'll talk you through it."

While Hartley sorted out the technicalities Luthi logged on to her PC and opened up her e-mails. Ninety seconds later the one from Hartley arrived. She clicked and opened up the programme. "I'm currently looking at the screen," she said, holding the mobile to her ear with her left hand and operating the mouse with the other.

"Good. Enter yesterday's date in the search bar, and, not forgetting they are five hours behind us, enter 1.10 p.m. Now, fast forward the recording." He paused, giving Luthi time to complete his instructions. "As you can see, she left the island yesterday morning at 8.12 a.m. local time, presumably by boat, which then appears to have docked in Winthorpes Bay. She then travelled to VC Bird International Airport, maybe hidden in the back of a cargo van. The jet took off at 9.15 a.m. local time, and landed at Stanstead at 10.15 p.m. BST. It refuelled, taking off again at 10.55 p.m. The flight plan was indeed to Moscow. The signal, which is currently outside the Post Office, suggests it was driven there, just after midnight. I'm guessing one of the pilots handed the envelope to a member of the ground crew and asked them to post it. I'm having the CCTV checked within that area."

Luthi quickly rewound the footage to the beginning of the day. She wanted to see where Coleman had been. "Just a minute," she said, puzzled. "Where's Coleman's signal? He said he left the island at 7.20 a.m."

"His implant has malfunctioned. It's not transmitting at the moment."

She frowned. "Why hasn't it been replaced?"

"He's missed the appointments."

"How many appointments?"

"Four."

"Four! You know the procedure. If they miss two appointments they have to be immediately called in. No excuses. How come he's missed four?!"

"He claims he's too busy and that he has your authority."

"I bet he does!" She took a moment to calm herself. "How long has it been malfunctioning?"

"Seven months."

"Seven months!" She was livid. It simply wasn't good enough.

"Are you still there?" Hartley checked.

"Yes. Yes, I am."

"There's something else that has come to my attention."

Her sigh encompassed the annoyance in her voice. "Please enlighten me."

"Hobbs had two trackers assigned to her. One of them started transmitting on Friday evening. The signal came from Great Exuma. Remember they're five hours behind us, so it was probably activated just after lunchtime. Then yesterday morning at around 9.15 a.m. local time the signal moved across to Barnes' house, and it's been there ever since."

"I arrived at Great Exuma just after lunchtime on Friday. She didn't mention activating a tracker. And Woods had been brought there earlier that morning."

"Mmm…"

"Mmm… indeed," she echoed. "According to Coleman, Woods remains locked in the basement, and, if that was the case, then someone went over to Great Exuma after Hobbs had been abducted and took whatever contained the tracker. Coleman said Barnes and the Field girl were with him all day, across in Antigua. The only other person at her house is the oncologist. Why would she go over there?"

"Good question. And if she went there, did she see Woods? And if so, why is he still with Coleman?"

"Something is definitely amiss here. I need to have time to think this through," she said, her mind awash with various theories, the primary one being that the oncologist was working for another agency, possibly the CIA. But why hadn't she been informed? And if that was the case, what the hell were the CIA they doing poking around on the island?

"At least we know Hobbs won't divulge anything to Kozlov. Not for the first few weeks, anyway. So we do have some time before she'll crack."

"That is the last thing I need to worry about right now," Luthi snapped.

"I could arrange to have the oncologist brought in for questioning."

"Don't involve Coleman!"

"Obviously not." He sounded annoyed that he'd had to clarify that point.

"We definitely need to know exactly what is going on in that house. Therefore, yes, have the oncologist questioned, but you'll have to entice her away from the island before you can do that."

"I'll think of something."

"Good, and I'll have a chat with Mr Coleman. Perhaps set him a little test to check where his loyalties actually lie."

At 8.30 a.m. local time, Kozlov arrived at the house. Barnes opened the gate and met him at the entrance doors, inviting him in and explaining that Woods and Zoe were waiting for him in the ocean room.

When everyone was together, Woods spoke first. "How's Faulkner-Brown?" he asked, slipping the Kindle he'd been reading into his jacket pocket.

"Complaining about the heat, the bugs, the lizards, and the fact that the tree frogs have kept him awake all night."

"Perfectly normal then," Barnes observed.

"Yes, his excursion into the sea hasn't dampened his grouchiness," Kozlov replied, glancing over at Woods.

"He tripped over Ben's tricycle," Woods said, raising his hands in a gesture of innocence. "I wasn't anywhere near him."

Zoe grinned. "Are you sure *you* didn't place it there, knowing his large girth would prevent him seeing it?"

He smirked back at her.

"What's the news on the decoder?" Barnes asked Kozlov, wanting to move things along.

"Delivered to the shop at 8.50 a.m. UK time. Mustafa Ahmed signed for it and my delivery man entered into a short conversation with him. So we have a recording of Mustafa's voice, which has been checked against Cody's footage and we can confirm that Mustafa isn't Haziq."

Barnes spotted Woods frowning. "Where is the package now?" he asked.

"Still at the shop."

"Last night Cody told them that he urgently needed it," Zoe asserted. "Kaleem immediately telephoned Haziq with that message."

Kozlov nodded. "We didn't pick up on any telecommunications between the Ahmeds last night. And no-one in that family has been to Sheffield Hallam University."

"That suggests the shop is merely being used as a drop-off point," Woods offered.

"Yes, we're watching it and them. Not long after the decoder was delivered Mustafa Ahmed sent a text message to an unregistered phone, saying simply, 'it's here'. But there hasn't been a reply to the text, so we're expecting someone to collect the package and then take it to the house. The tracker will identify where."

"What about other communications from the unregistered mobile?" Woods asked.

"Nothing. No calls to or from it, and no other texts. It was connected to the network this morning for three minutes at 10.00 a.m. UK time, presumably checking for the messages. The signal was traced to Dewsbury Bus Station. We've accessed the CCTV, and there are simply too many people there to identify the phone user."

Barnes' concerns were multiplying. "How many deliveries or collections have been made to the shop since 10.00 a.m.?" she wanted to know.

"I'd have to check," Kozlov responded. "But the tracker is still transmitting from there. Are you suggesting it's been detected, removed, and the decoder has already gone from the shop?"

She nodded slowly. "That's what I would have done."

Kozlov curled his lip. "Tell Cody to let us know the second it arrives," he instructed Zoe, who jumped up and hurried off out of the room.

"I'm developing a really bad feeling about this," Barnes said, looking to Woods for support.

"I know what you mean. What are your thoughts?"

"This is a set-up. We're being led down the garden path. Although it's possible to launch a nuclear weapon, it simply wouldn't reach its target. At first we thought they were a bunch of amateurs, now I'm not so sure, and if they're not, they'll know that what they are proposing would fail."

Kozlov's nod made her feel easier.

"But Zoe couldn't find any indication that Luthi was involved," Woods added.

"She isn't," Kozlov clarified. "I'm absolutely sure on that."

"I think this is a phantom attack," Barnes said, trying to clarify her thoughts, "made to look as realistic as possible, and draw the intelligence services in."

"Meanwhile, another attack is being planned that is totally off the radar," Kozlov offered, nodding again."

"You think we've been wrong footed?!" Woods asked.

Zoe appeared. "Yes, you have. Cody received the decoder two hours ago. Obviously someone at the shop removed the tracker."

"So what's the plan?" Woods asked.

"Good question," Zoe responded, flicking up her eyebrows.

"Firstly, even if it's a phantom attack, we still need to find Cody and Zen," Barnes replied, trying to instil some importance and urgency into that necessity.

"Then we can have the house closely monitored and the terrorists identified and watched. We can look into their communications. See who their associates are. Then we'll be in a better position to decide if their planned attack is serious, or, as you say, a phantom one," Kozlov added.

"In the meantime Zoe can search for other suspicious activity on the web and attempt to identify if it is linked to a terrorist cell," suggested Barnes, as Zoe's smile reassured her they were on the same page.

"I'll ring McLean," Woods said, getting up out of the chair. "We'd narrowed it down to three people studying an electrical course while Cody was at Sheffield. With a bit of luck he could have an answer."

As he left the room Barnes switched her attention back to Kozlov. "What are you planning to do with Hobbs?"

"Keep her out of the way."

"It will be interesting to see what Luthi does next."

"What are her options?" Zoe chipped in.

Kozlov smiled. "She'll know Hobbs will be able to resist questioning, but that eventually she'll succumb. Therefore she'll want to increase the pressure on you two to speed things along."

"I'm half expecting her to ring me," Barnes said. "I suspect she'll threaten to stop Woods' medication if Hobbs isn't released."

"How are you going to play that one?" Zoe enquired.

"Explain that if she does, then Woods is as good as dead, and therefore we'll stop assisting her."

"Why don't you tell her that you've uncovered Faulkner-Brown is behind the kidnapping, and that he's preparing to blackmail her. Then she'll need your help more than ever," Kozlov suggested.

She liked the idea. "I'll do that." She looked up as Woods re-entered the room grinning.

"Right," he said, rubbing his hands together. "McLean has an address in Ravensthorpe. It's a mid-terrace property on Calder Road, not far from the traffic lights at the junction with Huddersfield Road. The exact Chinese take-away meal that Cody described, was delivered to that address on Tuesday 22nd at 6.55 p.m. UK time. The property is owned by Aali Farooq, whose cousin and younger brother are in Syria fighting for the Islamic State militants. One of his other cousins, Gamal Farooq studied Electrical Engineering at Sheffield University when Cody was there. He works for Wakefield Council."

Barnes watched him hand Kozlov a piece of paper, presumably with the address and the names written on it.

"What have you told McLean?" Kozlov wanted to know from Woods.

"We think it's a set up. I've told him to hold fire. We've got until 5.00 p.m. UK time tomorrow, then Foster's involving SO15."

Kozlov clicked his tongue. "That doesn't give me much time."

"Well, it's all we've got!"

Kozlov folded up the piece of paper and placed it in his top pocket. "I'll give it my best shot," he said, standing and heading out of the room.

"And I'd better get back to monitoring the web," Zoe said, following him. "I'll start by looking at the Farooq family."

Barnes sensed Woods' trepidation. "We'll get them out alive," she said. "That has to be our priority. Even if it is a phantom attack, we want Cody and Zen set free."

"The trouble is we're 4,000 miles away. I'd feel easier if I were in Wakefield."

"But you're not, you are here with me. We'll sort it together. Stop worrying!"

Aliona appeared. "Sorry, excuse me. I go St John's, collect package. It arrived today. Special delivery. I need sign with ID. Would you like me take Benjamin? He's asked for more pirate things from shop."

She caught a glimpse of Woods looking expectantly at her, no doubt thinking she'd refuse. "Certainly, you can take him. He'll love it," she replied, smirking at Woods who'd held up a finger to attract Aliona's attention.

"Could you get me a pirate's hat and an eye patch, and maybe a toy cutlass, so that I can have pretend fights with Ben?" he asked.

Aliona looked at Barnes, who smiled and nodded. "It's okay, Aliona, Mr Greg's allowed a plastic sword too."

Luthi's call to Coleman was made at 5.05 p.m. "Where are you now and what are you doing?" she asked, tapping her fingers on her desk.

"I'm on the other side of the island, keeping an eye on Barnes and Field."

"I need you at Great Exuma. I'd like to speak to Woods again."

"Okay, I'll ring you back in fifteen minutes."

Luthi closed the call down and looked quizzically at Hartley. "Well?"

"He's on the opposite side of the island; the phone signal confirms it."

"So he's telling the truth. Let's see where the phone signal is when he puts Woods on the line."

She waited patiently for ten minutes, and then Hartley drew her attention by waving and beckoning for her to come over to his laptop. "Look at this," he said, frowning. "The tracker registered to Hobbs, is currently on the move. It appears to be heading back to Great Exuma."

"So I see," she said, the wry smirk spreading slowly from cheek to cheek. "I'd hazard a guess that the tracker is on Woods. Coleman's taking him from Barnes' across to Great Exuma. The phone signal when he rings me with Woods, will no doubt confirm that. Then after the call I'd wager the tracker will be travelling back across to Barnes'. What do you say?"

"If that happens, I'll have Coleman's balls for breakfast."

"Not so fast," she said quietly. "Let's see what the oncologist has to say later today."

"That's why they've kidnapped Hobbs, to get her out of the way."

She nodded. "And that's why Coleman doesn't want a replacement."

"They are all in this together," stated Hartley.

"It would appear so. Thank God, Hobbs put the tracker on Woods. Now we'll turn the tables. It's time we took the initiative."

Woods arrived back at the house at 1.30 p.m. local time and went out to the pool area, where Barnes was sitting thinking. She looked up as he approached. "What did Luthi want?" she asked, eagerly.

"Firstly, to question me about what I'd heard when Hobbs was abducted, and then she asked if I'd heard anything after that."

"And you said no?"

He nodded. "She said she'd be speaking to you later today."

"Anything else?"

"No."

"No! Don't you think that strange?"

He scowled. "It was just routine questioning."

"Was Kozlov listening to the conversation?"

"Yep, Coleman put it on speaker phone and Faulkner-Brown listened in too."

"What did they think?"

He shrugged. "They didn't really comment. Faulkner-Brown muttered something about her megalomania."

She stared across the ocean, fixing on the horizon. She had that gut feeling you have when something terrible is about to happen. She understood Kozlov had already placed the house in Ravensthorpe under surveillance, and that his people were awaiting further instructions. They were on standby, ready, should the need arise, to go in and rescue Cody and Zen. Meanwhile, Zoe was frantically delving in to the activities of the Farooqs, trying to find anything that would support Barnes' theory that this was a phantom attack.

"What was that?" Woods said.

She refocused and listened.

"There, did you hear it?" he said.

"It's Zoe, she's calling for us. She must have found something."

Together, they hurried inside, and went up to the computer room. "What is it, Zoe?" she asked, quickly catching her breath.

"Look at these seven texts, sent last week between an unregistered number which I've traced to the Jammu and Kashmir region of Pakistan, and Gamal Farooq." She twisted the screen.

How's the shadow?

Good. When will you be ready?

Sami has placed the cake in the oven.

Do we have a venue and a date for the wedding?

Plymouth. Saturday 3rd October. Stay away.

What about the helpers?

Dispose of them after the wedding.

While Woods paced around the room Barnes stared at the screen. Both were deep in thought, but refocused when Zoe spoke. "It's taken me ages to find these connections, but I've also uncovered that Gamal Farooq was at university with Sami Zaman and that the two of them became good friends. Sami Zaman recently worked at Devonport Dockyard, undertaking maintenance works."

"There are twelve retired nuclear submarines moored at the base, eight of them still containing their nuclear fuel," Barnes chipped in.

"And on Saturday 3rd October the base will be packed with people, as it's having a commemorative celebrations day," Zoe added.

"We need to let Kozlov know about this," Woods said.

Barnes pulled out her phone and pressed his contact number. "Hi, Zoe's found something. You may need to take a look at this."

"Okay, we'll all come across. Give us half an hour."

She slipped the phone into her pocket. "They'll all be here soon," she reported.

"What else do you know about Sami Zaman?" Woods asked Zoe.

"He too has been in contact with the same unregistered number in Pakistan; three calls - all made over the period when he was working at the dockyard."

"I don't suppose, by any chance, that there is a transcript of the calls on GCHQ's systems?" Barnes asked.

"Can't find one, which suggests that they are well and truly below the radar."

"The cake must be a bomb," Woods announced.

Barnes rolled her eyes and looked at Zoe. Neither commented.

"They're going to blow up the dockyard," he continued.

"And the quarter of a million people in the surrounding area," Barnes added.

Twenty-five minutes later the intercom receiver sounding meant Barnes had to go and answer it. She assumed it would be either Kozlov, or Aliona returning with Ben. "I'll let them in," she said, running over to her bedroom. "Hello," she answered, when she reached the receiver. Kozlov announced himself, Coleman and Faulkner-Brown. She opened the gates, and went downstairs to meet and greet them. "Come upstairs and take a look at this."

Faulkner-Brown was the slowest up the steps, and Kozlov and Coleman were already in the room with Zoe and Woods when he finally ascended the top step, panting and taking a moment to recover, before following Barnes into the room. "What have you dragged me all the way up here to see?" he demanded.

Zoe moved away from the desk so the three men could read the screen.

"What do you think?" Woods asked.

Faulkner-Brown answered first. "I think Miss Field is a very clever young woman."

Zoe totally ignored the compliment. It was as if she didn't even recognise his presence in the room.

Nonetheless, Kozlov stood, appearing subdued. Then he clicked his fingers, as though he wanted everyone's attention. "I think we've got these conversations on record."

"Between the unregistered mobile and Sami Zaman?" Barnes checked.

"Something rings a distant bell here. Let me make a quick call and check this out." He strode out of the room and Barnes could hear him speaking Russian. She knew exactly what he was saying and to whom; the others in the room appeared unaware that he was speaking to the President. There was the briefest of conversations and then he returned. "You were right, Maria. The attack on The White House is a phantom. The one at the Devonport Dockyard is real, and the one we need to prevent!"

"Thank God you two are here," Faulkner-Brown said, looking at both women.

Barnes smiled at him. "Thank goodness we're all here. Now we can sort this." She stopped speaking when her phone vibrated. She fished it out of her pocket and glanced at the display. "It's Luthi," she said.

"Put her on speaker phone," Kozlov ordered.

She complied and then answered. "Hello. What do you want?"

"Hello, Maria. Are you well?"

"Get lost! How's Woods?"

"Why don't you ask him; I presume he's standing next to you?"

She scowled and looked across at Kozlov.

"You see, Maria, if I had arrested Coleman, it would have taken forever to get him to talk. But oncologists aren't trained in that specialism. Aliona's been very accommodating, and she came with a bonus. If you give me a few moments, I'll be able to connect you to your little bundle of fun! Are you missing him?"

Woods stormed across and snatched the phone out of Barnes' hand. "Listen, Luthi," he snarled. "If anything happens to that child, you'll have me to deal with, and I'll destroy every fucking sinew of your wretched existence!"

The line went dead and Barnes stared at Kozlov. "What have I done?" she said, mortified.

Chapter 16

Tuesday 29th September

Barnes fought to control her emotions, but it was a battle she was losing. She needed to remain focused. Her son's life depended upon it, but she couldn't stop anguishing about him and what he would be doing right now. Would Aliona be with him or might he have been taken away from her and placed with people he didn't know? She knew he was unlikely to have been fazed by that; he loved meeting new people, but not knowing exactly what had happened to him gnawed at her soul, and the feeling of emptiness in the pit of her stomach was physically excruciating. She looked up to see Kozlov towering above her. He had clearly reverted to his *I'm in charge mode*.

"It's important that you remain calm, Maria. We'll get Benjamin back safe and well. You have my word on that."

There was absolutely no doubt in his words, and she believed him. What else could she do? But where was Ben? He could be on a plane heading anywhere.

"Luthi will ring again within the hour," Faulkner-Brown said softly, clearly trying to settle her nerves. "It's all about power and control with her. She won't be able to resist gloating and she'll have a list of demands."

"I knew this was going to happen," Woods said, pacing around the room, gesticulating wildly at Kozlov. "You should have known Ben would be in danger."

Barnes shook her head in disbelief. The statement, like a dagger, went straight into her heart. She bit hard on her lip.

"This isn't helping," snapped Zoe. "We are where we are. We have to face the facts and we'll have to sort it. We need to pull together."

"Yes we do," Barnes managed to say, as another wave of anguish washed over her.

"I'm trying to figure out how Luthi knew," Coleman said, looking to Kozlov.

"Before we solve that mystery, we need to get Cody and Zen safe. And we must concentrate on finding Benjamin," he replied.

"Yes," said Barnes, attempting to focus on the priorities.

"Luthi will probably now know most, but not all, of what's been going on, so speed is of the essence. Cody and Zen could be in imminent danger," Faulkner-Brown stated.

Kozlov glanced at his watch. "It's currently 7.30 p.m. in the UK," he said. "Zoe, message Cody, telling him we are preparing to storm the house and that it's an absolute necessity that he orchestrates for as many of the terrorists to be there as possible when we go in. That way, we can take them away for interrogation and place Cody and Zen in a safe-house. We'll make it appear as though the terrorists fled the property with the two captives. Do you know what time Kaleem, or Gamal Farooq, as we now know him to be, starts the night shift?" He was looking straight at Zoe.

"Usually 9.00 p.m." she replied.

"Right, that's when we go in."

"I'll message him now," Zoe replied, tapping away at the numbers on her keyboard.

Barnes spotted Woods frowning. Despite feeling as though every part of her was shaking, she thought concentrating on the discussion would help her. "When we divulge exactly what we have done, Luthi will want Cody and Zen out of the way and silenced, because they can testify that we have been helping them and trying to prevent the attack, whereas she'll want to implicate us."

"And if the house is empty when Luthi turns up, she'll think the terrorists got wind of her raid, and the old chestnut regarding someone close leaking her information, will resurface," Kozlov surmised.

"Are we going to tell Luthi everything?" Woods asked, looking concerned.

"We don't have a great deal of choice. Until we have Benjamin back, we'll have to comply with her demands," Kozlov answered. "When she rings I'll talk to her, and I'll decide what to reveal. I'll request that Maria be allowed to speak to Benjamin. Zoe, will you be able to trace the signal?"

Zoe continued to blast away at the numbers. "Yes," she replied, curtly, clearly annoyed at being distracted.

"Good, this is what I'm proposing: Coleman, Woods and I will rescue Benjamin, while Zoe, Maria and Faulkner-Brown stay here. You three can coordinate things and keep us up-to-date with what's happening."

"He's my son!" Barnes insisted. "I want to rescue him!"

"No! You need to stay here, Maria. Your judgement isn't sound. You are too emotionally involved. Benjamin thinks the world of Woods and as soon as he spots him he'll happily comply with our instructions."

She looked at Woods. "He's right, Maria. I'll make sure he's okay." He placed his arm gently across her back.

"Where do you think he is?" she asked, fighting to stay in control, knowing no-one in the room really knew the answer.

"I have a hunch he'll still be on Antigua or somewhere very close. I'll organise to have a helicopter flown in and on standby here, and as soon as Zoe gives us the coordinates of the call we can be airborne. If he's anywhere on the mainland we'll be there in less than ten minutes."

"Thank you," she said.

"You can thank me when we have him back here. Right now I need to make some urgent calls."

Kozlov hurried out of the room and Coleman strode straight across to Woods. "Show me the Kindle," he demanded. Woods took it out of his jacket pocket and gave it to him. Coleman pulled a penknife out and prised the device apart. A small piece, the size of an English one pound coin, fell to the floor. Coleman picked it up and examined it. "That's how Luthi knew," he said, placing it on the tiled floor and stamping hard on it. "There was a tracker hidden in the Kindle."

Woods went ashen. "I'm sorry, Maria. I had no idea."

"You weren't to know," Faulkner-Brown said, being surprisingly considerate. "You're not trained to look out for that sort of thing."

"No, but *he* is!" Woods snapped back, pointing his spindly finger at Coleman.

"Be quiet!" Barnes shouted, trying to listen to what Kozlov was saying out on the landing. He was speaking in Russian on his phone.

"What's he doing?" Faulkner-Brown wanted clarification. "I can't understand a damned word."

"He's sorting things out. He's currently requesting the helicopter. There's some issue with the availability of a pilot."

"I can fly it," Coleman said, smirking.

"By the time you've reached the bloody airport and then flown back here we'll have lost the opportunity," Faulkner-Brown grumbled.

Before Barnes had a chance to respond, her phone vibrated. "It's Luthi," she said.

"I'll get Kozlov. Don't answer it yet," Coleman said, rushing out of the room.

Kozlov strode back in and nodded at Barnes. She tossed the phone, still vibrating, across to him, and he caught it one-handed. He flicked it on to speakerphone.

"Yes, Luthi, what do you want?"

"Ah. Kozlov, I presume. I don't think we've met."

"I asked what you wanted."

"How's Maria?"

"How's Benjamin?"

"If you tell me how Maria is, then I'll reciprocate."

"I'm not playing games. Tell me what you want or I'll terminate the call."

"No you won't, because if you do that Barnes will never see the child again, and..."

Kozlov hit the red button. "Don't worry, Maria. She'll ring back. She obviously hasn't got the full story. She's needs more information and *we'll* have to play for time."

"What about the helicopter?" Woods asked.

"They've sourced a pilot who lives fifteen minutes from the airport. He'll fly it straight here." He turned to Coleman. "You and Woods go out to the tennis courts and direct him in when he arrives. Maria, do you have any white paint?"

She nodded. "In the garage."

"We'll paint a large H in the centre of the courts," Coleman offered. "Come on," he beckoned to Woods, who followed him out.

Kozlov passed the phone to Barnes. "Luthi will want you to sweat, so she'll leave it a while before she rings back. Don't panic. She won't touch Benjamin until she's got the full picture. I'll finish sorting things out. Zoe, have you had any response from Cody?"

She spun round in the swivel chair. "With a fair wind and a little bit of luck you should have all four terrorists there when you go in. Sahib and Abbas are already there and Kaleem will be arriving at nine. Cody's requesting that Haziq visits them urgently."

"Good, I'll update my team," he replied, striding out through the door, leaving Barnes and Zoe alone with Faulkner-Brown.

"We can turn this to our advantage, Maria," Faulkner-Brown said.

She nodded. "I've already worked that out. But first we need to free Cody and Zen, capture all four terrorists and, most importantly, bring Ben and Aliona home."

Cody jumped when the bedroom door flew open. Haziq strode in, looking quite annoyed. "Why do you want me to see, young man?" he asked, going across to where Cody was sitting staring at the PC screens. Abbas and Sahib, who had been draining the air from the radiator, stopped what they were doing and came over.

"I think we have a problem," Cody replied, his voice trembling. "I think someone is tracking what I'm doing. Look, when I input data there is a miniscule delay on screen. Watch closely or you'll miss it. Did you see that?" he asked, as he typed away on the keyboard.

Haziq leaned in.

"You have to have incredibly quick eyesight to spot it," Cody said.

"Can you two see anything?" Haziq asked Sahib and Abbas.

"I think I can," Sahib replied. "A fraction of a second delay. There!" he pointed at the screen.

Cody smiled inwardly. He'd made the whole thing up. There wasn't a delay. "I think we should change proxy server, otherwise they might be able to trace where we are," Cody said.

"That's why the tracker was in the decoder," Abbas said.

"Shut up," Haziq barked.

"W… what tracker?" Cody asked, fearing he'd receive Haziq's wrath for questioning him.

"There was a tracker in the decoder, but we outsmarted them. They'll not find you here."

Cody started shaking, only this time he was play-acting. "They will, they'll find us and we'll all be going to jail. We need to move to another house. Please," he begged.

Haziq sighed. "What time does Kaleem arrive?"

"Nine o'clock usually," Sahib answered.

"Get him on the phone and tell him I want him over here now!"

Sahib pulled out his phone and left the room.

"How long will it take to pack all this stuff up?" Haziq shouted.

"A couple of hours," replied Zen.

"I want Kaleem to see this first. If he concurs, then we'll move to another of my properties and set up again."

Sahib re-entered the room. "He was on his way, Boss. He'll be five minutes."

"Good. We'll see what he has to say."

The following few minutes passed without incident, and while Cody worked on the PC and Zen lay on the mattress, Haziq, Abbas and Sahib stood together in the corner of the room whispering. Eventually the door downstairs banged closed and indicated Kaleem's arrival. Cody listened as the footsteps slowly ascended the stairs; no doubt Kaleem was donning his mask.

"Hello, Boss," Kaleem said, as he entered the room. "What's up?"

Haziq did not get a chance to answer. There was an ear-shattering, nerve-gangling, boom from the ground floor room, followed by the thunderous sounds of footsteps racing up the stairs. Cody shrank back and covered his head, trembling for real this time, as he heard Kaleem chanting something incomprehensible. Eight heavily armed and completely masked men burst in, immediately knocking Haziq, Sahib, Abbas and Kaleem to the floor, and overpowering them. They pulled the four terrorists' masks off, handcuffing them in the process. "Which one is Aali Farooq?" the armed man, who appeared to be in charge, demanded of Cody.

"That one," Cody replied, pointing at Haziq.

"And which one is Gamal Farooq?"

"He is," Zen said, smiling and pointing at Kaleem.

"And which one has the keys to set you free?" the man continued.

Cody pointed at Sahib.

The man holding Sahib felt in his pockets and retrieved the keys.

"Right, get those four out of here," the one in charge ordered.

The terrorists were unceremoniously bundled out of the room, leaving Cody and Zen alone with the man in charge and three of the other armed men. "You two are coming with me. My colleagues will bring your equipment, and we're taking you to a safe-house, where you'll be looked after."

Cody looked at Zen. The relief on his face tinged with anxiety. It was 8.25 p.m.

Luthi's third call came in at 3.35 p.m. local time. Everyone was now sitting together in the ocean room. Zoe, her equipment attached to Barnes' phone, was waiting to trace the call when Ben was placed on Luthi's line. The helicopter was outside on the tennis courts, having been guided in by Woods and Coleman, who had since returned to the house.

Kozlov — who had just received the news that Cody and Zen had been freed and all four terrorists taken to be interrogated — was given the nod by Zoe, and he answered. The call was on speakerphone. "Hello, Luthi," he said. "Tell me what you want!"

She'd obviously become tired of wasting time. "I want to know exactly what you have uncovered; otherwise the child will be killed. . ."

He interrupted. "I'll tell you everything, on the proviso that Maria is allowed to speak to him and that you then let him and Aliona go."

"I'll let them go when I've checked out that everything you've said is correct."

"What about speaking to Benjamin?"

There was a pause.

"Drama queen," Faulkner-Brown muttered, under his breath.

"Of course Maria can speak to little Benjamin. She must be distraught, poor woman."

Barnes gritted her teeth and resisted the temptation of an outburst. She wasn't going to give Luthi the satisfaction.

"Right," Kozlov said. "In that case, I'll bring you up to speed." He spent fifteen minutes informing her about the house in Ravensthorpe and that Cody and Zen were being held there and forced to hack into the MOD's databases, with the aim of launching a Trident nuclear missile at The White House. He gave a brief outline of how they had been traced, omitting to mention the involvement of the detectives in Wakefield. He told her that they had become suspicious that the attack on The White House was actually a phantom, and said they believed a more sinister attack was being planned, and that the one on Ravensthorpe was a smokescreen. He failed to mention the — so far unconfirmed — attack on Devonport Dockyard.

"How near are you to uncovering the real attack?" Luthi asked when he'd finished.

Faulkner-Brown winked at Barnes.

"We only formed the view that this was a phantom attack earlier today. We haven't had a chance to further investigate that possibility; events have somewhat overtaken us. Anyway, when you capture the terrorists in Ravensthorpe, I'm sure you'll have that information before we do."

There was another pause. "You could be right. But here's the deal. You keep looking and we'll interrogate the terrorists. As soon as I have the answer, I'll free the oncologist and the child, but I also want Hobbs back." She paused. "I'm sure the Field girl will work her tiny fingers off trying to discover the truth if she thinks it will help her mother. Are you listening, Zoe? Get me the information before the terrorists give it to me and your mother goes free."

Barnes watched Zoe waving two fingers nonchalantly in the air. She smiled. That small gesture made her feel better.

"Right, I've given you what you want. Now place Benjamin on the line."

"It will take a minute or two to sort this," Luthi said. Then the line went quiet.

Kozlov nodded at Zoe and held his forefinger across his lips, indicating everyone should remain silent.

After ninety-five seconds the line crackled into life. Zoe hit the switch on her handheld receiver.

"Hello," Ben's voice echoed around the room.

Barnes wasn't prepared for the overwhelming emotions. She couldn't speak.

"Hello, Benjamin," Woods shouted.

"Mr Greg, how are you? And how are your headaches?"

"I'm fine. How are *you* and what have you been doing?"

"Playing real pirates. I've made some new friends."

"Are they looking after you?" Barnes managed between snivels.

"Hello, Mother, I'm being really good. Aliona's taken me to the shops and we bought lots more toys."

"Stay safe, Benjamin."

Zoe was scribbling away on a pad. She ripped the top page off and handed it to Coleman. She gave Kozlov the thumbs up and he waved for Woods to follow. The three men hurried out of the room.

"Is Aliona with you, Sweetheart?" Barnes asked.

The line went dead. Clearly there wasn't going to be any discussion regarding specifics.

"Well?" Faulkner-Brown muttered, looking at Zoe.

"English Harbour! They must be on a boat. That's why Ben said he's playing *real* pirates."

"How long in the helicopter?" he asked

"Six or seven minutes."

"Fantastic! Even if they weigh anchor and immediately sail off, Kozlov should see them heading out of the harbour."

Barnes nodded. "He sounded fine," she managed to say.

Woods and Coleman were sitting in the back of the helicopter, behind Kozlov and the pilot, who coincidently turned out to be Patrick, the man who had flown Woods and Zoe around the island when they'd first arrived in Antigua.

"So we are heading down to the South Coast and English Harbour?" Patrick asked, over the headsets.

"Yes," Kozlov affirmed, as the helicopter rotas gained speed and they rose up above the tennis courts. "Please can we take the quickest route?"

"Roger that," Patrick confirmed. He then outlined his intentions to Air Traffic Control and, on their confirmation, the helicopter swooped to the right and headed over the mainland.

"ETA?" Kozlov checked.

"Approximately six minutes," replied Patrick.

Woods looked across at Coleman, who held a camera with a telephoto lens, in readiness to take photographs of the harbour. He, in turn, pulled out the small pair of binoculars from his jacket pocket and prepared to focus in on the yachts. Figuratively, he had everything crossed for a successful outcome, and, notwithstanding Barnes' loathing of the word hope, he hoped against hope that they would find both Ben and Aliona. The most likely scenario, based on the coordinates Zoe had given them, was that they were being held on a boat or small craft, moored somewhere in the harbour. Concern that it may have sailed off as soon as the call had ended, was negated somewhat by the speed of the helicopter. Listening to the child's voice, and seeing his mother's reaction, had stirred deep-seated feelings, and he was having difficulty separating these out from what needed to be done, whereas Kozlov and Coleman appeared calm and focused. There were no signs of either of them being anything but detached from the emotional turmoil. They were clearly absorbed in the job in hand. Throughout his career as a detective Woods had used that skill. On countless occasions he had been able to set aside his feelings and concentrate on the details, but now things were different. He was personally involved, and that connection drove his desire to seek retribution for Luthi. He had meant each and every word when he'd told her that if anything happened to Ben, he would destroy every sinew of her wretched existence. Revenge, as he had said many times to his colleagues, was a destructive force.

"We are approaching Shirley Heights," Patrick announced, over the headsets. "Now, if you look over to the right, English Harbour is the smaller of the two bays. Falmouth Harbour is the larger, slightly to the right."

"Can you reduce altitude slightly so we can take a better look at the boats?" Kozlov requested. "Not too close to arouse suspicion, but enough for us to get a few good pictures."

"Will do."

The helicopter swooped and Woods quickly focused his binoculars. He scanned the various crafts, desperately looking for a glimpse of Ben or Aliona. Unfortunately, because of the previous weekend's fishing festival, there were numerous boats moored in the harbour, making his task more difficult.

"What about the yacht heading out to sea?" Coleman said, pointing south-west. "Please could we fly over that?"

"Affirmative."

Woods' concentration switched to that. He steadied his arms on the door rail and refocused. Coleman too was frantically taking pictures of the craft, and Kozlov held a pair of high powered binoculars.

"That's them," Kozlov's voice boomed over the headsets. "I can see Benjamin waving from the cabin window. Don't get too close. Fly seawards, making it appear we are sightseers going around the island," he told Patrick. He then pulled off the headset and quickly pressed the keys on his mobile, making a call.

While he spoke in Russian, Woods caught sight of Ben's tiny hand waving wildly. "Get a picture of him," he shouted to Coleman, forgetting to press the button on the microphone.

As the helicopter flew out and then headed west along the south-coast Kozlov was still speaking on his phone. Eventually he finished and re-donned the headset, turning to face Coleman and Woods. "I'm getting my people on the ground to keep track of where the yacht is sailing," he confirmed.

"I have the name and identification number," Coleman said. "We'll be able to follow it from the marine boat tracker."

"Provided it is switched on," Woods said, this time remembering to press the button.

"Bearing in mind the time, and the fact that it'll be dark in just over an hour, I suspect it'll be heading up the coast, possibly to Carlisle Bay, where it will moor for the night," Kozlov put forward.

"Should we head back to the house and decide how we're going to play this?" Woods asked.

"Night-time assault?" Coleman suggested.

Kozlov nodded. "Wait until we know where it's heading." He turned to Patrick. "Please could you fly us back to the house?"

"Roger." Patrick spoke to Air Traffic Control, informing them of his intentions, and then, on their approval, flew back across the mainland to Long Island. When he landed on the tennis courts Barnes was waiting, looking fraught. The three men left the helicopter and came across to her.

"We've seen him," Woods shouted, giving her the thumbs-up, as Patrick took off. "He's on a yacht. We can track it!"

She nodded, but he was unsure if she had heard him. Once the noise had subsided he repeated it. He deliberately omitted to tell her that the man sailing the craft had a Kalashnikov hung round his shoulders. "Kozlov thinks they may be heading to Carlisle Bay," he added, trying to reassure her.

"We'll go inside and let Zoe check where it's actually heading," Kozlov said.

"We can sail to Carlisle Bay now, on my cat," she said.

Woods looked straight at Kozlov and shook his head dismissively.

"No, Maria, when we know its exact location, Coleman, Woods and I will carry out the assault. I'm proposing that we board the vessel just before dawn tomorrow. That way we'll have the element of surprise on our side."

"Are they armed?" she asked.

"No, Maria, they're not," he lied.

Chapter 17

Wednesday 30th September

Woods waved to Barnes as he, Kozlov, and Coleman set off in her catamaran, heading to Carlisle Bay. It was quite dark, being 3.45 a.m., and the estimated travel time to their destination was just over an hour. Coleman was at the helm, using the boat's electronic navigating systems to guide him to their destination. The previous evening Zoe had been unable to trace the actual course of the yacht Ben and Aliona were being held on, due to the fact that that craft's marine boat tracker had been disconnected, as had the satellite phone Ben's call had been made on. However, one of Kozlov's men on the headland had been lucky enough to be able to follow the boat's progress through binoculars from the coast road, and he confirmed it was now moored in Carlisle Bay. Surveillance, in the form of night-vision binoculars, had identified two male agents and one female agent holding Ben and Aliona captive. More importantly, it had established that during the hours of darkness no-one was keeping watch from the boat. Kozlov's plan therefore entailed sailing quietly into the bay and mooring up approximately 200 metres from the target vessel. They would then use the dinghy and paddle stealthily across to the boat, embarking silently and using the element of surprise to overpower the three officers on board.

Now, as the catamaran reached open water and choppy seas, Coleman pushed the lever forward, slowly increasing the engine's speed. The plan was that as he neared Carlisle Bay he would gradually reduce power and drift in, if necessary using the sail to assist, but this would be dependent on tide and wind direction.

Meanwhile, Woods and Kozlov were sitting in the cabin drinking coffee, and had just been discussing the finer points of the plan. Zoe had downloaded the specification of the yacht from the boat builders who had manufactured it, so they knew the internal layout and where the four bedrooms were. Now Woods watched as Kozlov reached for the holdall that he'd carried on board, and unzipped it, pulling out an aluminium handgun storage case. He flicked it open and Woods spotted two semi-automatic pistols, complete with silencers, and several ammunition magazines.

"Are you able to use one of these?" Kozlov asked, without looking up.

"I've not been trained in the use of firearms, but I'm pretty sure that, if needs must, I can aim and pull the bloody trigger."

Kozlov took one of the weapons and loaded a magazine into the butt. "Come outside and I'll give you a brief demonstration, then you can try."

Woods followed him out and after paying heed to what he'd witnessed he clasped the gun with both hands and, adopting the shooting stance position, he prepared to fire out into the ocean.

"Slowly squeeze the trigger and hold the butt firmly. Get used to the recoil," Kozlov instructed.

Woods did just that, surprised by the rapidness of firing and the powerful throwback.

"Now, do it again, only this time imagine you are aiming straight at someone's chest. Someone, who, if you don't kill them, will certainly kill you," Kozlov said, with ice-cold conviction.

Woods did as instructed. "Was that better?" he asked.

Kozlov nodded, but looked far from impressed. "Hopefully, you won't need to use it, because Coleman and I will be taking the lead."

Woods laughed. "Hope demonstrates weakness," he said, remembering Barnes' words.

Kozlov gave him a knowing look. "Let's go inside and get ready," he said.

Barnes handed her phone to Faulkner-Brown, informing him it was Luthi calling. It was 3.55 a.m. local time, 8.55 a.m. in the UK.

"Hello, Luthi," Faulkner-Brown said, quickly placing the call on speakerphone.

"Rupert, how good to hear your voice again. How are you?"

"How do you think I am?"

"Belligerent, quarrelsome and obnoxious!"

"Only in your presence, Dear. Now what can I do for you?"

"Where's Kozlov?"

"Out. He has more important priorities than sitting around waiting for you to call."

"Where's Maria?"

"Sitting here with me; I'm the go-between."

She sighed, and Faulkner-Brown winked at Barnes.

"Well, Mr Go-between, could you inform her and Kozlov, that when we entered the house in Ravensthorpe it was empty. And when we simultaneously raided the homes of Aali Farooq and Gamal Farooq they too had disappeared."

"What!"

"You heard me."

"Are you saying Cody and Zen have never been in that house?"

"No! It appears they all left in a hurry. The equipment was gone, but there was evidence of their presence. I've got a team of forensic officers combing every square inch of the property. And I have another team at Cody's house and one at Zen's."

"So where are they now? Any ideas?"

"That's my question to you."

"Have you knocked on doors? Did anyone see anything in the street?"

"Yes, we have. The problem is that most of the residents either claim not to have English as their first language, or they simply will not help."

"So what do you suggest we do?"

"I would like the Field girl to re-establish contact with Cody."

"She's a woman," Barnes snarled, quietly under her breath.

"Are you serious?" Faulkner-Brown scoffed. "The last communication with Cody informed him that the good old British Intelligence Service were about to rescue him and arrest his captors. Suddenly, he's moved elsewhere! I doubt he'll ever trust Zoe again. My God, you were only told about this twelve hours ago! Is your security that lax?"

"What are you suggesting?"

"If you need it spelling out, I'm suggesting that we ought to think very carefully before divulging any more sensitive information to you. How many people at your end knew about this?"

"I'm not answering that," she snapped, an air of superiority apparent in her voice.

"Then there is no more to say on the matter. I presume you are searching for the Farooqs and interrogating the family members. Or, would you prefer us to pop over and do that for you? It appears that things have certainly gone downhill at Vauxhall Cross since you took hold of the reins. This would never have happened in my day, young lady!"

The line went dead and the grin on Faulkner-Brown's face widened as he chuckled away to himself. "I enjoyed that," he said. "Wait until she receives the news that Benjamin and Aliona have been freed."

Barnes smiled, but she felt ill at ease; she couldn't stop worrying that the attempt to rescue Ben would not go smoothly. Yes, Woods, Coleman, and particularly Kozlov were all capable individuals, but their mannerisms before they left had caused her disquiet. Either they were not telling her everything or they too were uncertain about the outcome. The next few hours would provide the answers. Little did she know that it was going to be a memorable day, but all for the wrong reasons!

As the catamaran reached the bay, Coleman cut the engines and drifted slowly into position, quietly lowering the anchor and making sure it was held. In the moonlight Woods could see the yacht rhythmically bobbing slowly up and down as the waters lapped at its sides. It was less than one hundred metres away. His heart rate quickened as he placed the handgun, with its safety-lock securely on, in his pocket. He donned the bullet-proof vest, put on the gloves, and pulled the black balaclava that Kozlov had given him over his head. Then he watched Coleman and Kozlov, similarly all in black, silently lowering the dinghy off the back of the catamaran. Kozlov boarded first, Coleman second, and finally Woods. Not a word was uttered as Kozlov skilfully paddled the dinghy in the moonlight towards the yacht. Coleman had donned a backpack, and Woods presumed it to contain handcuffs and other paraphernalia for restraining the three agents on board. When they reached the yacht, Woods stood and carefully tethered the small inflatable to the bow rail. He then held on to the rail to steady the dinghy so Kozlov and Coleman could board. Kozlov then held out a hand to assist him. All three took out their weapons and flicked off the safety catches. Kozlov crept to the cabin door and placed an ear to it. He listened for several seconds and then tried the catch. It was locked. He motioned to Coleman, who drew back and then kicked hard at it, smashing it open. Kozlov rushed down with Coleman and Woods following close behind. Kozlov barged through the door to the bedroom cabin on the left, and yelled, "Police! Get down on the floor!" Coleman did the same at the bedroom cabin on the right. Woods could hear the quiet thuds of firearms discharging behind him as he smashed through the door into the right bow bedroom cabin. He punched the light switch, refocused his eyes and stared at the female agent sitting on the bed with Ben held close to her side and the barrel of her gun placed on his temple. He quickly removed his balaclava.

"Mr Greg," Ben shouted, excitedly. "Are we playing bandits and robbers?"

Woods aimed at the centre of the woman's chest. "Let him go," he ordered.

She moved Ben so that he now acted as a human shield in front of her. "I think you realise that it is you who needs to put your gun down. That is, if you want the child to survive. If you pull the trigger, and by some miracle manage to hit my head, the last thing I'll do will be to ensure he dies." She glanced down at Ben, her intention clear.

Woods analysed the woman's facial features, desperate to gauge if it was a bluff. The staid look gave little away in the quiet moments. He slowly readjusted his aim to her forehead. "Is that a real gun, Mr Greg?" Ben asked, breaking the silence.

He nodded, his stare fixed firmly on the woman's eyes. The realisation slowly struck home: he had little choice other than to comply with her demands; the risks were too high. Reluctantly he bent down and placed the gun on the floor.

"Now kick it away from you," she said.

He obeyed, not sure of his next move. Then Kozlov and Coleman appeared at his side, both pointing their pistols straight at the woman. "Put down the weapon," Kozlov said, firmly.

"No chance! What have you done with my colleagues?"

"They're subdued in their cabins. Now place your weapon on the floor."

"Is Aliona safe?" Woods asked, playing for time, trying desperately to figure out a plan that might resolve this.

"She's fine," Coleman replied, maintaining his aim. "She's waiting on deck for Ben."

"The only way for you to walk away from this is to let the boy go," Kozlov asserted, calmly.

"I want to see my colleagues."

"That will not be possible," Kozlov replied.

Woods sensed the tension rising.

"That's because you've killed them," she claimed, pulling Ben in close. "Sit still!" she demanded of him, as he fought to free himself from her grip.

Kozlov's eyes narrowed. "If you fail to comply with my instructions, then my bullets will smash through your cranium killing you outright. Simultaneously Mr Coleman's bullets will strike your weapon, knocking it out of your hand. Now, for the last time, put the gun on the floor."

Woods' nerves were almost frazzled. Facts flashed through his mind, one after the other. He knew Kozlov's reputation wasn't built for compromising. There was no way he would back down. The line had clearly been drawn. Surely she would comply. Surely she wouldn't choose the alternative. Would she?

"You'll kill me no matter what I do, so say goodbye, Ben."

Woods spotted her index finger tightening on the trigger. His was a split second decision. Desperate times called for desperate measures. He had to try to save Ben. Mustering every single part of his might, he lunged himself forward onto the bed straight at the woman. His momentum, his determination, and the enormity of the consequences of his failure, kept him moving. As he made contact with them his right arm snatched at Ben's pyjamas and he hurled the child off to the side. A fraction of a second later his body crumpled hard into the woman's chest. He heard and felt a multitude of bullets whizzing past him into the female's body, but the pain, heat, and shock kicked in as he realised her last act had been to discharge her weapon up into his neck. The bullet had torn through his head. He was vaguely aware of Kozlov and Coleman pulling him off the blood-soaked form of the dead woman slumped on the bed.

"Stay with me, Greg." Kozlov's voice echoed distantly in his ears.

Dizzy, fighting for life, and knowing he was losing a large amount of blood, he looked up into Kozlov's eyes. He knew this was the end; his last hurrah. "Tell… Maria…" He coughed blood out as he fought to speak; the pain intensified and nullified his senses. "Tell… Maria… I… I…" The numbness overwhelmed him, and it fell dark and silent.

Kozlov glanced up at Coleman, who was holding Benjamin in his arms, attempting to shield him from witnessing the trauma. "Take him to Aliona," he ordered. "Then get back down here. We need to move fast. Give me the backpack!"

Coleman slipped it off and passed it to him. "Come on Ben, we'll go on deck. Aliona's waiting to take you back to your mother."

"What about Mr Greg? I want him to come with me."

"Mr Greg has gone to sleep with the angels," Coleman replied.

"Wake him up!"

"We can't wake him up, Benjamin. He'll sleep forever now."

"No-one sleeps forever."

"Your mother will explain," Kozlov said, nodding at Coleman and indicating he didn't have time for this conversation.

While Coleman disappeared off, Kozlov unzipped the backpack and carefully removed the package. He placed it on the floor and set the timer for ten minutes. He took one last look around the room, picking up Woods' gun and balaclava and placing them in the bag. He turned as Coleman reappeared. "We've got ten minutes," he said, thrusting the backpack at him.

"Right, let's go."

They hurried up on deck and helped Aliona and Ben into the dinghy. The little boy was clearly subdued and quietly complied with their instructions. Coleman then untied the leash and jumped in with them. Kozlov was the last to exit from the yacht. Coleman pulled the starting cord and the inflatable's engine fired into life. He twisted the throttle and made his way back to the catamaran where everyone quickly, at the behest of Kozlov, boarded. The dinghy was secured to the diving platform and Coleman started the catamaran's engine and then drew in the anchor.

Meanwhile, Aliona took Benjamin down into the cabin bedroom to settle him.

Kozlov glanced at his watch. "Come on," he urged, as Coleman pushed the lever forwards.

The craft moved, swinging around and sailing towards Old Road Bluff and the bay's entrance. As they neared the rocky outcrop an almighty explosion and a flash of light filled the skies.

Kozlov regarded Coleman at the helm. "He was one of the good guys," he said, knowingly, as the thousands of tiny fragments from the yacht splashed into the water nearby and an acrid smell filled the air.

"He had some bottle. To do what he did took guts."

Kozlov nodded. "Yes it did." He looked eastwards. The first shards of daylight were beginning to glisten on the horizon. "Maria will be devastated."

This time Coleman nodded. "Do you want to ring her and explain?"

"No! I need to do this face-to-face. It's not going to be easy."

Barnes had spent the past hour watching through the ocean room windows for the catamaran's return, and, as it sailed up to the jetty, she stood there waiting for them. First, Aliona appeared on deck, holding Ben in her arms. He waved excitedly at his mother. The emotions of the past twenty-four hours swept over her and she instantly felt the warm sensation of relief. She smiled and frantically waved back at him. She noticed Aliona's downcast appearance, and assumed it to be regret at having divulged their plans. That didn't matter any more. They had got him back. That was the most important thing. "Hello, Sweetheart," she shouted, grinning. Then she noticed Coleman, who looked as if he was deliberately avoiding eye contact with her. Kozlov came up on deck as Coleman tied up; he too seemed troubled. What was it? Aliona handed Ben over to her and she hugged him, kissing his forehead. "It's so good to have you back, Sweetheart." She looked around, expecting to see Woods emerging. "Where's Mr Greg?" she asked.

"Sleeping with the angels. He'll sleep forever now," Ben replied.

The expression on Kozlov's face hit her like an express train. "No!" she cried out. "No! He can't! He can't be!" Then she heard something behind her and looked back at the house. Zoe was running down towards them. Coleman shot past her and met Zoe before she reached them. He grabbed hold of her and forcibly walked her back towards the house.

There was a sudden ear-shattering scream, followed by Zoe lashing out at Coleman, who didn't attempt to defend himself. He allowed her to beat him. She yelled obscenities as she punched him in the abdomen and kicked at his legs. Still, he did not try to defend himself. He was clearly allowing her to vent her anger on him.

Barnes turned as she felt someone lightly touching her on the shoulder. It was Kozlov. "I'm so, so sorry, Maria. He saved Ben's life. He didn't deserve to die."

The tears flooding out blurred her vision. She squeezed Ben so tight that he said she was hurting him. She immediately loosened her grip. The last time she had had feelings like this was when Peter Glendale had brutally raped her. "Where is he?" she said. "I want to see him."

"The boat exploded and sent Mr Greg up to heaven," Ben answered.

"What!"

Kozlov shrugged. "Maria, let Aliona take Ben inside, and then I'll explain."

She handed the child over, not really knowing what she was doing. Everything appeared distant and removed from her, somehow surreal. Kozlov took her hand and led her to the end of the jetty, where, in a daze, she listened to what he had to say. She rubbed at her eyes, trying to dry the tears. Kozlov offered her his handkerchief, which she used and then blew her nose and regained a little of her composure. "This all started with the bombing of a boat."

"Yes, ironic that it should end that way. Listen, I'm going to fly you and Ben out of here, back to Russia where you can be looked after."

"No you are not!" she said, defiantly. "I'm going to finish this! I'm not walking away from it now. We're going to bring Luthi crashing down."

"Then I'm going to organise protection for you and Ben. There's no telling what she will do now."

She looked up as Faulkner-Brown waddled along the jetty, coming towards them. "I take it Woods didn't make it home," he said.

"Don't you dare say anything derogatory about him," she warned. "Otherwise you'll be taking another dip in the ocean."

He half smiled. "All I was going to say was, what a great shame. He was one of the most honest, hard-working, intelligent and determined people I ever met. It truly is a sad day, and I'll really miss him."

"Not as much as I will," she replied, staring out across the ocean.

Chapter 18

Wednesday 30th September – Thursday 1st October

By 9.00 a.m. local time, a modicum of calm had descended on Barnes' house, mainly due to the combined efforts of Kozlov and Coleman, taking control and prioritising what needed to be done. Kozlov had been using his phone virtually all time since reaching the house. He'd received updates from the interrogation of the four terrorists. He'd organised the presence of a number of armed guards, who were due to arrive on the tiny island later that afternoon, and he had received the news that Sami Zaman had been located in one of the Paris suburbs and been brought in for questioning. Kozlov had kept Barnes up to speed with developments, and emphasised the importance of focusing on the plan and not dwelling on the tragic events earlier in the day.

Now, once again, he obviously needed assistance. He came across, looking business-like, and she forced a half-hearted smile. "What would you like me to do?" she asked, timorously.

"You need to ring McLean, explain what has happened and ask him to go and see Woods' wife. She needs to be told, and it's better if someone does it face-to-face."

"I know," she replied, getting up. "They'd separated. Neither she nor his daughters had seen much of him over the past two years. They didn't even know about the tumour."

"But they need to be told, Maria."

She shrugged and snatched her phone up from the coffee table. He was right, of course he was, and using McLean was better than her having to break the news to Pamela and the girls.

"You also need to inform McLean that Luthi has taken over the investigation surrounding the terrorists in Ravensthorpe. Therefore there is no need for Foster to involve SO15. Tell him Luthi raided the house this morning and that the terrorists had fled, taking Cody and Zen with them. She has everything in hand now, or at least that's what *she* thinks." He winked at her.

"I'll thank him for his assistance," she said, wandering outside. She spotted Ben and Aliona sitting by the pool, so she decided to walk around the gardens and go and sit on the bench seat overlooking the tennis courts. It would be quieter there and she could make the call in private. Her thoughts at the moment were a mixture of deep sadness surrounding Woods' death, and deep regret that another three people had also been killed. Kozlov had explained that the agents had been murdered, one, to prevent them testifying that he, Coleman and Woods were at the scene, and two, to prevent Luthi discovering, in the short-term, that Benjamin had been rescued. Although Barnes understood his motives, she couldn't reconcile the further loss of life. It didn't sit easily on her shoulders.

Nevertheless, as she made her way through the fig trees, she spotted Zoe sitting alone on the seat. She meandered up and noticed the redness around her eyes. "Are you alright?" she asked, knowing the answer.

"No I'm not. I think I'm going to fly home. Aliona's talking about leaving today, and you don't need me anymore. Kozlov and Coleman have everything in order, and, as far as I'm concerned, there's no point to any of this now. He'd be alive if I hadn't brought him here."

Barnes settled on the seat next to her. "Yes he would, but he was dying and we gave him a chance; you saw how he improved when Aliona sorted his medication. If he could have had the treatment it might have saved him."

"But we'll never know."

"Zoe, none of this is your fault. If anything, it's me that has to shoulder the blame. But one thing is for sure, if he had been alive now, he would have been insisting that we see this through. Luthi is within our grasp, we've turned the tables, we can bring her, and the people she protected, crashing down, and we owe it to him to do just that. It's what he would have wanted."

"And what about me? Have you thought about that?! You know full well I want to see Faulkner-Brown behind bars. Woods did too. He was going to help me. I'm here because of my mother. You and Faulkner-Brown are as thick as thieves. I can't compete against the pair of you."

Barnes let out a long and purposeful sigh. "He isn't a bad person, Zoe. He's funded schools and colleges in some of the poorest areas of Africa, and he's helped hundreds, if not thousands, of disadvantaged children. He believes that education is the only way to solve famine, conflict, and prejudice. He's not the person you or most others think he is."

This time Zoe sighed. "You may be right about that, but none of it helps my mother."

"Listen, Zoe, I'm tired of this too. I'm sick of the killings and I've decided to put things right. I'm going to speak to Faulkner-Brown and get him to agree with the British authorities, that, for immunity from prosecution, he'll testify against Luthi, thus proving your mother worked under their orders. This way, it'll reduce your mother's sentence, possibly getting her released immediately."

"And do you think he'll really agree to that?"

"I'll make sure he does. Besides, it works in his favour too - with immunity from prosecution, he'll be able to go back to the UK."

"Is that what he wants?"

"Yes, it is." She waited, with bated breath, for Zoe's answer. She reached out and touched the warm flesh of her exposed shoulder. "Please don't leave, Zoe. I value your friendship, and I'm struggling to come to terms with what's happened. We're stronger if we stick together. People think I'm some kind of wonder woman, and that I can deal with anything. The truth is I'm not. I'm fragile, desperately lonely, and I'm cracking up." Zoe produced one of her lop-sided, silly little grins. Barnes wasn't sure if this was empathy or disbelief, so she added, "He was one of only a few men I have ever trusted, and I'll miss him so much." Her voice quavered towards the end.

Zoe placed her arm around her and hugged her. "I'll miss him too, Maria," she replied.

"So what do you think? Will you stay or will you go?"

Zoe smiled. "Okay," she said, "we'll finish it together."

"Thank you."

Zoe got up slowly off the bench. "I suppose I'd better go and check what Mr Wonderful wants me to do next."

Barnes nodded acceptance. "Well, now I've the unenviable task of breaking the news to McLean."

"Good luck with that, and don't forget to ring Pauline. She needs to know too."

Zoe mooched back towards the house and Barnes hit the speed-dial button on her phone. "Hello, Pete. It's Maria. I'm sorry to do this over the phone, but I have some very, very sad news for you." She took a deep breath, knowing exactly how McLean would react to what she intended to say next.

At 2.45 p.m. Luthi's office door flew open and Hartley hurried in looking fraught. Luthi smiled; she had not been expecting him.

"Sorry to trouble you, but I thought you ought to know that we have lost all contact with the three agents on the yacht," he said, quickly.

"What was their last known position?"

"Carlisle Bay. All three implants, plus the ping from their mobiles, stopped transmitting at 10.00 a.m. this morning, 5.00 a.m. Antigua time."

Luthi scowled and was about to say something when Hartley received a call on his mobile.

"Hello," he said, frowning. "What's the latest?"

There was a long pause.

"I see. Well, keep me informed. Thanks. Bye."

He stared at Luthi, his expression pallid. "There are reports of a yacht exploding early this morning in Carlisle Bay. The Antiguan police are investigating. Apparently there are no signs of anyone surviving."

"Was it a deliberate attack?"

"Too early to say."

Luthi leaned back in her chair. "Could Kozlov have tracked the boat's position from the satellite phone signal?"

"When the child spoke to them the yacht was in English Harbour, so yes, they could have traced that location, but as soon as the call ended, the phone was disconnected and the boat sailed off around the coast. The marine tracker had been deactivated, so I doubt they could have known where they headed."

"That is unless they have someone giving them information, someone with access to the implant tracking system." She stared at Hartley, tapping her pen rapidly on the desk.

"Whoa! Don't look at me like that. I'm not leaking anything. My lips are sealed on this subject. You know they are!"

She paused, weighing up her options. "I'll ring Barnes and test the depth of the water. I have a feeling she and Kozlov will have been involved in this." She pressed a few buttons on her mobile and awaited the call's connection. "Hello, Kozlov. I'd like to speak to Barnes." She flicked the speakerphone button so Hartley could hear.

"That won't be possible. You'll have to talk to me instead. What can I do for you?" he asked, his voice calm and unemotional.

"How is she?"

"That's no concern of yours. More importantly, how is the search for Cody and Zen progressing?"

"It isn't. We've hit a brick wall."

"Well then, you'll no doubt be pleased to know that I have some news for you."

"What news?"

"Zoe has restored her contact with Cody."

"Where is he?"

"We haven't established his exact location yet. She is still working on that."

"Then tell me what he's said."

"I'll do that on condition that Maria is allowed to speak to Benjamin, now."

"Sorry, you are in no position to make demands."

"You're right about that, but Maria is going out of her mind with worry. Give us a break, and let her speak to her son. That goodwill gesture will restore some trust between us."

She pondered for a moment. "I've temporarily lost contact with my team; the phone must have died. I'm awaiting further communication from them. You'll have to bear with me. Meanwhile, tell me what Cody has said. I need to trace him, fast."

"I know you do, but I'm not happy that you appear to be oozing information, sensitive information. I don't want another fiasco. I'm not endangering him and Zen again. Understood?"

The frustration mounting, she tightly sucked in her lips. Kozlov was giving nothing away. On the face of it he appeared not to know anything about the explosion in Carlisle Bay, but he could be bluffing. "I'd like to speak to Faulkner-Brown," she said, playing for time.

"He's not here. Call me back when you've made contact with your team and Maria can speak to Benjamin. Then I'll bring you up to speed with what Cody has said." Kozlov terminated the call.

She looked at Hartley. "What do you think?"

"Hard to say."

Her annoyance boiled over. "Hard to say!" she exclaimed. "You're paid to evaluate and make judgements. For God's sake, man, I need some input from you!"

"Why don't you ring him back? Tell him the boy will suffer if he doesn't cooperate?"

She shook her head. "Because, imbecile, he's aware that I only have a hold over them while the child is safe and well. He knows I won't carry out the threat until I've got what I want."

"Then we are running out of options. We need someone on the ground, someone who can report back!"

"I couldn't have put it better myself. You go! Get the next flight out. No, do what Kozlov would do, charter a jet and fly out there today. It's an eight hour flight." She glanced at her watch. "If you get your skates on you should be there well before midnight, 7.00 p.m. in Antigua. Ring me the second you reach Great Exuma."

"How am I supposed to get access onto the island?"

"We own the damned house! You fool! You'll have free access. You can go and knock on Barnes' door. See what kind of reception that creates. If you get the opportunity you can remove Coleman from the equation. Now leave me in peace. I need time to think!"

Hartley went towards the door, clearly troubled. He took hold of the handle and it appeared he was going to reply, but he left without saying another word.

When Kozlov finished speaking to Luthi he nodded across at Barnes. "She's fishing. She's presumably aware that some kind of incident has taken place in Carlisle Bay, and that her agents' implants have stopped transmitting. She'll think we've had a hand in it. Therefore I'm muddying the water and keeping her confused."

"I understand what you are doing," she replied.

"The good news is that the Farooqs and Sami Zaman are singing like frightened little canaries. We now have the identity and location of the man in Pakistan who masterminded both attacks. Even though he knew the one on The White House was unlikely to succeed, it was more about the shock waves it would send around the world. As for the bombs planted in Devonport Dockyard, we have their exact location and the planned time of detonation. We've also been given the names of several others involved in terrorist cell groups stationed around Europe."

"Your guys are experts at making people talk."

He chuckled. "People tend to comply, after a few, long, painful hours with us."

"I can imagine."

"Oh, and that reminds me. Paula Hobbs agreed to sign an affidavit detailing all Luthi's recent underhand activities, including kidnapping Woods and blackmailing you. We're back on track, Maria. Things are starting to work in our favour again."

"Except for one gigantic mistake early this morning."

He nodded. "Woods knew the danger; his primary goal was to rescue Benjamin. And if it wasn't for his sacrifice we'd all be mourning the loss of your son, rather than him."

"Knowing that doesn't make it any easier."

"In time it will."

She wasn't convinced it would.

"Now, are you okay with Coleman and me leaving this evening?" he checked.

"Yes, you're needed in Paris. I'll be watching when you break the news to the world's media."

"Faulkner-Brown's staying here with you and Zoe, and we'll take Aliona to Paris in our jet, then she can fly on to Moscow. That way, there is no record of her leaving Antigua. Luthi will be none the wiser. We'll leave as soon as the guards are here."

"I really appreciate everything you have done, particularly rescuing Ben. I just wish so many people didn't have to die."

"Think about the alternative, and how many would have died if the terrorists had succeeded. Then consider how many lives we have saved."

She scrunched up her nose and decided not to comment.

Thursday 1st October

Luthi's buzzing phone awakened her at 4.15 a.m. She picked it up, expecting it to be Hartley with news from Long Island. However, it was Vauxhall Cross calling. "Hello," she answered.

"We have just received, as of yet, unconfirmed reports that former Detective Superintendent Greg Woods died yesterday morning." It was Geoffrey Ryedale; she recognised his gritty voice, and he was one of the officers who monitored social media sites, searching for anything of interest.

"Have you spoken to anyone at the West Yorkshire Police HQ?"

"Yes, the press officer. She claimed not to know anything about it."

"Where did you pick it up?"

"Laura, his daughter, posted it on Facebook, just before midnight. I've looked at his wife and daughters' telecommunications for the past twenty-four hours and they have made and received a significant number of calls. Something has definitely happened."

Luthi's thoughts spiralled. "Thank you for the update. Keep monitoring their activity. Let me know what happens." She finished the call and laid her head back on the crisp, clean pillows. She carefully considered recent events, attempting to piece them together. Finally, after several minutes' contemplation, she slid out of bed, pulled on a fluffy, white dressing gown and went over to the desk to make some calls. Top of the list was Jacob Hartley. "Hi. It's me. Are you at Great Exuma?"

"Yes."

"Well?"

"You're not going to like this. Things are definitely slipping from our grasp. Firstly, when I arrived I went straight to the Antiguan Police Headquarters in St John's. I spoke to the head of their CID, who is investigating what happened in Carlisle Bay. They've had divers searching the sea bed and indications are that a bomb was placed on board the yacht. They still haven't identified it yet, but I think it's safe to say it was ours."

"Have they found human remains?"

"Yes, scattered far and wide. It's impossible, right now, to tell how many people were on board and what gender they were. The officer I spoke with said it would probably be the end of the week before they would know for certain. Apparently, the fragments are too small to make a visual assessment."

"Jesus Christ!" she replied, exasperated. "Well, I've just received a call informing me that Woods died yesterday morning. So — clearly — he was involved in this." She heard Hartley sigh. "I assume from that reaction that you have some more troubling news."

"Yes, I do. As you requested, I went over to Barnes' hoping to find out what's going on. Unfortunately, when I pressed the intercom on the gates, two heavily armed guards appeared and left me in no doubt that my presence there was unwelcome."

"They must have the child back with them. Give me five minutes, and I'll ring Kozlov, then I'll call you back."

"Before you go, you need to know that the armed guards had American accents. They were definitely *not* Russian."

That particular gem of information hit Luthi below the belt, sending her mind reeling. "What the hell are the Americans doing at the house?"

"Like I said, things are slipping from our grasp."

"Right, I'm going to make a few calls, I'll have further instructions for you within the hour." She closed the call down and quickly scanned her contacts list, finding Cuthbert Fisher, the Deputy Foreign Secretary. She checked the time, but made the call anyway. After several rings it went to his answerphone. "Hello, Cuthbert. It is Beth Luthi. Something urgent has come up. Please can you ring me, ASAP?" She ended the call and then tried Brad Coburn, her equivalent in the CIA. Their last conversation, several months ago, had been somewhat curt - a fact she now regretted, particularly as she needed a favour from him. This call was answered by a squeaky-voiced young American woman. "Hello. This is Beth Luthi speaking, from London. Please could you put me through to Mr Coburn?"

"One second, Miss Luthi." There was an elongated pause. "Hello, Miss Luthi. I'm sorry, Mr Coburn is unable to take your call right now. Would you like to leave a message?"

"Ask him to contact me when he's free."

"Will do. Have a good day, Miss Luthi."

Finally, she phoned Barnes' number, and when she heard, "this person's phone is switched off; please try again later or send a text", she sensed the storm clouds gathering. She immediately punched in Hartley's number. Several seconds later he answered. "I think we need to start planting evidence linking Barnes and the Field girl to the terrorists in Ravensthorpe. I get the distinct impression I'm out in the cold; no-one is answering my calls and I smell a rat."

"What would you like me to do?"

"Find out if the child is with her. If the answer is yes, remove them both from the equation, and if Faulkner-Brown and the Field girl are still on the island, dispose of them too."

"I'll need back-up. The place is heavily guarded; I can't succeed single-handedly."

"Then improvise. Just like me, you're on your own from now on." She slammed the phone down on the desk, her frustration, anger and contempt clear.

Chapter 19

Thursday 1st October – Friday 16th October

Barnes and Faulkner-Brown were sitting together in the ocean room, the TV channel tuned to CNN, awaiting broadcast of the live press conference, to be jointly presented by the French Head of the General Directorate for Internal Security, and Kozlov, representing the Russian FSB. The press conference was scheduled to commence at noon BST, but for some unspecified reason it was running late; the current time in Antigua was 7.38 a.m.

Barnes looked up and smiled when Zoe came into the room. "What's Ben doing?" she asked.

Zoe yawned, clearly tired. "He's playing bandits and robbers with the guards. They are keeping an eye on him. He's lost all interest in pirates. He's pretending to shoot them with his hand, formed in the shape of a gun. He's asking for a toy pistol. He doesn't think you'll let him have one."

Faulkner-Brown chortled away, but Barnes didn't find it amusing. "Well he's right, he's definitely not having one. I'll speak to the guards. I don't want them influencing his behaviour."

"He's only playing," grumbled Faulkner-Brown. "The time to worry is when he starts running around with a real one."

Barnes smirked at him.

"He's taken quite a shine to one of the guards," Zoe reported.

Barnes scowled. "Which one?"

"Alistair Fairbanks. Tall, dark hair, looks a bit like Jonathan Plant."

Barnes' attention switched to the TV screen when Kozlov and the Head of the General Directorate for Internal Security appeared. Kozlov looked nothing other than statesman-like.

"I'd love to ring Luthi and tell her to tune in," Faulkner-Brown said, grinning. "But no doubt someone will have informed her that the FSB have handed four terrorists over to SO15. That will have been what the delay was. Kozlov wanted them in the care of the British just before the press conference. It will be interesting to see how long it is before Luthi goes on the run."

"Shhh…" Barnes snapped, flicking up the volume as the dialogue on screen began. Even though CNN were using an interpreter, Faulkner-Brown insisted she translate.

She sighed. "The French guy is explaining that earlier this morning several raids were undertaken in Paris, Brussels, Berlin, Oslo, Stockholm, and Copenhagen. A total of forty-two people have been arrested, in connection with a range of terrorist-related activities, and a further eighteen people are currently being sought. He's saying that the raids were as a result of an undercover anti-terror operation undertaken by the Russian authorities, which General Kozlov will now detail."

Faulkner-Brown rubbed his hands together in glee. "Here comes the interesting part. You'll have to translate Kozlov's words too."

She sighed again. "Kozlov is saying that the FSB was contacted by two British hackers, who had been abducted by terrorists stationed in the UK, and that they had been forced to access the MOD's databases, with a view to launching a nuclear missile at the United States of America." She paused. "He says the hackers didn't trust the British Secret Intelligence Service, and, in fear of their lives, preferred to contact the FSB."

Faulkner-Brown laughed out loud. "Go on, Kozlov, old boy, stick the boot in!" he cheered.

Barnes continued. "He's now explaining about Ben – he's saying that Luthi kidnapped the child of one of his team, someone very close to him, and used the child as leverage to get in on the operation. He's saying threats to kill the child forced him to acquiesce and reveal the full details, agreeing that Luthi could arrest the terrorists. However, due to her previous record on secrecy and security breaches, and the fact that his team were very close to uncovering a second, more deadly, terrorist plot, the decision was made to temporarily bring the terrorists into Russian custody, thus facilitating their interrogation, which ultimately thwarted an attack on Devonport Dockyard scheduled for Saturday afternoon." She paused again.

"Keep going," Faulkner-Brown urged. "I'm enjoying this. If only I was a fly on Luthi's wall!"

"A gigantic one?" Zoe queried. "No doubt she'd spot you. That is, if she could actually fit in the room with you."

He laughed, apparently unconcerned by the jibe.

"Do you want me to carry on, or not?" Barnes snapped, annoyed.

"Yes! I need to know what he's saying!"

"He's told them about all four terrorists being handed over to the British authorities this morning, together with the full details of the operations and terrorist plots." She drew in a large breath. "Now he's explaining that one of his team was killed by Luthi's agents, when he attempted to free the child. He says that despite this the child has been reunited with its mother."

"Here comes the torpedo, aimed straight at Luthi's starboard side!" shouted Faulkner-Brown, coughing in excitement.

"Correct," answered Barnes. "He's explaining that he has confidential files and information proving she was involved in covering up the criminal activities of several prominent people, in return for political favour and financial recompense. Furthermore, he has compelling evidence showing that her agents actually poisoned Vladimir Peshkov and then laid a false trail across Europe, attempting to link the murder to the Russian president. He says he has sent copies to the inquest into Peshkov's death, which, as we know, is currently taking place in London."

"Amen," Zoe said, pulling a wayward ringlet back behind her ear.

"Now they are taking questions. Do you want me to interpret those too?"

Faulkner-Brown shook his head. "Half of them have been primed to ask about Luthi holidaying in the Caribbean while her agents kidnapped a two-year-old child. It's just more fuel to stoke up the fire."

"Good! Do you think she'll already have tendered her resignation?" Barnes asked.

"Give me your phone. I'll ask her," Faulkner-Brown suggested.

"No! We're not stooping to her level."

"My guess is she'll be arrested before she leaves the building," Zoe offered.

"Whatever happens, she's finished. It's just a pity Woods isn't here to see it."

"Remember that if he were here, little Ben wouldn't be," Faulkner-Brown pointed out.

She produced an unconvincing "I know." Then she caught sight of Zoe giving her a nod in the direction of Faulkner-Brown. She knew exactly what the gesture indicated. The daunting task of convincing him to agree to testify against Luthi would come next.

Luthi gazed incredulously at the TV screen, as the hyenas from Europe's press were baying for her blood. She felt somewhat transfixed by Kozlov's mannerisms — his calm, cool, intimidating exterior, his "I'm in charge" linguistics, and his ice-cold stare — whereas now she needed to focus on what to do next. Her problems revolved around the fact that she had never been as shrewd as Faulkner-Brown; she hadn't kept detailed records and a catalogue of evidence each time she'd been instructed to cross the line. She had believed that her obsequiousness would save her; only now did she realise the gravitas of that mistake. But there were other mistakes too, catastrophic ones. Why had she believed that *she* could ever outsmart Faulkner-Brown, Kozlov, and Barnes? Why? Then she remembered. Freddy Williams! He'd been the one who had convinced her that together they could achieve virtually anything they wanted. Maybe he had been right, but Faulkner-Brown had put an end to that dream. Possibly *he'd* recognised the danger and that's why he'd murdered Williams. She would never know. The thought triggered another: maybe Faulkner-Brown had teamed up with Barnes, knowing full well that her guardian angel, Kozlov, would not sit by and see her in danger. That was it! Bloody Maria Barnes! Everything always came back to her. Luthi grabbed hold of her phone and used the speed dial function to call Hartley. "Hello," she said, when he answered. "Have you seen the news?"

"I'm sitting watching it," he said, in a serious tone. "I need to disappear, fast."

"I think we both do. Have you organised something special for Barnes and the boy?"

"Yes, it's taken care of. Only I don't want to be anywhere near Antigua when it happens. I'm flying out of here later today. I'll ensure I'm on the other side of the world when the balloon goes up."

"Good. I need to move quickly too. Otherwise I'll lose the opportunity. Don't contact me again. I'll look forward to reading about Barnes' demise in the papers." She terminated the call and rushed to pull on her jacket, just as the phone on her desk started to chirp. She glanced at it, noting it was her secretary. She grabbed her bag, and made for the side door, which led straight out onto the fire exit. She could use this without being spotted. As she hurried down the steps her heels clicked, echoing around the uninviting drabness of the bare concrete. Unfortunately she didn't hear the two uniformed officers from SO15 ascending. When they came into view she stopped and turned, only to see two more uniformed officers descending. It was too late.

Cody went over to the TV and turned it off. "That's it. You're free to go," he said to Zen. "They've agreed to drive you home." He offered out his hand.

Zen took hold of it and shook it warmly. He pulled Cody in and hugged him. "Are you sure about this?"

"Unlike you, I don't have a reason to go home. I don't have a beautiful girlfriend or anyone in my life. You know why I've accepted their offer."

Zen smiled. "So you can earn a living doing what you do best."

"And I don't have to keep looking over my shoulder, feeling anxious every time there is a knock on my door. I'll have the best equipment money can buy, I can learn to speak Russian, and, apart from the odd panic attack when my wires get crossed, I won't have to worry about anything ever again."

"Will you stay in touch with Zoe?"

"Yes, of course. Will you?"

"Yes, provided you explain how you two communicate."

Cody laughed. "Like all cryptography, it's easy once you know the keys."

"All I know for sure is that you use four numbers for each of the letters in a word."

"That's correct. The first digit denotes the day of the week the message was sent. For example: 1 Monday, 2 Tuesday, 3 Wednesday and so on up to 7 Sunday. The middle two digits denote the letter of the alphabet, but the day of the week the message was sent also has a bearing on these numbers. Therefore on Monday the letter 'a' is simply 02 rising consecutively to 27 for the letter 'z'. On Tuesday the letter 'a' is 03 rising consecutively to 28 for 'z'. Then so on until Sunday when the letter 'a' is 08 rising consecutively to 33 for 'z'."

"What about the fourth digit?" Zen asked. "I've noticed you only use either 0 or 9."

Cody nodded. "9, if the letter precedes a new word, otherwise 0."

"In other words, 9 denotes a space."

"Correct."

"So… today 'Zen' would be. . ."

"4300, 4090, 4189," Cody answered for him, in lightning speed.

"I'd have to write the numbers and letters down. I can't do it as quick as you."

"4300, 4190, 4099 created a programme that deciphers my messages and writes hers."

Zen stood thinking for a few seconds, and then said, "Zoe?"

"Yes. If you send her a coded message I'm sure she'll email it to you."

Zen nodded, but his expression became serious. "Look, Mate. Over the past few weeks we've certainly been through some shit together. I couldn't have done what you did. I owe you my life."

"And I couldn't have done it without you. We saved each other and we helped prevent thousands of people being killed."

There was a knock at the door and one of the men who had been looking after them appeared. "If you are ready, Mr Zen, I can take you home."

"I'm ready," he replied, heading towards the man. As he reached the door, he turned and smiled at Cody. "I think I'll eat gluten-free food from now on. It was the Chinese meal you ordered that led them to us."

"One of my better ideas," Cody shouted, as Zen closed the door behind him. After he'd gone Cody looked round the stark room. Suddenly he felt the isolation and fear strike home. He started to shake.

Zoe watched as Ben chased the guard, Alistair Fairbanks, around the pool. She could see Fairbanks was allowing him to nearly catch up, but managing to keep just a fraction out of his reach. As they ran, Ben was in hysterics; eventually he stopped to catch his breath. Fairbanks at this point was alongside where she was enjoying the afternoon sun on one of the loungers.

He slowed to a halt and pulled his dark glasses down a fraction and looked over the top of them at her. He smiled. "Do you think I'll ever tire him out?" he said.

"No chance. He'll spend all afternoon chasing you."

"He wants the gun. His mother told me not to have it on show when he's around."

"Where is it?"

He tapped the side of his trouser leg and winked at her. "Safely out of the way."

While he spoke, Zoe noticed Ben taking an avid interest in what they were saying. Suddenly the child picked up a tennis ball and threw it into the shrubbery behind her. Fairbanks immediately spun round and crouched, his weapon already drawn.

"Ha, ha, ha!" shouted Ben. "I know where you keep it now!"

Zoe grinned. "Better not let Kozlov know you were outsmarted by a two year-old."

Fairbanks shrugged. "It happens." He motioned that Ben should follow him. "Come on, we'll go to the catamaran and check things down there. You can show me round it; I want to see what it's like inside." He started jogging slowly away and Ben raced after him, singing, "I know where you keep your gun, do dah, do dah, day."

Zoe chuckled. Then she spotted Faulkner-Brown, in a haze of cigar smoke, swaggering towards her. She produced that lop-sided smile. He settled awkwardly on the lounger next to her. He was sweating profusely. "It's too damned hot," he muttered, dabbing his forehead with a clean, crisp, white handkerchief. "What's *he* doing with Benjamin?" he asked, pointing down the path.

"Going to check out the catamaran. Ben's taken a liking to him, and he's reciprocated."

"Keep an eye on him."

"Who, Ben?"

"Fairbanks! He's supposed to be guarding us and all he appears to do is play around with the kid. I don't know what it is about him, but something doesn't seem to add up."

"Well, he appears to have taken Ben's mind off Woods. It's as if he's forgotten him already."

"Kids are like that. They concentrate on the here and now. He won't forget Woods. In quiet moments he'll remember him, and he'll feel grief. Then his mind will flick to something else, something which at that very second is happening right in front of him. It's a sort of defence mechanism. You can learn a great deal from kids."

"Maria mentioned all the work you've done for disadvantaged children. I looked it up on the net. She was right; under that grumpy exterior is a decent guy."

He became flustered and waved the comment away. "I don't... I don't talk about that," he said, appearing embarrassed.

She got the message. "So what brings you out at the hottest part of the day?"

"Maria's spoken to me about your mother."

"And?"

"I'll do what she suggests. You might not know this, but your mother was my protégée. I had great hopes for her. Nothing that happened was my doing. Luthi used her as the scapegoat. At the time, if I could have helped, I would have. Anyway, I'll testify against Luthi and hopefully we can have your mother freed."

"Thank you. That means a lot. Like Maria says, you're not as bad as people make out."

"Oh yes I am," he said, grinning broadly. "Or at least that's what I want people to believe."

Friday 16th October

Two weeks and one day after the press conference in Paris, the dust began to settle. The British press had been having a field day — amid claims that the British Secret Intelligence Service weren't fit for purpose — and although the fuss was now beginning to subside, the calls for Luthi's resignation had not. She remained under investigation, awaiting an array of charges, as did several prominent people and politicians, the surprise package being that Jacob Hartley had flown into Gatwick a few days earlier, immediately surrendering himself to the officer leading the investigation. There were rumours circulating in the press, which claimed that a deal had been struck allowing him to testify against Luthi - although Kozlov doubted this to be the case, as he thought Faulkner-Brown's testimony alone would have sufficed. True to his word, Faulkner-Brown was back in the UK, currently wining and dining at Claridge's in Mayfair, his sworn affidavit already in the hands of the Crown Prosecution Service. Kozlov had spoken in depth with the head of CID at the Antiguan Police Department, explaining that when his team had rescued the child from the yacht, a gun battle had ensued, resulting in the deaths of four people: one woman and two men who had been holding the child hostage, and one of his team. He claimed that when his men left the boat with the child, a further two hostage-takers were still on board. Both were alive; it was assumed that they blew the yacht up to destroy the evidence. His false account fitted in nicely with the discovery of body parts, from three males and one female, in Carlisle Bay. It had been agreed that no action would be taken against him. No doubt his recent activities, and the fact that he had prevented a catastrophic terrorist attack on the western world, swayed the decision in his favour. Since then he had agreed that the armed guards stationed at Barnes' house could be released and they had flown out the previous day.

Now, only Zoe remained at the house with Barnes and Ben, and she planned to fly back to the UK this evening. Before she left she had one last task to complete: the equipment in the computer room needed closing down and packaging, and, because Barnes intended taking Ben out on the catamaran this afternoon, Zoe would utilise the time to sort out the equipment in readiness for shipping back to England.

Zoe's emotions were a mixture of sadness and regret, tinged with satisfaction and accomplishment. When she'd arrived at Woods' flat, on the morning of Tuesday 1st September, she never envisaged the rollercoaster ride she was embarking on. And she had never imagined that he would not be there at the end. That one fact, more than anything else, twisted at her soul. Nonetheless, she had achieved her goal: speculation now surrounded her mother and her early release from a prison cell. But was it worth it? Of course it wasn't worth it! For fuck's sake - Woods had died! How could it possibly be worth that? She stared at the equipment, and an overriding desire to smash it to pieces came over her. But what good would that do? She sighed and settled in front of the PC screen. She took hold of the mouse and moved to close the current programme. As she was about to click the top right-hand corner she noticed a flashing alert on the Taskbar. She frowned as she clicked on it. Then she stared at the message. It was in her code. She knew that because all the four digit numbers started with five, and today was Friday. She copied and pasted it quickly into her programme. Within seconds it had been deciphered. She read it and immediately panic set in.

   One of your guards was working for Luthi.
   I don't know which one.
   I intercepted a message from them to GCHQ.
   CXVI awaiting full power. AF.

"Oh my God," she said out loud. "There's a bomb on the cat! AF must be Alistair Fairbanks. And CXVI was the codename used by MI6 when they bombed the boat that killed the Mathewson family. Shit! They are ending it the way it started." She jumped up, sending the chair hurtling across the room, but took no notice, racing straight out onto the landing, and running down the stairs. When she crashed through the ocean room doors onto the terrace by the pool, she almost stumbled, but her momentum kept her moving. She could see the catamaran bobbing slowly towards open water. "MARIA! MARIA! MARIA!" she shrieked, at the top of her voice. She could see Barnes' figure at the helm, but she was too far away to hear her. She needed to attract their attention; in a few seconds, when they reached open water, Barnes would push the lever to full power. Zoe grabbed a white towel from one of the loungers and waved it frenziedly above her head. "BENJAMIN! BENJAMIN! FOR CHRIST'S SAKE, BENJAMIN, LOOK THIS WAY!" Then she remembered her I-phone. She threw the towel down and, with trembling fingers, she managed to find Barnes in her contact list. She pressed on it and waited for the call to connect. She urged it to speed up, but she was a few seconds too late. There was an almighty boom as the catamaran disintegrated in a huge ball of orange flames and smoke. She fell to the floor, sobbing. She couldn't face looking out over the water. The horror of what she might see prevented her from doing so. Her thoughts were destroyed, her body numb, as she lay in the foetal position, devastated and broken. After what seemed like an eternity, she struggled up and glanced out to sea. It was as if the catamaran had never existed. A few bits of flotsam bobbed about on the surface, with the mighty frigate-birds and pelicans investigating their presence. She shuddered and looked away. In a dark daze she headed back indoors, not really knowing want to do now. "I suppose I need to ring Kozlov," she said to herself, pulling her phone out. She tapped on his number and waited for the connection. "Number unobtainable." She tossed the phone on the table and slumped on the sofa. What was she going to do now? She shook her head in disbelief. Why hadn't she taken more notice of Faulkner-Brown? He'd specifically told her to keep an eye on Fairbanks. She'd thought he was scaremongering and hadn't bothered. She shook her head and decided to go up to the computer room, and the screen she had received the message on. When she got there she pulled the keyboard towards her, and then noticed a further message had arrived. She stared, and quickly deciphered it.

>Do not worry Zoe everything is not as it seems.
>We are okay.
>The world needs to believe we are dead.
>Please play along.
>Keep the first message as evidence, but delete this one.
>Sleep safe and well.
>Love M.

She grinned. "You bastard!" she said, but it was framed with more than a hint of admiration.

The extremely elegant-looking, fairly new and very expensive Princess 42 motor launch was moored in the shallow waters just around the headland from where the catamaran exploded. The two figures, wearing full-face snorkelling masks, made their way slowly towards the rear of the boat and the steps up to the diving platform. Barnes climbed on board first and then assisted her son. "Did you see the parrotfish and the butterflyfish?" she asked, as he pulled his mask off.

"Yes. Did you see the humpback whale?"

"No, Benjamin, because there wasn't one. Now take this and dry yourself." She handed him a towel. "But keep the life jacket on, because we'll be sailing on the ocean soon."

"Where are we going?"

"To start a new life on another island."

"What was the loud noise?"

"Our catamaran exploding."

"Did we send someone up to heaven?"

"I suppose metaphorically we did."

He frowned. "What does that mean?"

"It's a figure of speech. It means it didn't really happen. You see I want the world to think that you and I are in heaven."

"With Mr Greg?"

"Yes."

"Why?"

"So we can live without fear."

"Was it you that made the catamaran explode?"

"Yes, Sweetheart, it was me."

"Is that why the stiff lady was wearing a wig, so she looked like you?"

"Yes, and she was a mannequin, not a lady. Now, you need to explore our new boat. I understand there are lots of toys hidden on board for you. Why don't you go and find what General Kozlov has left you."

While Ben ran down into the cabin and started looking in the cupboards, Barnes quickly donned a tee-shirt and shorts. Then she climbed up and settled in the comfortable leather seat at the helm. As he'd promised, Kozlov had left the keys in the ignition. She pressed the starter and the engines roared into life. She flicked the switch to weigh anchor and when it was safely on board she pushed the power levers slowly forward, getting used to the new craft. It was powerful and responsive.

"Look at this!" Ben shouted, proudly showing her a toy machine gun.

"Benjamin! You're not having that. Throw it overboard!" When she saw his eyes watering and his sad little face, her heart melted. "Alright, you win again. You can keep it," she said, thinking Kozlov had done that deliberately to wind her up. "Anyhow, come and sit up here with me. There's something I need to explain. And put this on, to shield you from the sun." She tossed a small yellow baseball cap to him.

He pulled on the cap and clambered up beside her, machine gun in hand. "What do you need to explain?" he asked, pretending to shoot down a pelican.

"In a few months' time you're going to have a little brother or sister."

His face lit up. "Wow, someone for me to play with. Are you sure?"

She laughed. "Yes!"

He fidgeted around excitedly on the seat "What will we call them?"

She tweaked her nose. "If it's a little sister we'll call her Zoe, and if it's a little brother we'll call him. . ."

"Mr Greg?" he shouted, eagerly.

"Yes, Sweetheart. We'll name him after his father."

The End.

Printed in Great Britain
by Amazon